Praises for *Soviet Fairytales*

"Socialism with 'a human face' acquires a literal meaning in *Soviet Fairytales*. The author manages to penetrate the Iron Curtain of abstraction and shows the lives of ordinary people with their own dreams and aspirations not unlike those of their Western counterparts, at the same time casting a critical glance at the 'fairytale' that was the Soviet Union. A highly recommended collection of short stories to those who would like to know what life under Communism was actually like."

Deividas Zibalas, Lecturer, Faculty of Philology, Institute of English, Romance and Classical Studies, Department of English Philology, University of Vilnius, Lithuania

"*Soviet Fairytales* are a collection of stories from Dr Pranauskas that embody a period of time in Lithuania during the Soviet period that helps to express a generation on the brink of adulthood. With the power of these short stories, she has managed to help us understand the struggles, the yearning for a western life and all that comes with the concept of *the grass is often greener somewhere else*. I read her stories like I was being told a story, and that is rare these days. I loved reading the tales from *Soviet Fairytales* and cannot express how rewarding the world, and the characters are as they leap from the pages into your heart."

Ms Sandra Sciberras, Head and Senior Lecturer, School of Film and Television, Faculty of Fine Arts and Music, University of Melbourne

"With an intimate sense of detail, Pranauskas lifts the curtain on Soviet society to immerse the reader into the lives, loves, struggles, disappointments and tragedies of each fairytale's subject. All her stories lead the reader unsuspectingly from contentment and personal joys to exposing experiences of loss. It is clear the stories are not entirely fictitious; Pranauskas' fingerprint, elements of her own life, are visible within each tender and insightful tale. I closed the final page of *Soviet Fairytales* with a genuine feeling of insight into the lives of a country and people who had been strangers to me on the first page."

Stephanie Juleff, Producer and Journalist, Asia Pacific News Centre, Australian Broadcasting Corporation

"These miniature 'fairytales' conjure in their simplicity and unadorned directness Soviet-era Lithuania, its conflicted and teetering totalitarian values, in the midst of which very human and poignant lives underscore the universals (nonetheless) of love, loyalty, truth and survival. A treat to read."

Dr Zachary Dunbar, Senior Lecturer, Theatre and Performing Arts, Faculty of Fine Arts and Music, University of Melbourne

"The realities of the last several decades of the Soviet regime in Lithuania are the context of the stories by Australian Lithuanian writer Gražina Pranauskas, who spent at least half of her life behind the Iron Curtain, in the cage of the Soviet system that constantly shifted but never lost its essential feature: its will to control the life of the people. Her fictional stories are deeply rooted in realities that are quite difficult to comprehend, not only by the people of Western world but also by the younger generation of Lithuanians who have not witnessed how the Soviet system worked. I can only wish readers of this exciting collection of stories to embrace Pranauskas' literary imagination and engage with the lives of Lithuanians of a bygone age."

Prof Almantas Samalavičius, Department of Architectural Fundamentals, Theory and Art, Vilnius Gediminas Technical University, Lithuania

"As a person from the former USSR, I have read these stories with great interest. Delightful stories! It is amazing to see how profoundly different the life of young people was in the Soviet Union and in the West, and still how profoundly similar were the feelings and aspirations of young people in the East and the West. Congratulations!"

Dr Joseph Jordania, Lecturer, World Music, Melbourne Conservatorium of Music, Faculty of Fine Arts and Music, University of Melbourne

"I have really enjoyed *Soviet Fairytales*, and wondered which stories came from the author's own experience and which ones from friends, family and acquaintances. There are so many sad moments, but also so many beautiful ones ... it's been quite an honour to read. Thank you."

Ms Liliana Braumberger, Service Delivery Manager (Acting), University of Melbourne

SOVIET FAIRYTALES

GRAŽINA PRANAUSKAS

ARCADIA

© Gražina Pranauskas 2019

First published 2019 by ARCADIA
the general books imprint of
Australian Scholarly Publishing Ltd
7 Lt Lothian St Nth, North Melbourne, Vic 3051

Tel: 03 9329 6963 / Fax: 03 9329 5452
enquiry@scholarly.info / www.scholarly.info

ISBN 978-1-925801-97-2

Cover design: Wayne Saunders

Contents

Acknowledgements .... *vi*

Author's Note... *viii*

Introduction: Soviet Way of Life Reconsidered .... *xi*

Love-grass Rings 1

Back to Herself.. 8

Army and Sex.. 15

The Forger... 25

Christmas Eve with Friends 41

Slip Up 54

Yuri Gagarin and a New Land 61

Acting Animals 73

Prince Charming... 82

My Soviet Passport.. 92

Dancing Figurines.. 104

One Night in Ossetia 124

I Want to Be Like Simas 143

Dreaming of Sweden... 160

About the Author *175*

Acknowledgements

I'd like to express my gratitude to people who made the publication of *Soviet Fairytales* possible. The greatest of these is my friend, Prof Ron Adams. Without his encouragement and support my writing may have never been as it is today.

I am also grateful to Prof Almantas Samalavičius from the University of Vilnius who has kindly agreed to write an introduction for this book that provides an informative and insightful overview on the twentieth century Soviet history.

Throughout the two years during which this book was written, I have engaged as many people as I could to read it and give feedback in order to sense how non-Soviet citizens may understand and interpret the *Soviet Fairytales*. They were surprised and shocked by discovering what was really happening behind the Iron Curtain. Among them a writer, Paul Dalgarno, who has appreciated my vivid characters and uncomplicated storytelling techniques cleverly underlining suppression and limitations of the Soviet citizens.

My special thanks to Liliana Braumberger and Stephanie Juleff for skillful editing.

I must acknowledge, too, my gratitude for the assistance given me by Nimity James, Janina Adelhardt, Sarah Hall, and Carina Claff for feedback and suggestions that enriched my stories.

I'm indebted to the Australian-Lithuanian Foundation for financial support and to my publisher, Nick Walker, who has released my book *Lietuvybė Down Under: Maintaining Lithuanian National and Cultural Identity in Australia* in 2018 and has made my *Soviet Fairytales* known in Australia and abroad.

Finally, I thank my husband, Peter, for being there for me during my personal journey into my past, and the past of those that lived and experienced daily struggles of ordinary Soviet citizens, constrained by the communist ideals.

Author's Note

Walking the streets of Melbourne, I now feel I am a proud Australian citizen. After thirty years, I've accepted the fate of an immigrant. However, my past is still challenging my identity. Growing up and maturing in Lithuania during its occupation, the Soviet Union keeps me attached to its twentieth century history. To deal with unsettled memories, drifting in and out my consciousness, in 2016 I began writing a sequence of stories named *Soviet Fairytales*.

My fictional stories, fed by autobiographical memories and imagination, remain deeply rooted in my homeland and are attached to historical, political and socio-economic discourses spanning from the 1940s to the 1990s. The process of constructing these stories allowed me to "return" to my childhood and youth, and rethink the effect of the circumstances that shaped me as a person. Surviving the communist ideals involved rationed goods and money shortages, thus forcing people to work in two or three jobs. For me, the benefits of extra income were irresistible, allowing me to travel around the Soviet Union to explore the Baltic States, to climb the mountains of Caucasus, Ossetia, and Altay, to sleep under the stars of Mongolian steppes or to visit Murmansk—the world's largest city inside the Arctic Circle. The opportunity to travel around the Soviet Union resulted in discovering different cultures and experiencing the hospitality of the locals. Although the citizens of the fifteen Soviet nations used their own language and retained their own national and cultural identity, visitors were welcomed in Russian—a compulsory language taught since my childhood—the only language of communication throughout the Soviet Union during those years of occupation.

My personal experiences not only enrich the *Soviet Fairytales* but also reflect on the lives of ordinary citizens. Encouraged to blend in while attempting to build a flawless society that does not tolerate disobedience, venereal diseases, disability or homosexuality, they are silenced by force. To show the existence under the red flag decorated with hammer and sickle, each of my stories reveal the colourful mosaic of individual thoughts, feelings and aspirations, trapped under the banner of communism. Readers should not be deceived by the light tone of the first two stories "Love-grass Rings" and "Back to Herself". With each story, unbeknown to me as I was writing, more political events come into play, raising the level of complexity and seriousness.

Within the pages of my fictional writing, I dwell on the collective "dream" of exploring the world behind the Iron Curtain. My physical presence in Lithuania made me an insider from 1957 to 1989. Using my insider's memories, after thirty years in Australia I have created a narrative, reflective of my past and written while geographically detached from my homeland. Undeniably, my memories formed under these particular historical, political and socio-economic discourses, are "reimagined" in my new home. At the same time, connection between the two countries is strengthened by including stories such as "Dancing Figurines" or "I Want to Be Like Simas" where my characters live in Australia. These and other stories are crossing the boundaries between "there" and "here" in trying to show the consequences of imprisonment, deportation and family separation due to the totalitarian Soviet regime.

Soviet Fairytales intertwine the significance of the Soviet cosmonaut Yuri Gagarin becoming the first man to leave Earth's orbit in 1961; 1940s deportations to Siberia; ongoing spying and KGB interrogations; forbidden Christmas celebrations and punishment for dissemination of religious publications. These events highlight the tragic Soviet past, hidden from the citizens of the postwar generation who grew up under the Russian flag with their own nation's history removed from the school curriculum. The power of the Soviet regime is felt in the stories "My Soviet Passport", "The Forger" and "I Want to Be Like Simas". The societal views on venereal diseases, homosexuality and disability are addressed in "Slip Up" and "Prince Charming", while "Christmas Eve with Friends" reveals consequences of deportation and suppression of religious celebrations. At the same time, the harshness of the political environment is softened by emotions where people in love are ignorant to their politicised existence. Examples of the fairytale events are portrayed in each of my stories, most romanticised in "Love-grass Rings", "Army and Sex" and "One Night in Ossetia".

My own desire to understand the withheld twentieth century Soviet Lithuanian history gave birth to "Dreaming of Sweden" where the main character, sheltered from her historical past, deals with the discovery of her homeland being occupied by Russia since 1940. This revelation results in her burning her schoolbooks and, in 1989, becoming one of two million people in Lithuania, Latvia and Estonia who joined hands across the three countries to mark fifty years of Soviet occupation in the "Baltic way".

In these fairytales, readers will find Lithuanian words, with unfamiliar symbols. They should not be intimidated. Being one of the oldest languages of the Indo-European group, originating from Sanskrit, today Lithuanian language is based on the Latin alphabet. Therefore, Lithuanian words are pronounced as they appear in text.

The process of writing fourteen *Soviet Fairytales* consumed me, and I was constantly missing my tram stop on the way to work and home. Hopefully, my readers will enjoy them as much as I did!

Soviet Way of Life Reconsidered

By Almantas Samalavičius

I happened to be born in Lithuania back in those days when it was still Soviet and I spent half of my life in a captive society before it spectacularly collapsed in 1990. Lithuania was the first country to break with the Soviet regime, soon followed by two other Baltic states.

Life in the Soviet dominated part of Europe was far more different from life in the any part of the Western world—so different that it is quite difficult for any present-day reader to imagine what complex and complicated forms it took and what inhabitants of the Soviet realm had to endure. Formally the Communist Party of the Soviet Union had always claimed that the Union of the Socialist Soviet Republics was a vanguard state where the hegemony of the proletariat (the working class) was firmly established. Accordingly, this vanguard state was destined to lead the way for the rest of the world until the capitalist system would finally collapse worldwide, giving way to the dream of a better life already embodied by the socialist republics of the Soviet Union paving the way for the paradise of Communism. As it is well known these days, in reality the Soviet system was anything but paradise. More than that—it was an oppressive totalitarian/authoritarian regime maintaining a tight control over people's life and thoughts to a degree hard to imagine for people raised and educated in democratic societies. Strange as it may seem, the Soviet Union was viewed extremely positively in the circles of the Western Left. In a notorious pamphlet written shortly before WWII and eventually expanded into a large book, Sidney and Beatrice Webb praised the Soviet system as a project that humanity was destined to face in future. According to these authors, the Soviet Union was the first country in the world where social equality was not only introduced and but also assured:

> It is claimed that the whole social organisation of Soviet Communism is based upon a social equality that is more genuine and more universal than has existed in any other community. To engage in socially useful work, according to capacity, is a universal duty. It is a distinct novelty in social life that there should be no exemption from this duty in favour of the possessors of wealth of the owners of land, the holders of offices, or those having exceptional intellectual or artistic gifts or attainments, the geniuses or the popular favourites. Work, like leisure, has to be shared by all able to join in social service. There is only a single social grade in the USSR, that of a producer by hand or by brain; including, for becoming producers, and those so aged or so infirm as only to be able to look back on the work they did in their strength. This is what is meant by the "classless society", in which each serves in accordance with his ability, and is provided for appropriately to his needs.[1]

The authors went as far as to suggest that Communism was a new type of civilisation and consequently a cornerstone for worldwide Progress. Elsewhere in the pamphlet, the authors go so far as to claim that

> It is a distinctive feature of the social arrangement of the Soviet Union that, to a degree unparalleled elsewhere, they provide for every person, irrespective of wealth or position, sex or race, the poorest and weakest as well as those who are "better

off", in all cases equality of opportunity for the children and adolescents, and increasingly, also a common and ever-rising standard of living for the whole population. This is well seen in the sphere of education. Other communities, especially during the past century or two, have striven to create educated, and even cultivated classes within their nation. The Soviet Union is the first to strive, without discrimination of sex or race, affluence or position, to produce not merely an intelligentsia but a cultivated nation.[2]

Though from the current perspective all these enthusiastic and largely overcooked statements seem to be nothing more than falsification of reality, it is possible to understand such distorted images of the Soviet Union before WWII, with contacts between the Soviet regime and the rest of the world very limited and entrance into the Soviet realm highly restricted, even to its Western admirers. What is more difficult to comprehend is the continuation of the same kind of adoration after WWII, when news about the atrocities of the Soviet regime, with its growing network of Gulags, were penetrating the Western domain. And yet, influential European intellectual publications of the Left continued to praise the supposed "achievements" of the Soviet Union. The highly esteemed French journal *Les Tempes Modernes*, associated with the circle of philosopher Jean Paul Sartre, wrote in 1950, when the exiles to Gulags in Siberia and other regions of the USSR were in full swing:

> There is no country in the world where the dignity of work is more respected than in the Soviet Union. Forced labor does not exist there, because the exploitation of man by man has long since been abolished. Workers enjoy full fruits of their own labor and are no longer forced to depend on a few capitalist exploiters. Forced labor is characteristic of the capitalist system because in capitalist countries, workers are treated like slaves by their capitalist masters.[3]

Ironically, the so-called slavery of labor in what the author calls the "capitalist system" was nothing compared to what people forced to perform compulsory work at the Soviet Gulags had to endure. One can get a true picture of what were the horrible conditions at the Soviet labor camps were during the period while reading for e.g. the account of Dalia Grinkevičiūtė, whose manuscript was eventually published in Lithuanian under the title of *Lithuanians at the Laptev Sea* and eventually translated into English under different titles.[4] Curiously enough, Sartre himself, who wrote a brilliant introduction to the book by renowned Algerian anti-colonial fighter and author Albert Memmi, was totally blind to the colonisation policies of the Soviet Union even after being an eye-witness to its realities during his famous visit to the USSR back in 1954.

These extremely naïve (if not openly cynical) views of the realities of Soviet life were challenged by the publication of *The Gulag Archipelago* by Alexander Solzhenitsyn, which reached English and French audiences almost simultaneously in 1974, exposing the atrocities of Soviet labor camps that proved to be no less inhuman than the ones established by the German Nazis before WWII. The publication of *The New Class* by Yugoslavian dissident Milovan Djilas in 1957 further exposed the inherent ills and self-delusions of the Communist system. Though the author was imprisoned for his writings, the book enjoyed enormous popularity and was translated into some 40 languages as an eye-witness account of how the system of Communism worked in practice. Despite of the fact that it first and foremost dealt with the Yugoslavian experience, it was instrumental in triggering the understanding about the totalitarian origins and ways of other Communist regimes, notably the Soviet. Among many other things, Djilas demonstrated to Western readers that despite claims of creating a society without social classes, the Communist system in fact created its own class of a power elite that enjoyed enormous social privileges over the rest of its population. With the English translations of these authors (meanwhile Solzhenitsyn was decorated with Nobel Prize as early as 1970), it was no longer possible to close one's yes on what was happening in the Communist realm, most notably the Soviet Union.

It is generally known that many things were subject to change after the so-called Khrushchev's thaw, even though the old-style Soviet functionaries managed to retain their powers and introduce policies that eventually paved the road to the so-called stagnation period. While during its final decades of existence the Soviet regime became milder, with fewer people physically exterminated or facing long-term imprisonment for their allegedly anti-Soviet activities as was customary during the Stalinist era, it still maintained its essential features. Dissidents and critics of the system were periodically attacked, tried and eventually sentenced to lengthy terms of prison, with those who repeatedly refused to obey the Communist power structures imprisoned for decades, like one of Lithuania's longest serving political prisoners Balys Gajauskas,[5] or detained in the mental asylums that existed until the collapse of the Soviet system in the last decade of the twentieth century. As anthropologist Catherine Verdery acutely observed in her timely autopsy of the Communist system, "The socialist societies of Eastern Europe and the Soviet Union differed from one another in significant respects—for instance, in the intensity, span and effectiveness of popular support or resistance, and in the degree and timing of efforts at reform."[6]

After the brief revisionism of Khrushchev's thaw provided a short-term illusion that a "socialism with a human face" was possible, the inhabitants of the Baltic republics, occupied and eventually colonised at the end of WWII, were forced to abandon their hopes about the essential transformation of the Communist regime. Persecution and imprisonment of dissidents continued, and censorship that had become somewhat lax during the reign of Nikita Khrushchev soon gave way to more brutal control of any published work and a centralised agency of censorship called GLAVLIT, which took care to control every written word that was published in the Soviet republics. All media were subject to the control if this agency and not a single article that appeared in the daily press or journals could be published without the *imprimatur* of the Soviet censors. The degree of censorship varied depending on the period: extremely harsh during the first post-war decades until Khrushchev's reforms, control over content reclaimed by his successors, and once again liberalised during the years of *perestroika* initiated by Mikhail Gorbachev. In real life, of course a lot depended on the personality of the censor. Some of the employees of GLAVLIT were bluntly following their instructions, while others were somewhat more lax, closing their eyes on the occasional slips or ambiguities they encountered.

Of course, many essential features of the system were undergoing change. As Milovan Djilas had already exposed in the nineteen sixties, the principle of equality about which Communism boasted was soon abandoned in practice, various privileges given to Communist party members, especially their leading cadres. As Lithuanian cultural sociologist Stanislovas Juknevičius has quite accurately observed, the founding element of the myth of equality was finally removed as the ruling issued by the Communist party's Central Committee requiring that salaries of any Communist should not be excessively higher than any worker of his or her enterprise was abandoned and "the distance between those in power and common ordinary citizen grew larger, instead of 'exploiters' and 'proletariat' new social groups came into being—those of party's leadership and the common folk. Originally having attempted to end the inequality between the rich and the poor, Communist became a new privileged caste."[7]

At the same time, a culture of scarcity prevailed throughout the existence of the Soviet Union. Though in theory it was claimed that everyone should be rewarded according to his or her needs, common ordinary inhabitants of the Soviet space lacked even the most essential necessities of daily life, meanwhile leading members of the party had access to specialised shops providing goods unavailable for other citizen. As Catherine Verdery has emphasised, "A result of the padding of budgets and hoarding of materials was wide-spread shortages, for which reason Soviet economics was called economics of shortage. Shortages were somewhat relative, as when sufficient qualities of materials and labor for a given level of output actually existed, but not where and when they were needed. Sometimes shortages were absolute, since relative shortage often resulted in lowered production …"[8] People were forced to obtain essential goods in a number of illegal or semi-legal ways, bribing officials or purchasing them in the black market. In many cases, some products were readily available, but only for those who had some access to officials distributing the goods and sufficiently well-off to bribe them. In the later phases of Soviet rule it was sometimes possible to bribe KGB officials in order to get the permission to travel to the Western countries, as witnessed by the persuasive memoir of the late Lithuanian medical doctor professor Kazys Ambrozaitis, who although a former prisoner of the Soviet Gulag, nevertheless managed to bribe his KGB supervisor to be able to visit his relatives in USA during the period of Gorbachev's perestroika.[9] Such events would have been hardly possible in earlier times, but a decade before its dissolution the Soviet system was getting more and more cynical and corrupt.

Some Lithuanian researchers have attempted to capture the essence of the last decades of Soviet rule by introducing the notion of boredom and such concepts as the "aesthetics of boredom" or even "society of boredom".[10] However, I would be inclined to debate the notion, as boredom was most likely peculiar to the ranks of the power elite rather than common ordinary citizens who were under constantly surveillance and controlled by the authorities and their law enforcement agencies. I myself was subjected to 2 hours interrogation by a KGB officer after a failed attempt to enter the border security of the Neringa region, and one of my teachers who supplied me with some banned titles in the nineties was detained for several months in KGB headquarters in Vilnius after some illegal texts he copied and gave to others were found in his possession. All this seems hardly to fit into the category of alleged "boredom"! The culture of the last decade of the Soviet regime is aptly summarised by Juknevičius, whose overview of the social tendencies of the Soviet era concludes that

> Larger and larger segments of society realised that in a material domain, the shortcomings of socialism were far greater than its benefits. People lived in the conditions of constant shortage; even most essential practicalities were scarce, and attempts to get access to goods far exceeded the

joy of acquiring them; besides the better quality of material life had clear limits; even the richest people realised that even despite their efforts they will never live like rich individuals in the West: they will never own yachts, villas or airplanes. Things got even worse because of gerontocracy that was eventually labelled as "years of stagnation" by official propaganda. An idea that one was destined to spend one's life under conditions of regular shortage was driving large parts of population toward desperation.[11]

Soviet society and culture were full of contradictions and thus often it is somewhat difficult to grasp the true meaning of certain phenomena. Nevertheless, I do believe that it is still possible to make certain distinctions between the truth and lies. In this sense, I tend to agree with Vaclav Havel, who commenting on the Communist regime in Czechoslovakia in his topical essay *The Power of Powerless*, famously claimed that people there lived "in lies".[12] This kind of interpretation of life under Communism has been criticised by Alexey Yurchak, who claims that such attitudes "share a crucial problem: although they provide an alternative to the binary division between the recognition and misrecognition of ideology, they do so by providing another problematic binary between 'truth' and 'falsity', 'reality' and 'mask', 'revealing' and 'dissimulating'".[13] The reason I can't agree with Yurchak's assessment is that his attitude opens the door to a relativist position and a revisionist justification of the Communist regime bordering on nostalgia.

Yale scholar Marcy Shore insightfully notes that,

It is not by chance eastern European dissidents so often spoke about truth as if it were something tangible, solid like the keys in the pocket. Havel was not alone in the conviction that the ontological reality of truth was proven by the experience of the ontological reality of lies. In centering a philosophy of dissent around the distinction between truth and lies, eastern

European dissidents drew not only upon the philosophical references of Central Europe, but also upon a rich tradition of Russian literature. After 1968, the communist regime resembled Dostoyevsky's Grand Inquisitor who had only one secret: he did not believe in God. For Dostoyevsky, Gogol, Tolstoy and others, to take pen to paper was to search for truth of human existence.[14]

On the other hand, authors who embrace postmodern relativism like Alexey Yurchak seem to be hardly aware (or ignorant) of this kind of essentially different existential positions.

The realities of the last several decades of the Soviet regime in Lithuania are the context of the stories by Australian Lithuanian writer Gražina Pranauskas, who spent at least half of her life behind the Iron Curtain, in the cage of the Soviet system that constantly shifted but never lost its essential feature: its will to control the life of the people. Her fictional stories are deeply rooted in realities that are quite difficult to comprehend, not only by the people of Western world but also by the younger generation of Lithuanians who have not witnessed how the Soviet system worked. In any case, these stories are a challenge—urging readers to break unfamiliar codes in order to understand the epoch that seems to be finally over. Her stories bring back the memories of the not-so-distant Soviet past and deal with a wide range of themes, from peculiarities of sexual life to persecution of any religious activities to the traumatic experience of deportation. The stories are sometimes sad, sometimes funny, but one way or another they are built on the author's first-hand experience of Soviet life and its omnipotent institutions of total control. They provide glimpses into a historical period when people behind the Iron Curtain tried to live their own lives no matter how difficult or desperate the political and social situations were. I can only wish readers of this exciting collection of stories to embrace Pranauskas' literary imagination and engage with the lives of Lithuanians of a bygone age.

Notes

1. Sidney and Beatrice Webb. *Soviet Communism: A New Civilisation?* Left Review Pamhlet 3d, London: The Left review, November 1936, p. 10.

2. Ibid., pp. 12–13.

3. Quoted by Karlis Račevskis in his article "Toward a Postcolonial Perspective", *Baltic Postcolonialism*, Violeta Kelertas (ed.), Amsterdam and New York: Rodopi, 2006, p. 171.

4. See, Dalia Grinkevičiūtė. "Lithuanians by the Laptev Sea: Siberian Memoirs of Dalia Grinkevičiūtė", *Lituanus*, Vol. 36, No. 4 (Winter 1990) or *A Stolen Youth, A Stolen Homeland* (translated by Izolda Geniušienė), Vilnius: Lithuanian Writers' Union, 2002 or more recently published as *Shadows on the Tundra* (translated by Delija Valiukėnaitė) by Peregrine Press, 2018.

5. Accused and sentenced for his involvement in anti-Soviet resistance and dissident political activities after WWII, Balys Gajauskas was detained in Soviet Gulag during 1949–73 and then again served another lengthy term in prison during 1978–87.

6. Catherine Verdery. *What Was Socialism and What Comes Next.* New Jersey: Princeton University Press, 1996, p. 19.

7. Stanislovas Juknevičius. "Komunistinis Aukso amžiaus mitas: ištakos ir raidos ypatybės", *Sovijus: Tarpdalykiniai kultūros tyrimai*, 2018, Vol. 6, No 1, www.sovijus.lt, p. 20.

8. Verdery, *What Was Socialism and What Comes Next*, p. 21.

9. See Kazys Ambrozaitis. *Gyvenimo keliu.* Vilnius: Vilniaus universiteto leidykla, 2007.

10. See Agnė Narušytė. *The Aesthetics of Boredom* (the original 2008 volume in English translation), Vilnius: VDA Publishers, 2010 and Tomas Vaiseta. *Nuobodulio visuomenė* (in Lithuanian), Vilnius: Naujasis židinys, 2014.

11. Stanislovas Juknevičius. "Komunistinis Aukso amžiaus mitas: ištakos ir raidos ypatybės", www.sovijus.lt, p. 22.

12. Vaclav Havel. "The Power of Powerless", *Living in Truth*. London: Faber and Faber, 1986, pp. 50–1.

13. Alexey Yurchak. *Everything Was Forever, Until It Was No More.* New Jersey: Princeton University Press, 2005, p. 17.

14. Marci Shore. "A Pre-history of Post-truth, East and West", *Widening the Context. A Eurozine Anthology*, Vienna: Eurozine, 2018, pp. 124–5.

Love-grass Rings

Loreta spent her evenings near the sea. She walked bare foot, carrying her shoes, sinking her toes into the rough sand. The shivering sensation from the freezing waves splashing above her ankles made her alert. She took a deep breath anticipating the waves as they rolled towards her, carrying broken shells, shiny pebbles and smooth pieces of glass onto the yellowish shore. May's sun hung on the horizon, tingeing the clear sky with light pink, burgundy and purple. With her feet exposed by the moving sand, she stretched her hands into the distance, took another breath and brushed the salt residue from her cracked lips. She smiled to a bow-legged man with evenly-shaped eyebrows and discheveled hair as he walked by. *It's Romas.* She laughed as she shook her head and considered how she'd observed most men being taken aback by her strong, curious gaze. Running her fingers through her caramel bob, she stood still for a while to watch him struggling to walk against the wind. He didn't turn. She was not sure if she should follow.

She developed a crush on Romas in grade eleven, but not openly and she was convinced that he didn't realise it. She kept his photo between the pages of her exercise book. He had an athletic body, and when he spoke he held his head to one side, leaning towards the person he spoke to, listening intensely. Maybe he did it because he wanted to be at eye level, but it displayed warmth and affection—girls loved him for his kind personality. Loreta's girlfriends felt disappointed he didn't single out any of them, paying equal attention to them all. She kept her love for him deep in her heart. He followed her home once and gave her a bunch of field flowers. She dried them upside down on a cord string and touched or kissed them each time she was there looking for clothes. Another time, accidently bumping into Loreta, he complimented her on her electric blue eyes. After finishing high school, Loreta went on to study to become a nurse. She learned that Romas underwent his vocational seamanship training at the Maritime School.

*

One day Loreta and Romas met on a busy street of Klaipėda. He suggested they find seats in a nearby café. Dressed in his white and blue sailor's uniform, he stood out from the others. He chatted away about his experiences of living and studying at the Klaipėda Maritime School and apologised for wearing his uniform. He said it was compulsory to dress in uniform inside and beyond the school grounds, but today he was an off-duty sailor. He was so proud of his uniform, wanting to wear it all the time. He knew how to navigate a ship, how to read the weather forecast, how to sail, undertake mechanical repairs and maintenance jobs, and how to handle the dangerous cargo.

"Seamanship to me is security at sea and maritime safety," he said. His confidence impressed her, while she listened to his deep voice. She pinched herself under the table to make sure she wasn't dreaming. She thought she should discard her dried flowers still hanging in her wardrobe—he was in front of her in person! She learned that he was about to sail to Morocco, and would take three months catching, processing and preserving fish for canning on the ship.

Loreta noticed how broad his shoulders were. She thought his freckles, covering his nose and arms, resembled her yellow dotted dress. She had never noticed before that he had a rather oval face, and mentioned that he looked much fuller than when they were in high school. He laughed, explaining how he had put on some weight because he needed to be strong while tossing rats overboard. She cringed at the thought of a rat biting his lip or a part of his ear in his sleep ... she looked into his eyes shining with intensity and, in reply, he touched the tips of her cold fingers. They kissed after emptying their champagne glasses. He suggested they go to his place, but she said she'd prefer to go to her home. She sensed that he didn't expect such answer as he smirked with approval. Why would she go to his flat? What if he only wanted to sleep with her and nothing else? She had heard that men, no different to whales, would rather go deep into the ocean for krill, even if it meant risking their lives. Why hurry things along, spoiling their encounter?

They strolled around the town until midnight and he kissed her on her lips at the door of her flat.

"Sorry, I cannot make any promises. Soon I'll be sailing on rough seas, winds and storms, and it's no good making any plans. I don't want to have a girl onshore waiting for me, missing out on her own life."

"I understand."

"I'm glad you do. Besides, how long could anyone wait for me? It would be selfish on my behalf to let that happen."

"Maybe not," she said casually, but wanting to scream, "I want to wait for you!"

Ignorant to her thoughts, he added, "The seaman's life is adrift. Can you imagine how after stepping on land with my 'sea legs', I sway to and fro for a few months, unable to adjust to even surfaces?"

"I don't know how you can you do it, then? How can you risk your own life?"

"Well. I need to think of the future, to save money, and this job pays well. I know that you'd want to have nice perfume, jewellery, designer clothing …

"Not necessarily."

"You'll be the first! All women do. It's one of many expectations this sailor must consider."

She held her breath, listening to his words, and imagined being his girlfriend, waiting on shore for his return, passers-by eyeing her clothes which Soviet Lithuanian women only dreamed of, following her around with envy. Before they parted, she promised to get him nausea tablets to fix his "sea legs" problem. He smiled and kissed her on the cheek. Each time he went to sea, she heard him saying "No letters", but upon his return he would find her, and she would enjoy his company once again. She loved his endless stories about sea lions and sharks trying to hop onto the deck, and about the freezing temperatures in preservation containers that made fish stiff and slippery. She enjoyed the make-up, pure wool scarf, a watch, and other gifts he brought from Spain and Africa. They would go out to the best concerts and theatres, have meals in the best restaurants, dance to live music, never forgetting to raise their glasses to those at sea. He added once that he may not go back, but he was tipsy and she wasn't sure if he was serious or not.

Out of the blue he wrote a letter to her about rats trying to get into his bed and bite his nose in the middle of the night. Maybe he was joking but it was enough to frighten her as she tried to remind herself he gave "No promises while at sea". Even though she was worried—his writing appeared shaky, sentences incoherent and words hard to work out—she didn't reply to his letter.

*

Loreta looked into the mirror to admire her shoulder-length hair, set in big curls. Her tight dress showed her curvy body and her stilettoes made her look taller. She raised her eyebrows, pinched her cheeks with her cold fingertips, sighing with satisfaction. She put her pink lipstick on and checked her watch loosely hanging around her wrist. Finally, friends began to arrive for her twenty-fifth birthday celebration. She saw Romas with her girlfriend Daiva but had no time to contemplate it. After all, she hadn't seen him for a year, even though at their last date he'd given her a bottle of Christian Dior perfume in a pink box. He must have been serious about their relationship in the past but today she wasn't sure. Maybe he'd forgotten about her? Maybe he was serious about his new relationship with Daiva and Loreta had been left out? For now, she closed her eyes and enjoyed the strains of "Happy birthday" and the popping of champagne corks.

Before leaving the party, Romas approached her and kissed her on her cheek. He quietly told her that he truly missed her. But all she could think of was his words told hundreds of times … "No promises". Daiva found them chatting in the hallway, holding hands.

At twenty-six, Loreta began regular walks along the beach front, filling her evenings after her day job at the hospital. A man was walking well ahead of her. When she caught up with him, struggling to hurry against the wind, he hesitated but slowed down and eventually stopped. She knew it was Romas from his ash-blond hair and bowed legs. But he looked different— his bulky body, expressionless face and squinty eyes were something she had never seen before. His embarrassment and momentary silence startled her. His words made her shiver.

"It's all about expectations, isn't it?" he said, spitting on the sand. "My friend Rimgaudas hanged himself at sea after learning that his girlfriend left him. It seems that life is not what it's supposed to be!"

While she tried to find the right words, he spat again, turning his face towards the sea and purposely walking away. She saw him swaying to and fro. She stood speechless for some time, thinking about the last nine years she'd spent in love with a man who had so many dreams to fulfil, who wanted to live the life of a sailor in the endless waters of the world. Instead, he told her, he was catching, gutting and stuffing the fish into tins. Now he had lost his friend. To her, he was a young moon that showed his face in cycles, resurfacing with a shining smile before vanishing into a void, his heavy words echoing behind: "No promises while at sea". Why should she value the gifts he gave her each time they met? Was he sincere or did he just pretend to be? Was he still a whale wanting to dive deep for krill?

*

Three months later, a bunch of field flowers was delivered to her at work without a note. She thought, how typical of Romas. Returning home that night, she found him sitting on the staircase in front of the door of her flat. She sat next to him for a while, but they didn't talk. She inhaled his pleasant, cinnamon-scented aftershave. He was so close and yet, so distant. With his constant absences at sea she hardly knew him anymore. Once she invited him inside, he opened up about his expectations and the expectations of others. He said that the sea was too much to handle, that he was a failure.

She shook her head, and kept repeating "No, no, you are not, you are not. You are just a human being, why should expectations matter?"

Clumsily sipping his coffee, he said seeing her at the beach front made him realise that he was sliding backwards. He put on more weight, got depressed and drank what captains and sailors drank—rum and wine. They had to keep their spirits up. Group drinking helped bonding, preventing self-harm. He apologised for misbehaving at the beach and walking away, explaining he wasn't himself.

"I always loved you but didn't want to admit it," he said. "When I was at sea, loneliness saturated my body and pierced through my bones, making me cold and hopeless. During such moments, my only wish was to have you, to live with you on shore, and to regain my sense of permanency. There is no permanency at sea. The presence of gushing water, splashing and spraying all over is frightful. I thought I was going mad, especially when I saw Rimgaudas' body buried at sea. I imagined sharks hanging around below the deck, waiting for him …"

*

They sat on the bench near the sea, holding hands and swinging their feet. They listened to the sounds of the screeching seagulls.

"Do you recall a song about a young woman waiting for her boyfriend's return from his work at sea?" Romas asked.

"Yes, I do," said Loreta.

"While she patiently stood at the edge of the water, the seagull sang her a song of love," he recalled.

"And the part of the song was that once she got sick of waiting, she left the pier and found another sailor?"

"Sure she did."

Clearing her throat, Loreta sang quietly:

> Listen, sailor,
> You stayed at sea too long,
> And I forgot about you.
> So, I found someone else instead.

"Did you?"

"No. For me it was different. I have loved you since school," she said.

They looked at each other and smiled. He moved closer to her and she put her head on his shoulder. They watched the transparent waves turn into amber and aqua shades, playing on the surface of the rising water. They followed the slow disappearance of the glowing oval into the distance. They wandered into the dunes and made love-grass rings to fit each other's fingers.

Back to Herself

Lijana's dark curly hair and wide eyes were often discussed among the boys at Kretinga High School. In year ten, she wore the shortest uniform in class, ill-suited to heavily bowed legs. But she wasn't fussed what other students thought of her appearance. Her dark-brown gaze could kill. An ex-student Darius, five years older than us, invited Lijana for a motorbike ride one day. We saw him at the front of the school waving to her to come for a ride, but she refused. A couple of evenings later, I spotted them together, riding towards the park. She wore a short white dress, white shoes and a scarf, loosely tied around her neck, which covered her grin as the motorbike swerved on the bumpy road, their bodies swaying side to side. I followed them with my eyes, squinting until couldn't see them anymore, thinking what a thrilling life they had.

I heard the two were married soon after Lijana completed high school. They had twin daughters. Darius was working at a fox farm and there were various rumours about him. Some said he was breeding and selling foxes at the local market. Some said his assistant Jonas was doing all the work while he was off on business trips around the Soviet Union. Others gossiped about his love affairs, and that Lijana wanted a divorce.

Years later, I met her occasionally in Palanga between my studies in the capital, sharing details of my geology course and complaining about the lack of privacy living with my aunt. She was interested to know if I had a boyfriend, and I said there was no time for such a thing. I did my homework at the university library, then carried my heavy notebooks home. Lijana spoke of her troubled marriage, admitting she wasn't in love. This revelation shocked me—I fancied Darius. Every female student fancied him! I couldn't understand why she had children with him. Forcing a faint smile from her narrow lips, she admitted her daughters were born by accident, during the time she was on speaking terms with Darius. Sometimes they would make plans to join his uncle in West Germany where he'd escaped to during the Second World War. Other times they would empty a couple of bottles of wine and would relax in each other's arms in front of the television. She said these were rare occasions of happiness that produced Sigita and Jurgita. Lijana wished she'd never given in to his charms and hadn't been blinded by the clothing and jewellery he bought her to prove his deepest feelings. Once they exchanged their wedding vows, he'd changed, treating her as an unwanted puppy to which he used to devote his attention. He was busy running the business, drinking with clients, travelling around the country and beyond. She was bringing up her young family, sharing her doubts about their future with her parents.

It was painful seeing her worried face, listening to her wondering why her expectations were far from fulfilled. I tried to comfort her in a soothing voice, but she started to cry, her tears running down her cheeks and into her slightly open mouth. She wiped her face, clutching her white hankie between her short fingers as if it was her last hope, as if it was a sail that would take her on a different journey.

*

Five years after finishing high school, we had a reunion. When Lijana entered the classroom, I thought she was somebody's partner, but surely not the girl I remembered being the classiest in school? Learning it was her, I had to hold onto my chair. Her loose dress well covered her heavy body. She brought her husband along, and they sat next to each other as if they were strangers. He had an angelic face with a severe tan. Did he spend a lot of time on the beaches of Sochi? He sat erect, his milky eyes glaring around the room. During the evening he chatted to any available woman he could find, while we badly gossiped.

"Why did she marry him? Isn't it obvious she didn't love him?"

"Have you heard about his latest affair with a history teacher?"

"Just seeing him flirting makes me so sad."

"What happened to her? Look how she's let herself go!"

Overwhelmed with everybody talking at once, enquiring, questioning, sharing what they'd been doing since they left school, Lijana and I decided to catch up the following day. She seemed intrigued in my work at the Palanga Surveillance Office that investigated metals and minerals, gas, oil, water quality, and measured the level of hazardous materials around the seashore. But when I spoke with dedication to my topic, I could sense she was getting bored, steering our conversation elsewhere. She admitted how much she envied my life as a spinster. She was jealous of my freedom. She remarked that, in her opinion, the word "spinster" may not be attractive, but the life led by one definitely is! Oh, how wrong she was—I hated being a spinster. If only she knew how I wanted to find a husband. But what chance did I have with my black-framed, unfashionable glasses, slipping down my small pointy nose, hiding my Mongolian eyes? What chance did I have with my owl-mouse appearance that made me look bold and unattractive at the same time? With a strong sense of bitterness in her voice, Lijana spoke of Darius' absence. He was always too busy for her. She was left with maternal responsibilities that tied her down, making her lose her self-esteem. She was insulted hear me say that children were the only thing in her life. She mocked me, saying "how would you know."

Some months later Darius was jailed for possession of marijuana. Lijana moved from their rental property by the fox farm to her parents' flat with her daughters. She began a bookkeeping course, which she completed in two years, and worked as an accountant. She met another man. I passed them occasionally in the forest, holding hands. Once, I was walking the parallel pathway when I recognised them through the alley of fir trees. Younger than her, medium-build, he passionately caressed her dark hair and they kissed on the lips, before he left her standing in trance. I thought he may have been an athlete, preparing for a running competition—he ran so fast! I thought she could never catch up with him, and she didn't attempt it. She spotted me instead, waving her hand and calling my name. She said she came from Kretinga by herself to take some time from her family chores.

Ten years after completing high school, I received another invitation for a class reunion at a restaurant in Kretinga. At the entrance I caught up with Lijana who looked different. Had she had a face-lift? Her visage was smooth and wrinkle free. Her fake eyelashes framed her captivating eyes. She wore a black knee-high skirt, a pink blouse, and a burgundy jumper over her shrunken frame. Now she had long, light hair and instead of a wedding band, wore a ruby ring. When I approached her to complement her on her looks, she took me aside and discreetly pointed to a man sitting at the table of ten. She said his name was Leonas and he was here with her best friend Rita. I recognised his straight posture and his unruly hair from previously seeing them together. Revealing that he was her boyfriend, she made me promise to keep her secret to myself. Seeing her husband looking our way, we went to our tables.

Darius was sitting next to Lijana quietly with his head down. Somebody told me he'd been unemployed since getting out of jail. I was most curious about the new Darius. His muscular body made me keep glancing his way. I recalled how our hearts had missed a beat when as schoolgirls we saw him turning up after class on his slick motorbike, waving to us warmly with a gloved hand. He'd tune the motor to the highest possible pitch, heavy clouds of smoke billowing, checking his reflection in the side mirror while waiting for Lijana. How he had aged now, and gotten fatter. How had she regained her confidence, and where did the money come from while he was in jail for four years?

During our meal she got up and before making a toast, hugged her old school friend Rita, a single tear running down a pert cheek. She talked about the meaning of friendships that took her back to her childhood and youth, where they felt real and unbreakable. She paused and looked at us, quietly sitting around the table. She acknowledged her family, comparing it to a permanent fixture and the essence of her existence. We cheered loudly.

I plucked up my courage to say how the passing years changed us and brought yearning for our school times when we didn't have a heavily-loaded cart of experiences pressing down on our shoulders today.

"Yes, let's drink to that," was heard from the surrounding tables, and we stood up with champagne flutes in our hands, clinking them and emptying them together on a count of three. We clapped while the waiter replenished our drinks, wishing each other good fortune. I saw Lijana quickly exchanging glances with Leonas, adjusting one of her loosening curls, heavily blinking her extended eyelashes.

*

I watched Darius getting up from the table, following him outside. He lit his cigarette and slowly blew a couple of even rings of smoke into the air. I coughed.

"Sorry Jone, I feel foolish." I didn't know what to say and looked down at my shoes.

"I've known you for a long time and feel that I can trust you."

"Of course you can trust me," I replied, swiftly licking my lips, smoothing the lipstick that may have smudged after the meal. I could hardly believe he was actually speaking to me.

"It's just a thing, isn't it? She gets all the attention, but nobody asks me how I feel.'

"What do you mean?"

"Did you hear her pitiable speech?"

"Hm. It was alright, I thought."

"She didn't say anything about me. As her husband, I should've been mentioned and praised."

"But I thought you were included as 'part of a permanent fixture and an essence of her existence?'"

"I don't know where she'd found these words, but she forgot that everything she is having today is mine."

"I'm sure Lijana is grateful."

"No, she isn't," he said, obviously irritated, dropping his unfinished cigarette on the ground, squashing the lightly smoking bud with his elegant shoe. "She wants a divorce."

My heartbeat increased. I thought I'd faint and fall into his strong arms. Instead I leaned against the wall, watching the wind messing up his few wisps of his hair. He spoke through his teeth how he had buried all his savings under the apple tree. Now he worked out where she had been getting her money all these years. How she pretended to have no knowledge of the money, quickly moving in with her parents and leaving his helper to look after the foxes. "When I didn't find my savings, she dared to blame Jonas for the theft of five thousand rubles I risked my life for! "She must have digged it up."

"But I thought husband and wife have no secrets from each other," I said, my words obviously upsetting him, making him throw his cigarette lighter over his shoulder. He squeezed his fists, and his face tightened. I thought he would punch me. He took a deep breath instead and looked right into my squinting eyes. I moved my glasses up with unsteady fingers, breaking in hot sweat, unable to control my shivering body. I felt nauseous, as if someone came from behind and cut me at my knees—they were bending further and further down.

"She's got this boyfriend, you see, convinced he is better than me. She pretends that he gives her things, clothes, rings, and wants to take her away from me. But if fact, it's her that makes him stay, playing the game of the lures. She knows how to tie the man down!"

"Are you sure? I haven't seen her with anyone while you were away," I lied, trying to lift the heaviness of our unexpected conversation. Without attempting to, I lowered myself even more, looking up at his tall posture.

"Anyway, it's none of your business," he said, spitting something out on the grass. Then, he nervously waved, not looking at me, and blended into the darkening evening. I was shaking with fear and excitement, yearning for the sound of his croaky voice and the sight of the dragon tattoo on his neck.

*

I remained in a mesmerised state for a while, glued to the brick wall, contemplating his sudden departure and now confused at the extent of the gossip circulating during the years. After hearing his words, I told myself it wasn't anyone's business what happened between them. People move on with their lives, even though we may not want them to. I returned to the restaurant to mingle with the others as we raised our glasses to long-lasting friendships. In the distance, Lijana was dancing with Leonas, their bodies and lips touching in the heat of a slow dance. Her pearl necklace shone on the dimmed dance floor. Such a happy snapshot to keep in mind for the next reunion, I thought, unable to take my eyes off the loving couple.

Army and Sex

As I turn the narrow street corner in the Old Town of Klaipėda, I bump into a young man. We apologise to each other and talk about how pleasant it is to walk on cold cobblestones on a summer afternoon. Edgars introduces himself as a Latvian from Riga, serving in the Soviet Army in Klaipėda. I joke that at least he is only two hundred kilometres away from home. I say I know a woman, Rima, whose sons are both serving in Afghanistan, fighting in the Soviet-Afghan war. Edgars lifts his eyes to the sky and thanks God he isn't there. He has heard whoever goes to Afghanistan either dies or comes home injured. He repeats my name Audra twice and is surprised that it means storm. He tells me I'm the most beautiful woman he has ever met and compares my eyes to cornflowers. We speak Russian, regretting that Lithuanians and Latvians can't speak each other's languages. Edgars invites me to a café nearby with weatherboard shutters and polished floorboards. A solidly-built woman stands near the entry. She looks us up and down and her expression is angry. Her heavy make-up, more suitable for the evening, is smudged and traces of her red lipstick mark the cigarette she is holding between her thick fingers.

Edgars follows me to the table, and we sit down facing each other. We order two glasses of hot sweet wine, boiled with cinnamon sticks and orange peel. Once it arrives, we sip it through straws. Glancing towards the bar, Edgars tells me about prostitution in Moscow. There, prostitutes work in full view of the platforms at large suburban train stations. They sit with their legs stretched out and their prices written on the soles of their shoes. I'm shocked hearing these details and how he talks about these women so openly. It's a little dark in the café and I hope he can't see my reddening face.

"It's disgusting," I say but he assures me that only a few men approach prostitutes during the day. It's too conspicuous. They wait for nightfall. He suggests that something similar could be going on in this café. We observe how the woman we met at the door swings with the bar stool from side to side. How she adjusts her straight, bleached hair and flirts with a man in uniform. So eye-catching is his hat, that I decide he must be the captain of a ship. Edgars confirms it, and I turn my attention to the other women at the bar, all dolled-up, wearing high heeled shoes, their bright lips uttering stiff German phrases. The one we already met keeps glancing towards our table, and eventually comes over. She suggests we should get out of this place as it's for foreigners only. As she looks at us, she leans forward, purposely scratching the surface of our tabletop with her fingernails. She puts her elbows on our table. Her huge breasts are barely covered by a red blouse with a few top buttons undone. When Edgars points out he is Latvian, she bursts into a harsh laugh, and replies that he is not a westerner and should take me elsewhere. We watch her making her way to the bar, purposely moving her shoulders forward and backward. She is wearing stilettoes to make her legs look longer and her leather skirt is hardly covering her bottom.

As soon as our bill is paid, we leave. I want to find it funny but I can't. Edgars wants to kiss me but I'm too upset. For the first time in my life I saw real prostitutes, operating right under my nose. I used to cross the cobbled streets of the Old Town unaware of the business going on in this café! We cross the road as the Post Office clock strikes eleven. Edgars needs to return to his base, and once we reach it by bus he sneaks through a hole under the brick fence. A man-made hole to enable soldiers to get in and out during their time off. He assures me the commanders have no idea that, once outside the army base, soldiers hide their uniforms under trees and change to civilian clothes before going to the heart of the city. We decide to meet in two weeks in the same spot where we'd bumped into each other. He asks me if I have a girlfriend to bring along as he wants to introduce us to his army friend Juris.

On the weekend, I visit my girlfriend Nida to tell her what's happened. After learning of our upcoming double date, she waltzes around the room. She looks in her wardrobe for a suitable outfit. It takes about ten minutes before she finally settles on a floral dress. With long lashes framing upturned eyes, she moves her perfect body to the rhythm of a tango, parading in her dress. She is surprised that at the age of twenty Edgars is well informed about sex. I agree. We are the same age as him but had never heard about prostitution in Moscow or Klaipėda until now. We never talked about sex at school. Nida wonders whether we have an operating prostitution ring because Klaipėda is a port where foreign ships dock. We are curious about the shady activities happening in the Old Town. As we dip dried bagels into our sweet tea, we contemplate a plan. We need a male companion to execute it, so we decide to call our mutual friend Justas.

The following evening the three of us enter the same café Edgars and I went to. We order coffee. It seems the chatting at the bar hasn't stopped. This time the Spanish sailors are conversing in English with brightly-dressed, heavily-accessorised women with stylish hairdos. They are obviously impressing the men who, sitting in close proximity, pat the women's backs and touch their legs.

The waiter returns with our coffee. As we're just about to drink it, a middle-aged man approaches to ask if he could join us as there are no free seats left. We nod. He introduces himself in Russian as Volodia and takes a place next to Justas. He orders his meal. Then he gazes sadly towards the bar. I ask him whether he is alright and he points at a young, dark-haired woman in a green, body-hugging dress. He says he loves her but as far as I can see she's enjoying the company of a group of Spaniards. He says they were lovers, but she's too pricy. The foreigners pay better and in US dollars. She doesn't want his rubles. We are surprised to learn from Volodia how the café clientele operates under the name of the Sixteenth Division. He explains that during and after the war there was a Lithuanian division with such a name formed to fight against the Nazis. They were brave fighters, but the division is no more. So, the local prostitutes adopted the name. Justas offers to buy some wine but Volodia grabs the waiter's attention and orders Soviet champagne. He says he wants to thank us for sharing our table. We toast the champagne to his better luck in the future. His eyes remain glued to Nadia—a Russian beauty born and bred in Klaipéda. Observing how women sit with their legs apart, struggling to articulate foreign words in their tipsy voices, makes me shiver.

*

I feel at ease meeting Edgars and Juris as they are extremely polite. Juris is taller than Edgars, but Edgars has broad shoulders and speaks with more confidence. Nida is wearing her floral dress while my white top and pants are contrasted by blue earrings and matching beads. Our friends are dressed in creased t-shirts and shorts. We venture around the Old Town and settle on a bar in a two-storey building. The entry is well lit and the waiter leads us to a table for four. We order hot wine. Juris and Nida talk about their relatives and friends. Edgars and I are consciously looking around for unexpected surprises. I spot Rima sitting in a corner table and excuse myself to have a chat with her. She is alone and her "hello" gives away her trembling voice. Her wine glass sits in front of her untouched. She is hiding her tears in an already soaked hanky. She tells me that her second son has been killed in Afghanistan. She buried him in the same grave as her first one, who was returned in a sealed coffin last year. How can one woman take so much? Why is she here? Does her ex-husband provide her with any support? She tells me she hasn't seen the bodies of either son as opening the bolted steel coffins is forbidden by Soviet authorities. This has been explained in the official letter glued to each coffin. Each felt so light. She suspects there were no bodies, just bits and pieces—could've been anyone's clothing and bones. I pat her hand and we sob. Edgars comes over and joins us. He introduces himself as a soldier in the Soviet Army and Rima looks at him with pity. She repeats her story. This time her eyes are dry and her voice doesn't tremble. She spits her words automatically as if she were firing bullets from a Kalashnikov—so loud that soon those around turn their heads, listening to her grief. Juris and Nida appear behind us. We take Rima home.

Rima's flat is filled with sympathy cards, flowers and open photo albums. I help her into the kitchen to make tea while she gathers cups, saucers and finds some biscuits. Sitting around her dinner table, we listen to her speak about her sons dying in Afghanistan—one in 1982 and the other in 1983.

"Stepas and Aras were enlisted in the Soviet Army and allocated to Afghanistan," she says.

Juris confirms with her that war started in 1979, and she nods.

"But why did my sons, my Lithuanian boys, have to die for nothing?" she sobs, taking a deep breath, pausing for a few seconds. "Just because the Russians decided to interfere in another country's politics? How many more young men will keep coming back in sealed coffins until the useless war is over? I search and search for answers but in vain."

While I pour the tea into our cups in silence, Edgars points to a photo in the album and asks who it is.

"It's Stepas, the older one," says Rima. I observe his open face and his light hair. She flicks through pages as the elongated figure of a sun-tanned youth is left behind. "Here they are—Aras, eighteen, and Stepas, nineteen," she says. Posing seriously for an official black and white photo, they stand erect, staring trustingly into the camera with their wide-open eyes. As we try to comfort her, her body shakes out of control. I hold her hand until she stops shaking and agrees to sip some tea. After the tea pot is empty and biscuits eaten one by one, I ask Rima if she wants us to stay. She shakes her head, adjusts her scarf around her tiny shoulders and straightens herself into a rigid pose as if preparing to fire a Kalashnikov.

We say our goodbyes and run down the stairs. We wander the streets of Klaipėda, annoyed by drunken voices coming from the nearby flats. We agree how spooky the unlit alleys feel tonight. Before our friends catch the bus to their quarters, they are curious how I know Rima. I tell them she was my accordion teacher for five years. Edgars kisses me on the cheek and Juris politely shakes Nida's hand. It's their first date, and they probably had no time to get to know each other.

We return from the bus stop and pass the city bridge where I spot a cluster of uneven ripples in the murky water of the Dangė. Nida admits Juris is not her type. She suggests we don't show-up at our next date, but I feel the opposite. If I don't go, I might not see Edgars again.

*

Weeks fly by and I tremble waiting at the corner of the cobbled street of the Old Town. In the distance Edgars' figure stands out. He is alone. It seems that Nida's and Juris' feelings are mutual. Edgars embraces me around my firm waist and presses his lips to mine. I can feel a pleasant gust of wind slightly rippling my cream, hand-embroidered knee-length dress. We stand in the middle of the side street and a group of cyclists pass us with cheers. I am in love. I know he is also serious. He has written to his parents about us. He tells me his father is a factory worker and his mother is a nurse. Both of his older sisters are married. I tell him about my sister, a night club singer married to a Ukrainian engineer, and that my parents are teachers. I'm lulled by his deep voice, at ease in his strong embrace. Edgars opens his backpack and presents me with a slightly wilted bunch of field flowers he gathered on the way. I kiss him on the cheek. He kisses me back. We don't go to any café and just sit on a bench and chat. We hold hands. Passers-by approvingly smile at us. A whooshing sound of maple leaves remind me of autumn, which brings with it a melancholy air. As we talk, I watch his clean-shaven face that I want to touch, but keep my hands on the sides of my dress, scrunching the embroidered flowers with my fingers.

The next time we meet, we go to the Post Office to call his parents. We wait our turn in a long queue to pre-pay for his eight-minute conversation to Latvia. Soon afterwards, a harsh female voice announces that Edgars Jansons' connection to Riga is ready in phone box five. He emerges from the phone box with a sweet smile. Once outside the building, he tells me his time in the army is coming to an end and he'll be leaving in six weeks. The rhythm of *six weeks, six weeks, six weeks* echoes in my steps—flowers, kisses, hopes and desires of a budding romance—all left to the wind to scatter.

Before his departure, Edgars doesn't want me to walk with him to his bus stop. It's our last evening together. We circle around the sculpture park nearby, reading the names of works created by local artists. One of them is a horse made of steel. Edgars jumps on the saddle and sits in a majestic pose. His rectangular face glows with satisfaction as he watches me from above. He makes noises with his tightly closed lips, imitating the gallop of the horse and swings an invisible whip in the air. His hair shines in the sun.

"Freedom, freedom, freedom," he repeats under his breath, bursting into careless laughter. The evening fades away. Our heads touching, we look up to the sky which absorbs purplish rays of the late summer sunset. He strokes my ginger hair, slides his hand down my heart-shaped face, then draws two big hearts with his index finger in the air. We promise to write to each other. We part at the bridge. I lift myself on my toes to see the top of his spiky head blurring in the distance. At first he walks unsteadily, turning back for a split second, and then increases his steps, taking the unsaid words I *love you* with him.

*

When the first month passes, I become suspicious Edgars has lost my address. Instead of writing to him myself, I wait another three months before making the decision to call him. I find a piece of paper with a phone number he gave me before leaving. At the local Post Office, I wait in a queue, pre-pay for my five-minute phone call and sit down. Some twenty minutes later a rough female voice announces: "Audra Viskontaitė! Riga, Riga, connection to Riga phone box six". I force myself into the narrow space, conscious people are looking at me. My cheeks are burning and a sense of shame overwhelms me. I shouldn't be chasing my boyfriend. Hearing Edgars' reassuring voice, I bury my pride. We talk as if nothing happened, as if he just left. He invites me to come to visit him and I agree to do so the following month. I hang-up the receiver with his words "I'll always love you" ringing in my ear.

After my overnight Klaipėda–Riga bus journey, Edgars embraces me with his long arms and gives me three stems of roses. He turns me around and passionately kisses me on the lips. Then we travel on a local bus to his dwelling. A woman, barely taller than a child, opens the door and he introduces her as Inga. I feel her piercing brown eyes following me around. She gathers her wavy chestnut hair into a ponytail and invites me to be seated at the coffee table. She finds a vase and roughly arranges the flowers. I learn she is a photographer and she shows me an album bursting with her client photos. The banging of pots and pans in the kitchen stops when Edgars brings us coffee and cake. I wonder who Inga is, and what she is doing here.

"We are gathered here today to celebrate Inga and Edgars' union," he says, keeping a straight face, passing the cups and plates with pieces of cake. I laugh, inhaling the faint aroma of the red roses he gave me just an hour back. *What a joker*, I think to myself, spotting identical gold rings on their fingers. As we drink our coffee, Inga beats him to the punch and says they just got married, proudly showing her belly. I hadn't noticed it beneath her loose jumper. I hadn't noticed Edgars' wedding ring at the station either. Inga bends her left-hand fingers one by one, counting to five—this is how long they've been together! I can't sense anything from Edgars' blank face, trying to deal with the realisation that after returning to Riga he didn't waste any time. As our relationship had been restrained to kissing, I had no idea he would hop into bed with a stranger ... a Latvian stranger. I was mistaken in believing he was a serious man. His knowledge about prostitution in Moscow now sounded suspicious. He had been there to explore his sexual desires in person for sure! Buried in my thoughts, I don't hear him approaching from behind and taking a seat close to me.

"It's alright," he says, when I jump and move away. "Inga went to the bathroom, and I want to apologise for what I've done. Apparently I got her pregnant at the party at my friend's place, on the very night I returned from Klaipėda. I was so upset leaving you behind. I must've been drunk.

"I see," I say, raising my eyebrows.

"I have a blurred vision of us sitting on a sofa, laughing, then burying myself in your open cleavage and calling your name."

"I wish it was me."

"Me too, Audra. Honestly, a drunken slip up has destroyed my life. My father found out about Inga's pregnancy and forced me into marriage. It's all my fault, forgive me."

I shrug my shoulders and give him a questioning look. "What am I doing here then?" I ask. As he opens his mouth to reply, Inga walks in with a bottle of Soviet champagne in one hand and two glass flutes in the other. She has a cynical look on her face, complemented by a fake smile. We drink to their happiness in silence.

*

Inga and I are standing in her darkroom where she shows me how she develops her black and white photos. Probably sensing my nervousness, she assures me that she knows about our romance, suspecting Edgars still has feelings for me. She wanted to meet me and to straighten things out. So, my call to Edgars and his invitation to visit him was something she approved. She dips film into a chemical solution and hangs already developed photos on a piece of string. When we come out of the darkroom, I look at her and wonder what their life will be without love. I haven't seen them cuddling, holding hands nor whispering in each other's ear as Edgars and I did. I want to bring them side by side, shake them by their shoulders, and ask: *Do you know what are you doing? Why? Why? Why?* But I continue to sit on a squeaking chair, holding my tears back, biting my full lips and watching her work.

When Inga leaves to buy some food, Edgars and I are finally alone. All I want to do is to sob in his arms. All he wants to do is to be with me. He wishes the drunken encounter with Inga never took place. He says the memory of my cornflower eyes has been waking him up at night. He caresses my face and gently plants kisses on my neck. Unwillingly pulling myself away from the heavenly pleasure of his touch, I dig my fingers into my palm, and beg him to leave Inga. We cuddle and kiss until we hear the noise of the rattling keys in the door.

The next morning, Edgars, Inga and I travel on a local bus towards the main terminal. People pass us in the aisle, shuffling their bags and counting their change. Inga is reading and Edgars is looking out the window. He sits opposite me. Our knees don't touch. I see his worried face reflected in glass. I put my finger to my lips and touch the contour of his lips on the window. The sun shines in my eyes and, as the bus pulls away, I can't quite make out his face.

The Forger

Vladas glued his broad shoulders to his seat, gazing out of the window. It was 10 am and he had half an hour to get to the heart of Klaipėda where his client was waiting. The slow speed of the bus stopping every few hundred metres made him fidget with the zip of his new black coat. Finally, he got off at the alley of oak trees overlooking the Town Square, walking the rest of the way to the prestigious Hotel Klaipėda. Seated in a red plush chair at a table for two, he amused himself with the attentions of an attractive brunette while she jotted down his order. Standing in front of him in shiny stilettoes, she wore nude stockings which made her full ankles appear more delicate. Placing her pencil and paper in her oval apron pocket, she slowly lowered her fake lashes. Turning on the tips of her pointy shoes, Vladas' imagination was stirred with what it would be like to kissed by her, her glittered lips leaving their mark all over his body. Sweat dampened his armpits. Smoothly swaying her hips, she maintained her model walk, not once needing to adjust the heavily-starched napkin hanging over her right hand. He had an extraordinary memory for faces and names, and she would be no exception. He stored her face in his memory, not just for her beauty but for the ever-present chance she might be a pretend waitress ... the KGB were everywhere.

Glancing over at the gold-plated wall clock above the bar, its hands frozen at 11 am, he checked his own watch and repeated under his breath in Russian "Vsyo budet horosho"—"All will be fine". He contemplated reassuring his client with either the words "All will be fine" or "Viskas bus gerai", but wasn't sure whether he knew English or Lithuanian. Piotr had spoken Russian on the phone so Vladas made up his mind to stick to Russian. He finished his orange juice at the same time that a well-built, middle-aged man approached, greeting him, "Zdravstvuyte *Doctor*"—"Hello *Doctor*". Vladas discretely pointed his thumb across the table where Piotr lowered himself heavily into a soft chair. Veronika, the waitress, balanced her weight from one foot to the other, patiently waiting for Piotr as his hand flicked through the menu, eventually settling on a glass of Georgian wine.

"What have you got for me?"

The man handed Vladas a manila folder containing a number of hand-written reports, signed and dated by the prominent neurologist Vilius Vilkaitis.

"How did you manage to get these?" asked Vladas, skimming through the confidential patient files. Piotr replied that the cleaner had got them for him. He pointed at the black fountain pen ink, arrogantly highlighting that Vladas should use the same colour in his forgeries. Vladas was an expert craftsman. His expression turned thunderous.

"I've done this hundreds of times!" Vladas said, snapping his fingers in front of Piotr's long nose. "My work is that of a surgeon."

His client rushed to apologise.

"Oh, I've heard you operate your magic pen with the same precision," whispered a red-faced Piotr, wiping sweat from his stocky face with the sleeve of his overly-tight jacket. Before replying, Vladas took a mental note of the unevenness of his eyebrows, sitting as they did too close to his darting beady eyes.

"The secret to a successful operation is using the right blade, or pen in my case, at the right time. But there is always a risk."

"Yes. Of course." Piotr paused. "How much risk?"

"Fifty rubles." Before Piotr had a chance to say anything, Vladas acknowledged the sizable amount—many workers were paid less than one hundred rubles per month.

"Comrade, six weeks working in the black market would surely cover the expenses?"

"I hope so," Piotr said, obviously surprised by Vladas' straightforward approach. It worked every time! He knew how to talk his clients around to *his* prices.

"We're talking about medical certificate with extensions, are we not?"

"Yes."

"Regardless of the quantity, the price will remain the same—fifty rubles each—half at the start and the rest when the job is done."

The men finished their drinks, settling on the time and date of their next meeting. They shook hands with closed-lipped smiles. Squeezing his tense fingers around the twenty-five-ruble banknote, with an image of bearded revolutionary leader Vladimir Ilyich Lenin, Vladas added in Russian "Vsyo budet horosho"—"All will be fine."

*

Vladas walked towards the giant statue of Lenin decorating the Town Square, its marble hand pointing directly at the red brick building of the Cultural Centre across the road. Stopping in front of the building, Vladas observed passengers getting on and off the overcrowded Hungarian-made Ikarus buses. Time and again he'd witnessed how the pairs of yellow buses, joined in the middle by the rubbery accordion bellows, maneuvered through the ice-damaged roads. Once, while on a bus, the forger had had the chance to enjoy the skills of a Charlie Chaplin impersonator. A professional actor, balancing in the middle of the turntable platform, adjoining the two ends of the Ikarus buses, had drawn a circle around himself with his walking stick. Then, hugging his arms around himself he had offered passengers his stick for support, eliciting a storm of giggles. Vladas, standing on the rotating platform, listening to the earthy noises of the rubber bellows expanding, twisting and folding into thick strips, admired the driver's 'figure-skating' skills. But such entertainment was only possible on a semi-empty bus. Most times passengers failed to push themselves into the expandable bellows or once on, struggled to squeeze back out at their destination, leaving with missing buttons and wigs, ripped stockings and broken heels. Vladas rarely used public transport, instead choosing to travel by taxi or on foot.

He wasn't a stranger to the Cultural Centre, the library being a preferred meeting place of his clients. While waiting he read the newspaper *Pravda*—The Truth—stuffed with articles about the diligence of the

Soviet system. The impression left from reading the daily news was that citizens of the fifteen Soviet republics, sturdily governed by Moscow, were thriving after building missiles for the last forty years, showing off heavy ammunition during the yearly May parades. As far as Moscow was concerned, the impressive size of tanks, rockets and technologically-advanced war planes maintained the Soviet Union as the most powerful country in the world. Such deadly devices came at a cost: the food stores were half-empty. Meat and poultry were always in great demand while imported fruit were almost non-existent. Such desire to frighten the world with ever-expanding weaponry came at the cost of basic necessities. People struggled to find toilet paper and kitchen appliances.

Newspapers aside, for Vladas the cozy library was a place to escape to. The stillness of the shelved, ready-to-borrow publications soothed him. He would read Mikhail Bulgakov, Maxim Gorky and Juozas Baltušis. He especially enjoyed a rare translation of Stendhal for the precise analysis of the psychology of his characters. He kept notes from Dale Carnegie's *How to Win Friends and Influence People* by his bedside, obtained through his sources, as the book was not available in the library. The library was Vladas' observatory. He envied those who had time to fully immerse themselves in biographies, short stories and novels, or those who were capable of getting lost between the pages of academic writing. He surveyed the entrance by listening to the opening and closing of the door. He heard the staff talking to the borrowers returning or checking out publications. He tuned into the subdued whisperings of personal affairs. He had developed methods of spotting, identifying and distinguishing those he could and couldn't trust. He knew how quickly people could turn against each other.

*

Settling down to work at a friend's hideaway, Vladas contemplated his life. Running a hand down a muscular thigh, he paused to gaze at his manicured fingers. Due to the delicate nature of the job he required smooth, flawless hands. A manual profession was absolutely out of the question. The skill of being ambidextrous was one he had cultivated from childhood and it now stood him in good stead. His heart responded to each carefully-crafted word with a joyful beat. As he worked into the night, he couldn't help thinking of his efforts to manipulate the Soviet rules. At the end of each completed forgery, he felt as if he'd climbed over the Iron Curtain to taste the sweetness of personal freedom. The jail bars, keeping him from the outside world until 1983, left him well exposed to the weaknesses of the Soviet system. He questioned himself. *Why don't I stop? I've already been in jail. But then, why should I? This occupation allows me to live as I please. I own my own flat, furniture, piano, aquarium. Any girl I desire is mine for the taking. I'll stop. One day. Should I do it soon?*

Concentrating on the unique letter incline, Vladas withdrew into his own world. His tiny writing transformed, blossoming into large, medium, narrow, broad, straight or uneven letters, whatever was required— all achieved with strokes from his Parker pen. The created texts looked indistinguishable from the original writing samples. Exhausted and worn out from working all night, he slipped off his chair and lay down on the piece of shabby carpet covering the floor.

The following morning, sitting at the base of Lenin's monument, Vladas reflexively checked his wristwatch. There was another hour before his next appointment. He walked up and down the main street, following coquettes with a longing gaze, pausing to chat to a passing acquaintance, reading and rereading the newspaper *Komjaunimo tiesa*. In the Truth of Komsomol he learned the names of schools of the Klaipėda region whose pupils were taken by buses to the *kolkhozes*—collective farms—to help with vegetable harvesting. He covered his mouth so as not to laugh out loud, recalling how nearly twenty years prior, in grade ten, he too had dug potatoes from the muddy fields with his bare hands. He worked at one of the twenty-six thousand government-owned farms throughout the Soviet Union. In reality, government property was regarded as people's property. So, Vladas and his classmates filled their burlap sacks with potatoes while one of the parents, waiting in his 70s model Žiguli close by, loaded the stock into his car and drove off to the fresh produce market. Later the boys were rewarded five rubles each. Reading the article, "Potato harvesting success", Vladas had no doubt that out of one hundred sacks of collected vegetables, some had ended up at the market.

Today Vladas was anticipating his second encounter with a man who reminded him of a rabbit. Approaching from the other side of Lenin's monument was Arūnas, his familiar short figure contrasted by his large ears and protruding top teeth. His squashed nose was festooned with tiny pimples. At the bottom of the concrete steps that carried skywards the gigantic immortal revolutionary leader, Arūnas paid Vladas for the forgery of his medical certificate extension. After they parted, Vladas went through his mental diary for the following week's appointments: by Monday 2 pm— create a Moscow Lomonosov University degree certificate; by Wednesday 4 pm—fake some Leningrad Conservatory academic transcripts; by Friday 10 am—complete the difficult falsification of a medical certificate. Having previously been caught, Vladas preferred working alone and not having to share his profits. His trusty companion from the past still remained behind bars. "Jail is a place for criminals, not for fraudulent copiers," he was told by wardens. Forgers of his kind were a rarity, and even in jail he'd had to do favours for both staff and outsiders. Once he had forged a divorce certificate for a prominent army officer to show to his lover who had wanted permanency in their relationship. Now both women were content. In these moments Vladas wondered whether he was a genius or a crook, whether he fulfilled or ruined people's goals and aspirations. In jail he hadn't expected to keep doing the very tasks that had sent him there in the first place!

Even though he had decided to never return to forgery, after his release the demand for his 'artwork' soon reached a peak. Admiring his long fingers, he dismissed any regret that he didn't pursue his dream of becoming a great pianist. He didn't want to admit lying to himself about why he had ended up as a forger. Looking on the bright side, he thought, his four-year from Srednevo Specialnovo Obrazovanie musical college had proved most beneficial in this line of work! Knowing what solfeggio, polyphony and score reading entailed helped in forging transcripts for music students. Clients gave him the freedom of inserting incomplete subjects or adjusting failed marks. As part of his own Music Diploma, he'd gone to great length to memorise the concepts of Marxist-Leninist doctrine in order to pass a political subject. Today, he diligently followed the principles of communist society: "From each according to his ability, to each according to his needs". Surely, in his craft, he was utilising his ability to work "to the greatest benefit of the people"! He was indifferent that not only ordinary people but also corrupted high ranking officials were using him for their benefits. *I am a fine cog in a machine, trapped because the work is too well paid to stop, to the point that I have stopped pursuing my dreams and my ego, and even when I'm caught, they will let me go again so not even "the law", as corrupt as it is, will put a stop to it.*

*

Vladas warmed a tin of tomato soup in a small pot on a gas cooker and ate it with a piece of thickly-buttered bread. Then, sitting in front of his huge aquarium he fondly watched his six goldfish sucking in flakes and pellets, gulping fresh water and showing their appreciation by letting out bubbles to float to the tank surface. He loved his fish for their inquisitive nature as they explored everything inside and outside the tank with their eyes— pink, white and black-shaded buttons that never seemed to look right at him. Brushing their delicate fins against the gravel, rocks and dark-green underwater garden, they reminded him of his own lifestyle. He caught himself leading a life both on the surface and beneath. In his surface life, he projected confidence, guided by Carnegie's teachings on self-improvement. In his other life it felt as if he was trapped in the body of a slippery eel hiding in stagnant waters. At times the extreme stress of the "dirty" rubles, earned through forgery, coloured his body with pus. He scratched himself at night, bloodying his silk sheets, throwing up from the thought he was a forger and a "dirty eel", but very much protected because the government had an interest in keeping him around. The names and faces of the people Vladas had falsified documents for haunted him. Once, he had a dream that the waitress Veronika, who had served him juice and coffee at the restaurant, was the lover of the First Lieutenant with the forged divorce certificate. Vladas woke up before the Lieutenant's wife choked Veronika with her necklace …

Vladas' conversations with himself or his fish were often accompanied by music. As a student, he had played and listened to music to find inspiration or unlock hidden emotions. But today he was no longer willing to share anything with others. He put on a tape of his favourite pop group Hiperbolė, stretching out on his plush couch. The male singer's reassuring voice encouraged him to keep looking for love and Vladas' body stirred in response. He yearned for true love. Having a woman for sex didn't count. Available women reminded him of his colourful goldfish. Each one had a unique personality, but all the same, were easily replaceable. For a long time now he had ached to feel the warmth of a woman who wished to be with him. If he trusted her enough, he hoped that she would embrace his secrets. Ideally, he wanted to shed the tough, ugly skin of the eel, to surface from the muddy pond and look into her eyes as a new man. If Carnegie managed to reach the heights of his career by believing in himself, so Vladas still had a chance! He had no doubt he would easily pass the entrance exams to continue his studies at the Vilnius Conservatory of Music. Just to prove this to himself, he opened the dusty lid of his second-hand piano. After warming up his fingers running through a few scales, he selected "Nocturne in E Flat Major, Op. 9, No. 2" to match his melancholic mood. He'd begun to play the piano at the age of seven, attending the government music school twice a week for seven years. He was twenty when he performed this particular Nocturne of Chopin's during his piano exam, impressing the academic panel with his sensitivity in projecting the desperate composer's love for fellow pianist Marie Pleyer. Sitting at his upright piano, he mused on how it was that the yearning for true love could still sing so strongly through the notes one hundred and fifty years after the piece was written.

The joy of being able to play his pieces by heart inspired Vladas to get up, shower, wash and dry his thick hair, brushing and styling it back with gel. Later that night, he dressed in designer jeans, matching shirt, dark-blue shoes and coat, and caught a taxi to a night club. The foreign sailors, delivering cargo to the port of Klaipėda, regarded Vėtrungė as their favourite place. Vladas was led to the only available table for four and soon other patrons filled the seats around him, two mature women and a young man. He looked at his companions with surprise, thinking they probably had mistaken the venue for a family restaurant. After sipping some wine, he left the table. He wasn't interested in the grandmother's affectionate ramblings to her daughter and grandson. He hadn't seen his own parents since he was jailed. They had rejected him. Having a family member in jail was regarded as a disgrace. Afraid of losing their jobs or neighbours' respect, they had disassociated themselves from their son, the fallen musician.

Reaching the far end of the venue where people were standing or chatting between dances, Vladas leaned on the panel of a see-through partition. He overheard a woman's voice on the other side, adamantly in saying that if nobody invited her to dance in the next ten minutes, she was going home!

"I don't want to keep standing here like a desperate object of humiliation, begging for men's attention."

Vladas smiled, listening to her companions attempt to calm her down.

"Snieguole, how else will we find suitable husbands?" one voice asked.

"Going out is the only way," assured the other.

Snieguolė sipped her cocktail through a straw, watching the dancing couples and adjusting her glasses. There was something about her that caught Vladas' interest. *It must be her femininity*, he decided. Peering through the gap in the partition, he eyed her skinny legs, exposed by her brief red mini dress which was complemented by matching heels. She finished her drink, bent down to leave her glass on the floor and said goodbye to her friends.

Vladas caught up with her.

"Would you care to dance?"

"Sure," she said, giving him a surprised look. Walking towards the dance floor they introduced themselves. The band was playing fast rock. Snieguolė, leaning backwards with each new sequence of beats, elegantly waved her bare arms in the air. So impressed with her moves, he kept count in his head so as not to miss a beat. Oh, how he wanted to kiss her long neck, daringly exposed by the low-cut dress. Snieguolė—this Snow-Maiden with her bright cheeks and white arms—he couldn't believe she was real. But she was! Each time he opened his eyes, there she was, vigorously shaking her lithe body.

She removed her oversized glasses, letting him in on her little secret—she only wore them to look older. He thought it a very clever trick, but deep down was pleased as young women with glasses were considered slightly damaged goods. As they continued to move, the whole room appeared to spin out of control and the chandeliers seemed to come lower and lower, down towards his head. He tried to count how many glasses of wine he had consumed, landing on three before remembering he'd consumed half a bottle of red before heading out that night. Steadying himself on his feet, he pulled himself upright. He didn't want her to find him unattractive just because he'd had a few drinks. Thoughts circled in his mind: *she's a delicate elk and I have to tread carefully not to frighten her off.*

They remained on the dance floor for hours, only returning to their seats to finish their meals. Before the end of the night, Vladas had moved to Snieguolė's table and ordered champagne for her and her friends. He offered to take them all home, but her friends didn't want to leave. In the taxi, he asked Snieguolė if she fancies to finish the evening with more champagne and strawberries at his place. She shook her head saying it was far too late for such things at two o'clock in the morning. Sitting close to her on the back seat, he tried to kiss her, but she quickly pulled away. *Such a jumpy elk*, he thought, taking her small hand into his. In her presence he felt like an imperfect, clumsy giant. Once they reached her dwelling in a block of multistoreyed buildings, he asked if he could walk her to the door to make sure she was safe. Standing under the streetlight, she found her keys and dismissed his suggestion. He wrote his phone number on a piece of paper and attempted to pass it to her. She didn't take it, justifying herself by saying she didn't have a phone. She suggested he could seek her out between the shelves of the Children's Library on the other side of the city where she worked. In turn he proposed a proper date for the following Saturday, meeting at the entrance of the Central Post Office in full view of the statue of Lenin. Giggling, she replied she was going away to Kaunas for a week. To his delight, she wrote down her girlfriend's phone number in case she wasn't back by then.

Vladas caught himself analysing Snieguolė's character, but even his extensive knowledge of psychology hadn't prepared him for love. He simply couldn't find the right words to describe her. Reason had no control over his budding feelings for this serious young woman. He calculated he was eleven years older than her and hoped the age gap wouldn't be an obstacle. He didn't look his age, receiving compliments at the gym for his perfect form and regularly cutting his hair in the latest fashion. Her unwillingness to be trapped by his charms and decision not to hop into his bed at the first invitation had completely disarmed him. Finding her surrounded by mystery, he had to remind himself to be patient.

The following week, while working on a series of complex forgeries, he struggled to concentrate. He strove to push Snieguolė out of his mind during the day, but at night her childish face, lilting voice and feminine manners made him yearn for her embrace. He fantasised about spending their winter vacations in the Mountains of Caucasus, relaxing together at the top resorts of Yalta, Sochi and Batumi. Lying in bed, he decided Snieguolė was not like an elk but a fragile gazelle, one with ringed horns that she was ready to use. Gentle yet stubborn and ready to defend herself. He couldn't wait for the end of the week, wanting to spoil her with an array of thoroughly planned entertainment as well as a simple gift.

On Saturday Vladas paced up and down in front of the Post Office, but Snieguolė didn't show. He made a call to Kaunas and discovered she had not yet returned having suffered a broken arm. He memorised the address of the hospital she had been admitted to. After leaving the public phone booth, he rested against the red brick building wall, blood rushing to his worried face. That night he caught the train to Kaunas, arriving at the hospital around eleven the next morning, carrying a bunch of tulips in his hands. Snieguolė greeted him with a faint smile, half sitting in her narrow iron bed, dressed in a flimsy, oversized hospital gown. She explained how she had gone to a disco with her friend Aldona and had slipped, falling on the pavement on their way home. Gripped by strong pain during the night, she hadn't actually realised she'd broken the bone. Vladas touched her swollen elbow, surprised it wasn't in plaster. She whispered she didn't have the twenty-five rubles the surgeon wanted for plastering. They both wondered why this wasn't done for free. As they spoke, she seemed in great discomfort, pulling at her brown fringe with anxious fingers. She hadn't been given any painkillers either. He tightened his fists, politely excusing himself.

At the reception he discovered that no doctors were present on the ward on Sundays, except the visiting doctor who popped in and out from another floor. He learned the name of the head nurse and the location of her office. Before charging there, he quickly ran down the stairs to buy some flowers. Then after knocking on the door, presented her with three long-stemmed roses. She found a doctor and finally, Snieguolė, signing her release form, was free to dress and leave.

Meeting her at the reception, Vladas adjusted her slipping floral scarf and buttoned-up her dark coat. He led Snieguolė into the lift by her uninjured elbow, carrying her medication and belongings in his other hand.

"I will take you to Klaipėda," he said. "My surgeon friend can see you as soon as we arrive." Realising there were still eight hours to wait for a train, they caught a taxi to her childhood friend's place. Bubbly, brunette Aldona wore a striped apron while she cooked them some pancakes, followed by cups and cups of tea. Vladas was taken aback that as injured as she was, Snieguolė was trying to joke. She recalled stories from working in the library and spoke of personal belongings being left behind.

"When scarfs, gloves, jumpers and hats get mixed up, parents return demanding their child's specific belongings. I find it funny how they tend to forget that style and colour of clothing is very much the same in every shop! Imagine the confusion in trying to decide what belongs to whom?"

Aldona agreed, putting down her knitting which she'd been occupied with since their arrival. She joked that it would be hard to claim her black scarf if she'd lost it, as most people wore black! By the time they had to go, tall, vivid-eyed Aldona presented Vladas with a completed scarf, expressing her gratitude in caring for her best friend. This touching gesture tightened his throat as he tried to thank her in a harsh, dry voice. He felt honoured to be in the company of these selfless women. He offered his own joke, promising not to let his new scarf join the ranks of lost clothes at the library, and a wave of laughter was shared by the trio.

The taxi driver let them out in the heart of the city. While waiting for their train, Vladas and Snieguolė had coffee in the Old Town of Kaunas. She was amused that the restaurant was named after the flowers he had given her at the hospital—Tulpė. After swallowing some painkillers, she admitted that his tulips, neatly gathered in a ceramic vase on their table had made her ordeal more bearable. Remembering the gift, he had intended to surprise her with on their first date, he reached into his shirt pocket. She smiled, instantly recognising her own silhouette well-executed in a neat ink drawing. She admitted to feeling overwhelmed by his endless attention: taking her around in taxis, paying for her meals, entertaining her and her friends with champagne. She couldn't help wondering why he was so kind, thinking of his gesture of racing to rescue her after her accident as too generous. After all, Kaunas was two hundred kilometres away from Klaipėda! He kept reassuring he was doing all this because he wanted them to be friends. Watching her biting her tiny lips, he wanted to kiss them into submission. Reaching for her fragile fingers, he held them tenderly in his narrow hands. He had weighed up the risks and the benefits before deciding to use this moment to tell her the truth about himself. He admitted being a document forger for one and only reason—to save money for his further studies.

She reacted calmly to his occupation and afterwards she stroked his shaking hands while he struggled to find words to overcome years of self-imposed silence. Throughout his monologue, she nodded her head encouraging him to continue, attentively looking into his dark, glinting eyes. Being able to release his emotions with confession eased his internal suffering, the sense of being trapped by his loneliness. After telling her all he could, he leaned back in his chair, not sure whether to laugh or cry when she asked him to add his silhouette to his gift. He withdrew his magic pen and within moments had added the right side of his face. In exchange, she promised to knit him warm winter socks, and once again they started laughing as they did at Aldona's place. Being surprised by her acceptance, he felt a huge sense of relief.

Vladas and Snieguolė boarded their night train, the joyful prospect of having a sleeper all to themselves dashed when a passing-by attendant warned more passengers were boarding at the next station. While helping Snieguolė to take off her coat, he admired her slim figure clothed in one of her mini dresses. He knelt on both knees to assist in removing her boots. He took the upper bunk but listening to her sounds of her discomfort, the pain of her injury coming into sharper relief at night, soft moans coming from below, he decided to come down. He inhaled the freshness of his tulips, sitting in a glass jar on a small table, then opened the curtain and blankly stared into the night. Holding Snieguolė's cold fingers as she lay in her bunk in complete darkness, he wasn't pleased when the new passengers switched on the light upon entering their sleeper. Once the elderly couple settled down and turned the light off, he shut his eyes. Thinking of Snieguolė's pain had him cursing and swearing to himself as he thought about the corruption endemic in the medical system. The deceiving communism principle to work "to the greatest benefit of the people" echoed in his head until he wanted to scream. *My gazelle, you should've charged at the Kaunas hospital medical staff with your curled horns, knocking them over for not looking after you! I'll look after you and protect you, always,* he promised to himself, unwillingly releasing her fingers and tucking them under the blanket. Once again he climbed up to his bunk, drifting in and out of bad dreams, coming down before dawn had broken. He sat on the edge of her bunk until she opened her eyes. Kissing her on her forehead, he whispered "I love you." Still sleepy, she whispered "Thank you for everything." She kept holding his hand tightly, despite for obvious pain.

At 6 am they made their way to the Klaipėda hospital, a couple hundred metres from the station. Within the hour, the doctor had completed his examination of Snieguolė's X-rays and plastered half of her arm. Vladas took her home by taxi. Her parents, already informed of everything, were most grateful to him. After spotting a telephone sitting on a small stool in the hallway, her father gave him the number.

He placed the number in his coat pocket and began to walk the forty-five-minute journey home. Forty-five minutes—that's how far apart their dwellings were. Forty-five minutes between embraces. Forty-five minutes away from holding her close and never letting go. Moving up the stairs to his flat, he memorised and discarded her number. He wanted to call her the moment he got inside.

*

The door of Vladas' flat was already ajar, two uniformed officers obstructing the entry. It was too late to escape another officer, coming up the stairs, pushing him inside.

"Comrade *Doctor*?" asked an old officer whose grey hair protruded from under his hat adorned with the red star.

"The same," Vladas said. He was certain there was nothing they could pin on him: no traces of documents, stamps, fountain pens, concealing powder, absorbing paper, bottles of inks nor chemical solutions. Having a small storage room five blocks away at his disposal, he never worked from home. He constantly changed his route to the place, travelling at different times and had never noticed anyone following. Unfortunately it hadn't been enough.

Vladas was given half an hour to pack under guarded supervision before they locked and sealed his flat, keeping the key. He was questioned at the police station, his interrogator being amazed by Vladas' ability to forge confidential papers in such quantities. The Special Bodies were proud of finding his secret hideaway with some of the highly sought-after forgeries still in progress. He was told that the KGB never failed. Confused and disorientated after repeated questioning, he stared at the dirty cell ceiling, seeing the faces of his clients in a long row, staring at him, pointing fingers at each other—*it was her, it was him, all of us were responsible for your arrest!* But another voice in his head told him *you are the victim of the system.* As the trusted owner of the room he utilised was at sea, and those, possessing his forgeries, would've been foolish to speak out, there was no other possible explanation! How ironic, he thought, he had almost been freed of his previous life, with a woman he loved. But just as soon as he had found her, his cheating past had finally entrapped him.

The following week, after returning from questioning Vladas sat in his cell, sighing heavily and shaking his head. Apparently, being too valuable to be put behind bars again, he'd be relocated to Novosibirsk—a far-reaching dot on the map of the Soviet Union. He would be there on assignment to continue with his current line of work. He had walked on hot coals covered by the red flag, decorated with hammer and sickle, and finally had burned his feet. Before his departure to the Siberian town, some four thousand five hundred kilometres from Klaipėda, Vladas wished to write a private letter. A letter to Snieguolė. A letter of regret of not being able to play her his best-loved Chopin to properly express his emotions. They'd allowed him to write his letter, surely sharing it around afterwards, mocking his graceful gazelle, laughing their heads off, and once everybody read it, hiding it away. But not before copying it. Not before creating a fresh, Snieguolė's file and putting a copy of his letter there. Not before marking the original letter as "supplementary material" and placing it into his file.

The police vehicle arrived at the train station, two accompanying officers boarding the train from Klaipėda to Vilnius with him. As the train began to move, Vladas' narrowed his eyes, following the rows and rows of identical red brick blocks of flats. He observed weary passengers trying to board overcrowded Ikarus, slipping and sliding in the late autumn mud. Curling his tingling lips, biting down to stop the tears, he focused on memorising the dark streets and alleys of his hometown. He imagined a policeman he'd done a favour for once, posting a letter on his behalf. He imagined Snieguolė opening and reading his letter. He imagined her holding it with both hands close to her wide eyes, filled with tears. He imagined her admiring his neat handwriting, then finding and kissing the drawing of their silhouettes. He imagined her gracefully packing her belongings, including hand-knitted winter socks for him, and following him in a few months. He imagined performing Chopin, playing to a concert hall on a grand piano.

Christmas Eve with Friends

When Lolita invited me to celebrate Kūčios—Christmas Eve 1982, I was honestly surprised. I asked her how one celebrates it. Offering no explanation—"You'll see, Vile!"—she assured me that I'd enjoy it. As I walked home that evening the snowflakes gently circled above my head, landing on my face and covering my handbag and my winter coat.

At 8 pm on the 24th of December, I approached a two-storey weatherboard house, containing six flats. The staircase leading to Lolita's flat was decorated with origami. In the corner of the lounge room a fir tree stood decorated with angel figure shapes. There were round balls and colourful lollies dangling on pieces of string, and tiny pieces of cotton fluff imitating the snow drops. I was introduced to Dainora, Mindaugas, Nijolė and Liuda, chatting near the tree. Lolita's mother Dana wore a black and white dress and welcomed us to the table. The herring with beetroot, herring with onions and eggs, potato salad, grated carrots in oil, bean salad, apple-cinnamon salad, and a reddish-brown, white-stemmed boletus mushrooms with fried onions released a pleasant aroma, making me hungry. As we complimented on every dish for its presentation, Lolita said they also made šližikai—croutons—by sizing and baking plain flour dough bits, and adding water and poppy seeds.

Arriving guests filled all twelve seats. How extraordinary, I thought, after being told that we'd be having exactly twelve dishes. And the dishes kept coming: poppy seed milk—sort of an eggnog—for dipping the šližikai in, kisielius drink made from frozen cranberries, strained and thickened with starch, with added sugar. Waffles and an apple pie completed the dishes. I felt embarrassed when Lolita's mother crossed herself but seeing everybody doing it I joined in, mumbling under my breath, not knowing the words of the prayer. We then shared the blessed wafer, wishing each other a good year. Before starting our meal we had to reach under the tablecloth and find a dried rye straw. While searching for the straw, I noticed that the table was improvised from a long wooden board with homemade frames— two on each end of the table and one in the middle where I sat, bracing its sides with my slightly bowed legs. My straw was the longest one, which meant I'd live to a very old age.

The lounge room was quite spacious, fitting all of us, and there was still room for a shabby sofa and a television set. The discoloured drapes and dim lighting made the room darker. Three people were pictured in a black and white photo hanging above the sofa, Lolita pointing to her parents and herself as a baby. Somehow the trio looked tense. The ordinary crockery on the table and bare surroundings didn't match the culinary spread. When I asked Lolita how they could afford such an extravagant meal, she replied that she and her mother prepared for the occasion by gathering and freezing berries and mushrooms, by helping themselves to vegetables at the collective fields where Dana worked, and by stocking up with hard-to-get items such as green peas and mayonnaise during the year. "There is no shortage of flour, so šližikai and cakes are easy to make!" We both agreed that making pancakes for unexpected guests was one of the greatest ideas—flour, egg, pinch of salt and water—how easy was that?

"Kūčios has always been celebrated in our family," she said, moving away from me to chat with other guests.

I joined my friends Jolanta, Nora and Ignas, engaged in discussing Dostoevsky's *The Idiot*. The book portrayed the nineteenth century Russian Count Myshkin—a naïve, compassionate, innocent and kind noble. After spending four years in Switzerland, he returned to his homeland but continued to dress and act as a foreigner—becoming an "idiot"—the outcast of society.

"I'm sure at this very moment we would be viewed as idiots by Moscow but hopefully they won't find us out!" Dana said, passing us on her way to the kitchen.

"Ah, it would be nice to go to Switzerland, or anywhere to the West," Ignas remarked, and we echoed his words.

"I suppose I am lucky my husband is at sea," said Nora. "At least he brings me French perfume, coffee, clothing and earns reasonable wages." She was wearing Wrangler jeans and a bright purple jumper with matching earrings. Strolling through the main street of Klaipėda with her, I noticed how her fashionable look always attracted male attention. Tonight she shone as a distant star. In comparison, the rest of us were ordinarily dressed—men in worn-out suits, and women in black dresses or plain tops and skirts. My dress was decorated with metal studs.

After a couple of drinks, everybody became more talkative, Ignas getting into the spirit of telling jokes. Jokes about Soviet Union leaders were well received. We heard how one day Nikita Khrushchev was greeted by the morning sun with "Good morning, Comrade Khrushchev!" When the evening approached and the sun didn't say anything, he asked "Sun, why did you not greet me in the evening?" The sun replied "Ha, I'm in the West now and you cannot reach me!"

Conversation returned to the subject of travelling outside the Soviet Union. Soviet citizens who were allowed to go abroad for a visit were cautiously screened. The tourist delegations visiting Czechoslovakia, Hungary or East Germany were organised by Inturist Sputnik. Each group of Soviet tourists carried identical Sputnik bags which alerted the shopkeepers of their approach. Having visited Germany earlier in the year, I shared my experiences. I recalled how fourteen out of fifty performers were selected to go there as part of a song and dance group called Disvytis. We made the one-thousand-kilometre journey by train. Oh, how frightened we were when the train was stopped in the middle of the night, so our passports could be checked! When Russian officials randomly opened our bags, I was sick with worry of being caught with extra foreign currency sown in a seam of my national dress.

"How much did you have?" Nora asked.

"One hundred Deutsche marks."

"And how long did you stay in Germany?"

"Ten days. The money I had was just enough to buy some clothes and presents but those who had fifty marks for spending felt greatly disadvantaged."

"What happened on the train? Did they find your money?" everybody wanted to know.

"No. They didn't touch my bag. I sat quietly, reading my book, shivering all over inside. After searching through other luggage and not finding anything suspicious, the soldiers left our sleeper."

"You were lucky," said Jolanta. "But it seems the danger was real."

"Yes, it definitely was!" I replied. "Finally, after our train was separated in half, we were out of Lithuania. Our group entertained residents of a nursing home in East Berlin; the concert was held in a garden setting. All those old people were sitting in wheelchairs … it really surprised me. Over here we're supposed to believe Soviet citizens are so strong. Why don't we ever see disabled people? They must exist!"

"They simply don't go out," Nijolė said.

"That's right," said Nora, telling us how three years ago her uncle lost both his legs in a car accident. "Since then, his disability prevents him from leaving his apartment. It's on the third floor, and there's no lift."

"How does he manage?" Ignas asked.

"His sister moved in with him to help out."

"My father's parents are very old. They live in a government dwelling, walking with each other's help," Liuda said. "They don't want to go to a nursing home where they will be separated against their will. There, they'd be forced to share accommodation with nine other patients of their own sex."

We agreed that to leave the elderly to die in the nursing home would be a disgrace in the eyes of neighbours and family members. Somehow the clinking of our glassed sounded subdued. I continued to share how after a few concerts around Berlin, we were taken to the heart of the city by bus. How, while window shopping, my friend Aurelija and I were left behind, entering a clothing department store and observing salespeople pulling items from under the counter. That confirmed what we had already heard from others—the Soviet tourists were not welcomed here! As soon as they walked towards the shops, the marked down items were out of site. We hid our Sputnik bags in our handbags before entering and walked along the rows of clothing, speaking among ourselves in Lithuanian. Having never heard of Lithuania, the salespersons gave us a welcoming reception, convinced we were from Sweden.

"That's nice!" said Jolanta.

"Yes. It was. With our basic German skills, we were unable to explain who we really were. So, we smiled instead, pleased at being taken for Swedes. They showed us reasonably priced items, encouraging us to try them on. We thought we were dreaming. I purchased a cherry colour jumper and Aurelija a pink skirt." Listening to my story, my friends couldn't agree more with the idea that citizens of Soviet nations should have their own identity in the West!

Secretly celebrating Christmas Eve at Lolita's place, we wondered why only non-religious celebrations such as New Year's Eve were greatly encouraged. There was plenty of alcohol in shops and spectacular fireworks were anticipated in each City Square where people gathered with Soviet champagne. At the stroke of midnight they collectively popped the corks, drinking around a central fir tree decorated with flickering lights. The New Year's Eve concert on television, called Novogodnij Ogoniok, provided great entertainment featuring prominent Russian singer Alla Pugacheva. She had frizzy hair and a gap between her front teeth. Iosif Kobzon with a stiff, wrinkle-free face loudly projected Soviet citizen love for the motherland.

Glancing around Lolita's lounge room, I spotted Sigis and Roma. Occasionally I saw them in a café called Pupelė, not far from Klaipėda City Market. The sign above the door, complemented by a drawing of a bean, corresponded with the meaning of the place. I would catch Sigis looking me up and down and I would feel angered by his unfairness to Roma. Our group consisted of an accountant Nora, painter Jolanta, teacher Lolita, and me—a swimming instructor. We ordered tea and coffee and shared our homemade sweets which made each gathering extra special. During the week, Ignas, the only man in our female company, unloaded cargo at the port of Klaipėda. He'd been studying off campus at Vilnius University, but even when tired or overworked he'd never miss our conversations. Ignas' favourite jokes were invented while watching the Soviet movie "Seventeen Moments of Spring", based on the novel by Yulian Semyonov. A fictional Russian spy called Stierlitz, played by Vyacheslav Tikhonov, infiltrates into the Nazi Germany intelligence services and belittles the Germans. Ignas chose to tell jokes about Stierlitz in Russian as the punch line didn't make sense in Lithuanian. He used a high-pitched voice to imitate a German officer's words, then playing Stierlitz with his droll, smart replies. Ignas, like the Stierlitz character, had straight dark hair and broad shoulders. He was tall and masculine with intense eyes, making us sigh as he spoke—*ahh, ohh, you say it so persuasively!* Once he told us about a judge walking out of his chambers laughing aloud. When his colleague approached him and asked why he was laughing, the judge replied:

"I just heard the funniest joke in the world!"

"Well, go ahead, tell me!" said the other judge.

"But I can't. I just gave a Soviet citizen ten years for it!"

We discussed the differences between a capitalist and a Marxist fairytale. This time, Lolita had an answer. "The capitalist fairytale starts with the words 'Once upon a time there was ....' but the Marxist fairytale begins with 'Someday there will be ....'"

We cursed the compulsory Marxism-Leninism subject taught at school and tertiary institutions.

*

Close to midnight we heard a loud knock on Lolita's flat door, and Lolita welcomed Santa up the stairs soon afterwards. She gathered us around the Christmas tree and seated him in the middle. Each of us had to entertain him. Some of us acted like children, circling around Santa's chair, some recited common childhood poems in adult voices and others told jokes with straight faces, making them even funnier. A popular joke, retold by Sigis, sounded very fitting on this particular evening.

"The Soviet man asks his neighbour, 'Why is our government not in a hurry to land our men on the moon?' The neighbour replies 'Because they may refuse to return!'"

Lolita shared her joke.

"The Soviet worker asks his supervisor, 'Is it true that under communism we will order food over the phone?' 'Definitely! And they will deliver it over TV.'"

Accompanied by Ignas on guitar, I sang about a crocodile falling in love with a swan. Sigis' cheering and clapping seemed the loudest, making me blush. Santa gave us small gifts. I couldn't recall ever having so much fun. But there was more! We were asked to take our seats at the table, and the light went off. In the presence of candles Lolita scrunched a newspaper page and lit it on a porcelain plate. We watched the crumbling shadows of the burning paper on the wall. The paper curled and twisted into the shape of a tall tower, Dana explaining that it meant Lolita would get promoted at work. We raised our thumbs up. Sigis' paper formed a house—he'll move into his own dwelling. We clapped. The remains of Jolanta's paper shaped into a cot—she'll have a baby soon. What an exciting prospect. Ignas' paper folded into a thick book—he'll be finally completing his psychology course. Remains of mine burned into a ring, and Dana predicted my forthcoming marriage. Taken aback, I watched the guests cheering me on. I looked at Ignas but couldn't catch his attention. Nora's paper folded into a boat, and we hoped her husband would be back from Spain for New Year. When Dana's paper turned into a coffin, she didn't utter a word until Lolita assured her it was a treasure box. We all agreed, making her relax.

There were no facilities inside the dwelling and after midnight we lined up at the creaking toilet door outside. There was quite a queue— Lolita's neighbours from other flats were before us, shining their torches around. We also brought torches because the toilet had no lights, and we hated sitting on the awkward hole. To pass the time we made snowballs and threw them at each other. Moving was the only way not to freeze in -29°C. Nijolė suggested that on returning to our dwellings we could put our family members' shoes into one bag, and then take them out one by one and line them up towards the front door. The person whose shoe ended up closest to the door would leave the household first. We were greatly intrigued by such a spell as most of us couldn't wait to start independent life! Jolanta told us that by writing the names of possible suitors on pieces of paper, folding and placing them under our pillows, we'd definitely find out the name of a future husband. All we needed to do was to select and unfold one of the pieces in the morning! As the toilet queue was hardly moving, we followed Lolita to the next house with a low fence. She squatted down and reached her arm across the low fence palings, asking us to count them. It was an uneven number, meaning she wouldn't marry next year. After managing to reach my arm across eight palings with the tips of my gloved fingers, a warm tingling sensation surged through my body. I took my woollen hat off and joyfully threw it into the air, feeling my golden curls getting damp in the snowfall.

Back inside, I caught up with Lolita in the kitchen. We commented on each other's fresh rosy faces, and sat down. I asked her why she was given such an unusual name. Dana, lighting the stove, explained how she read Nabokov's *Lolita* during her pregnancy. Liking the sound of the name, she gave it to her daughter.

"Does the Lolita in the book resemble your daughter?"

"No. My Lolita is shy, and a well-disciplined twenty-three-year-old teacher. She has no similarities with the adolescent girl whatsoever. Though I found the name Lo-li-ta soothing like a lullaby!"

I watched Lolita glancing at her mother and back at the newspaper she was flicking through with her thin fingers, before rolling her eyes at me. I wondered what Nabokov's heroine was like, regretting that I'd never come across his writing. Lolita kept blowing her long, fair fringe from her Madonna-like face. I didn't think she was shy and well-disciplined. On the contrary, she was always up to mischief. Once, she came to our café dressed as a gypsy, wearing some ragged clothes. Wanting to purchase a book, she stood near the book shop begging for money until she was chased away by a real gypsy called Rožė who lived in a derelict dwelling in one of the alleys of the main market. What would Lolita's mother have said to that if she knew? The queue outside the famous book shop at the entry to the market was always enormous. People were very keen readers of translated western or new Soviet literature, grabbing three to four books at one time. I would sacrifice food money for a good book, purchasing works by Balzac, Dumas, Dostoyevsky, Tolstoy and Baltušis. For us, sitting in the café with one beverage each for hours was an escape from the boring offerings of television, preferring to discuss new book releases, fresh theatre and opera productions over the regular dull offerings of German-Russian war movies.

Dana poured some tea into three cups. I spotted her husband's photo on the fridge with a black piece of ribbon over the frame.

"What happened to him?" I asked.

She spoke of her beloved Feliksas, a twenty-seven-year-old geography teacher who was arrested by KGB officials for keeping the *Catholic Chronicle* at home.

"Was he punished for reading the *Chronicle*?"

"Worse. He was caught for possessing and disseminating it among the believers."

"How could they take him away from you and Lolita?"

"They showed no mercy! Lolita was six months old then. I later learned how they tortured him and broke his fingers. They said they did it to deter him from writing his anti-Soviet rubbish."

"How could they?!"

"Well. Stalin and his followers had no feelings. He didn't hesitate to dispose of his own family members for non-compliance to his rule! My poor Feliksas died in Yakutsk Labour Camp. A man who survived deportation told me how he helped to bury him, some four hundred and fifty kilometres south of the Arctic Circle. The burial was carried out by taking the body outside the living quarters and covering it with snow—the ice was too thick to be broken. There is no grave. We didn't even have a chance to say goodbye," Dana said, her trembling voice drowning in the sounds of music, dance and laughter coming from the lounge room. She sighed before starting to slice her new bake. She gave each of us a sliver to try, and we approved of her moist, mouth-watering orange cake. Afterwards she pinched her cheeks with her chubby fingers, straightened her posture and carried the cake to the guests.

"My maternal grandfather vanished in the sixties, I was told," I said to Lolita.

"Maybe he too died somewhere in Siberia," she said, pulling her tight skirt down on our way to the lounge room. The word *died, died, died* stabbed my heart, the blood rushing to my throbbing temples. I thought she was right. He must have died. My parents would've told me if he was still alive. They talked little about the past, never mentioning his name.

*

At the start of the New Year I was browsing through my favourite book shop near the entry to the Central Market, surrounded by a few familiar faces. I noticed Ignas in the poetry section and made my way there. I took a random book from the display and pretended to read Brodsky's verses, but instead listened to Ignas' conversation with another person. She wore a black coat with a tight belt, accentuating her waist. I wondered why she was dressed in a man's coat before realising "she" was a male. Standing right behind Ignas, I watched him turning the pages of a book, deeply engaged in conversation with the younger man who had smooth, translucent skin and spoke quietly, awkwardly touching a brim of his hat.

"I want to manicure your fingernails tonight. Your toenails too," said Ignas.

"Sure, *my dearest*. Cannot wait for it," the man replied, and I nearly dropped Brodsky on the floor, before quickly leaving the shop. I didn't understand what it meant for two men to be talking that way, and never suspected Ignas of having a secret life. He used to tell me how he enjoyed sinking his fingers into my hair, how he loved my pining eyes that reminded him of the stormy sea, how he was besotted with my sweet lips while we kissed, stretched on the white sand of Smiltynė beach.

My icy tears seemed to freeze on my cheeks. It started snowing and I walked home on a thickening carpet of whiteness. Leaving my footprints behind, I kept turning around to wonder why they were covered so fast, as if the evidence of my daily existence was swept into the depths of the frozen earth. The passers-by were as much preoccupied with their thoughts as I was. For me, the year of the water pig was not fulfilling my dreams. I wished to love and be loved, but with Ignas out of the question, there was little hope. Women in their late twenties were called spinsters and their prospect of marrying was hardly realistic. Most available men got married after high school, and some of those who stayed free conducted various relationships at the same time. To get involved with a man who left his wife for another woman was a bad omen, as the folk saying went—"If he left his wife, he will leave his girlfriend too!" But another saying went "Ah, if only men of Lithuania weren't so attractive!"

The following morning, I threw away the tiny pieces of paper tucked under my pillow and ripped the one sitting on the bedside drawer with the name Ignas written on it. I went to meet my friends at our café, wondering whether he was game enough to show us his male friend. I met Rožė on my way, a familiar gypsy who grabbed my right hand to read my palm.

"No love lost with the one you thought was for you! There is another who is in love with you. Don't ignore his feelings!" she said, stretching her gloved hand in front of me.

I laughed, wished her happy New Year and gave her two rubles, quickly escaping her heavy presence. Sometime back another gypsy had lured the whole monthly stipend of forty rubles from Nora, and I didn't want to be caught. As I continued on my way, I slowed down, taken aback by Rožė's singing:

> Aina, raina, aina, raina, ainanai,
> Aina, raina, aina, raina, ainanai,
> Kur aš dėsiuos pasiklydus be namų,
> Svetimoj šaly tarp žmonių svetimų?

The sad melody reflected on a story, told by my friend Jolanta. Her relatives had escaped to Germany in 1944 and became Displaced Persons. After five years of living in the DP camps, they were resettled in Australia.

There they embraced their new life, built a house, purchased a car, had plenty to eat—money literally falling off their apple tree! But for some reason they didn't feel that they belonged.

> *Where would I be without a home,*
> *Surrounded by the foreign land and people?*

Rožė's words sounded so touching. I ran back, opened my purse and gave her my last ten rubles, wishing her to one day find her true home. She didn't say anything but her face lit up as she hurriedly hid the banknote in the folds of her long skirt.

With my loose change I ordered a cup of coffee, a more-costly drink for the occasion of the New Year at Café Pupelė. I wondered why being wealthy didn't make people happy, recalling the words of a Russian song proclaiming that "It's much better to have one hundred friends than one hundred rubles!" During my travels around the Soviet Union, even strangers were willing to help and share their last resources. We didn't hesitate to borrow salt, sugar, bread or flour from our neighbours, and vice versa. Communal sharing made us laugh at ourselves, living with constant shortages. I secretly wished to visit Finland or Norway but had my doubts it would ever happen. Recently learning that there was a Soviet informer among us during our German trip made me feel uneasy. Now each of the fourteen performers had a file to their name, describing their activities throughout the journey. My face burned thinking about telling others of the forbidden Deutsche marks, safely hidden in my skirt; of freely exchanging Soviet jokes; and of not complying with the curfew to return to the hotel before 10 pm! If the KGB had my file, what hope did I have to travel again? As for my friend Jolanta, she had a chance to join her relatives in Australia one day. She confided in me that given the opportunity to visit, she would never return.

Absorbed in my thoughts, I didn't realise Sigis, whom I'd met here on many occasions and seen at the Kūčios celebrations with Roma, was standing in front of me. He asked if he could join me and I nodded, watching him open his carrying bag and take out a small hyacinth.

"It's for you, Vile," he said, placing the pot on the table.

"But my birthday is in July," I said, hoping that in standing so close to me he was not hearing my heart beating loud and fast. "How about your girlfriend? Will you be also seeing her today?"

"I'll always be seeing Roma as she is my cousin."

Looking into his honest face, I relaxed, but not for long. Remembering that my friends would be entering the café at any moment now, I turned my worried face towards the front door.

"I begged them not to disturb us today," Sigis said, taking my fingers into his big warm hands. He admitted how much he'd wanted to do this since he first saw me here two years ago. We ordered lunch and watched the snowflakes sticking to the windows, wanting to wish us happiness.

Slip Up

How could I tell my wife about my condition? Vytas asked himself, closing the heavy door of the Skin and Venereal Disease Clinic behind him. He walked home slowly. Though the air was fresh with spring, he felt nauseated. "*Gonorrhoea, gonorrhoea, gonorrhoea* is the name of my new existence," he whispered to the birds chirping in the oak trees above. He looked at the muddy sky with patches of dark clouds gathering and his spirits sank. He took a seat on a nearby bench, stretched his long legs, crossed his ankles and placed his hands in his coat pockets. *I am not worth even the tiniest toe of my dear Rasa. How could I have been tempted to slip up? True, I have a little girl and a gorgeous wife, but in the past eight months, since Angelė was born, Rasa only lives for her.* He reflected on how it had come to this. He thought about how he wanted more attention, how he found he couldn't resist the charms of his fellow student. *This all happened because I couldn't resist Violeta. I'm so weak! I should have just written my part of the article like the other students and just gone home. But I chose to stay at her flat. It was going so well before I decided to have a drink with her.* He shook his head recalling how Violeta threw him out after hearing him screaming Rasa, Rasa, Rasa during the drunken sexual encounter.

Vytas watched the threatening clouds hanging over him. He was not sure whether he should return home, approach Rasa, tell her the truth or should go to his parents' place until his condition goes away? *Either way, what should I tell Rasa? What should I tell my mother?* He could just imagine her condemning him for marrying at eighteen, and starting university in the same year. *At least, living in Kaunas helps. Our flat—Rasa's flat—inherited from her grandmother, is so close to my Medical Institute. I wish I wasn't studying medicine as it makes me cringe to think how much I overstepped my professional boundaries.* The doctor at the Skin and Venereal Disease Clinic assured him that gonorrhoea was not a permanent condition. "It is curable with strong medication," he said. He had purchased some for Rasa as well, conscious he had infected her after his encounter with Violeta. But how could he tell her? He practised his lines aloud.

"Good evening, my sweetheart. I brought some pills for you to swallow to punish you for my unfaithfulness, but don't worry, you should be fine in a week or so."

While sitting on the cold bench, he found a piece of paper in his coat pocket and began scribbling Rasa's name on the page. He closed his tired eyes and imagined the passers-by with angry looks, shaking their heads and pointing their fingers at him. His body shivered and teeth shattered from an inner chill, spreading from his neck to his toes. He moved his auburn fringe away to check his forehead, making sure that while he was day-dreaming no stranger attached a label with the word *gonorrhoea* written on it. He felt like an absolute bastard. Heavy thoughts made his glistening eyes water. He kept moving his pen between his shaking fingers, trying to concentrate on what to write.

*

As he approached home, he saw Rasa strolling with a pram. Her short, chocolate-brown hair shone and her face was glowing. She looked comfortable in her heels, the colour matching her dark coat. Her scarf was caught in the wind, partially covering her round face. He wished she wouldn't see him but she did, rushing towards him for a kiss. He stopped her from touching him, making her trustful eyes squint. Biting her lips, she asked him what was wrong. Forcing a tiny smile, he suggested they talk at home. He helped Rasa to carry the pram with a sleeping Angelė to their second floor flat.

While Rasa was feeding her, Vytas packed his study books and some clothes. Rasa heard the front door closing and hurried to the kitchen window. She was taken aback to see straight-postured Vytas transformed, hunched and unsteady as he walked away with his carrying bag. She found his set of flat keys sitting on a table with a note that she read rapidly, her chest tightening. It contained an instruction on how to cure gonorrhoea, followed by his confession of recently contracting it. She thought it was out of character, especially his unconvincing explanation of being too drunk to remember how it happened. Vytas hardly drank!

It would be too embarrassing for you to seek help at the Skin and Venereal Disease Clinic I visited today. I asked the doctor to prescribe you the required medication, and you should be fine after taking it for ten days. Please go and see doctor Juozas Skvernelis afterwards. He knows our situation.

No *I love you*, no *goodbye*—Rasa couldn't imagine a worse thing her high school sweetheart could've done to her! Living in the same neighbourhood, they had been inseparable since grade one and, in grade ten, promised each other to always be together. She was brilliant in mathematics and he was good in biology, often helping one another to study. Rasa's parents were impressed with Vytas' manners, being not in the least surprised when he came to propose to her in front of them. They got married after the last school bell rang in May 1980.

They should have been having their supper together now. Instead, Rasa was reading instructions on how to take the necessary medication. She didn't have any of the symptoms listed there. She had no burning sensation while urinating and no yellowish discharge from her vagina. She ran to her neighbour Brigita, living two flights of stairs above, and told her what happened. Brigita also had a baby and kindly agreed to share her milk until Rasa finished her course of medication. She was not going to risk passing the infection to her little one.

*

Two weeks later, Rasa visited doctor Skvernelis at the Skin and Venereal Disease Clinic. He examined her and ran some tests. It took three more agonising days waiting for the results to discover she was fine. One evening Vytas turned up at the door. After the doorbell rang, she saw him via the looking glass but didn't let him in, asking him to wait for her under their balcony. She had been warily preparing for this very moment and once she found him standing there she started throwing his shirts, pants, and underwear at him. Defending himself with his outstretched hands, he was still hit with his own shoe on the side of his head. They didn't say anything to each other but their tense faces and silent glances were more potent than shouting and screaming. Lastly, Vytas' suitcase was dropped in front of his feet. He gathered his belongings and stuffed them inside. He looked up before leaving, disgusted by the lifting corners of curtains and drapes in the adjourning flats. His ears tuned to the loud music and angry conversations coming from the open windows of the multistorey building. Rasa's window was closed.

He went to Violeta's place and abused her for passing gonorrhoea to him, telling her to fix herself up before she infected someone else. He discovered she had already taken precautions. Following a few more angry exchanges, they embraced, and then sat in the presence of a burning candle before falling asleep in each other's arms.

*

In the morning Rasa took Angelė to the kindergarten and went to work at a book shop in the heart of Laisvės alėja. The famous stretch of the so-called Alley of Freedom was crowded with shops, cafes and people. After having her lunch at the canteen, she enjoyed strolling past the Music Theatre and window shopping. On the morning she initiated her divorce proceedings in court, she walked the main pedestrian street leading to the famous church Soboras. The massive columns and round domes stretched a good fifty metres high and, standing before them, she felt tiny and vulnerable. She had heard people whispering at her book shop that Soboras was closed during the First World War. It reopened in 1919 without the church bells. Apparently, the Germans found them in one of the five domes, cut them down and transported them to their country. After that, a Lithuanian garrison occupied the building until 1939, keeping ammunition there and greatly damaging the interior. No wonder the government debated as to whether they should demolish it. Luckily the gigantic Soboras survived and was reorganised into an art gallery, attracting locals and tourists alike.

Rasa watched as a group of Russians were guided through the heavy wooden door inside the Roman-Byzantine style building. She loved coming here and spending time among the majestic paintings. The voices of the tourists echoed off the main dome, bouncing around like her thoughts. She could've stayed with Vytas. She didn't have to let him go, but she was brought up with high expectations of herself and others. If Vytas could choose Violeta over her, he had little or no respect for women. "I will survive," she said firmly, not worried that she was overheard by passing strangers.

Divorce proceedings were painless and quick. Rasa and Vytas were separated on the grounds of his extra marital affair. He had no child visitation rights, deemed unfit to be a father. The judge decreed that he did not have the morals of an upstanding Soviet citizen, and he walked out of court in great distress.

*

Vytas was strolling along the Laisvės alėja pedestrian strip, noticing Rasa making her way to the fountain. Once she sat near the water he joined her, smiling at her surprised face. They looked at each other for a long time without speaking. He finally tore himself away from her anguished face. He opened his briefcase and showed her his new article, published in a health magazine. "Prevention of Venereal Diseases" was a good name for an article, she thought. He asked her if she wanted a copy and she shook her head.

"I gather you moved from working on children's illness to adult diseases."

"Yes, given personal experience …"

"We both learned so much in the past two years."

"What about us, Rasa? Did you forgive me?"

"There is nothing to forgive. Yes, we spent years together, but then we took different paths and made separate journeys."

"Are you happy?"

"Yes, and you?"

"I suppose so. Violeta is a good woman. She cares about me very much."

Do you care about her? Rasa wanted to ask but simply sat, watching the streams of water rising up and falling down with force. Children were laughing and playing with bubbles. Tiny, medium and huge bubbles, detaching themselves from the waterfall, floated towards the edges, multiplying, rolling, bursting, and eventually turning into the creamy mash. She saw the fountain as a symbol of the rises and falls of her life, Vytas' life, and Angelė's life. The bursting bubbles reminded her of troubles she faced with him. The noise of cascading water made her aware of dissolving time. At this very moment she yearned to rewind the clock.

"The fountain reminds me of the cycle of life. Don't you agree?" she asked.

Lost in his thoughts, Vytas didn't hear the question, and said, "Violeta is working tonight. Just as well, otherwise I may not have met you."

Rasa wanted to put her head on his shoulder and to gently stroke his thick hair, to look into his burning eyes and tell him how much she'd suffered since that awful night when the poisonous news entered their dwelling.

"How is Angelė?" Where is she?" asked Vytas, his body inching toward her.

"At her grandmother's."

He wanted to take her in his arms and kiss her rosy lips, and to tell her how much he missed her. Most importantly, how much he missed his little girl.

"She is nearly three now."

"I know. I have been paying her maintenance," he smiled. "Can I come and visit you sometime?"

"You are always welcome," she said, trying to hold her voice steady.

"How do you manage?"

"Our next-door neighbour helps me carry any heavy shopping to the flat, fixes leaking taps and does other jobs I cannot do."

Vytas wanted to scream—*But I can!*—his body stiff with the fear of losing her again. They parted by hardly touching each other's fingertips.

Watching her elegant figure and listening to the fading sound of her black stilettoes, he wanted to run after her, to take her in his arms, and to propose marriage again.

Yuri Gagarin and a New Land

Lina's childhood wasn't the one she wanted to have. Born in Soviet Lithuania in 1951, she had moved to the Russian town of Taganrog in 1956 with her family. Her father Zigmas, an ambulance driver, had decided to seek greater opportunities in Russia and secured his job before their arrival. Her mother Regina was a cook and easily found a job at a local restaurant. Taganrog was a heavily industrialised town with expanding aerospace, machine-building, engineering and military chemical factories. There were processors and traders of timber, iron and metal. Most importantly, Taganrog was one of the major ports of the Sea of Azov—the extension of the Black Sea—some one thousand kilometres from the city. Living in shared accommodation with three other families, Lina's family soon realised that people lived better back in Lithuania. With all industry in a state of development, including food, there was little or no money for essentials. Luckily, Lina's mother regularly brought leftovers from the restaurant to supplement their meals.

Lina was five years old when they moved. The following year her brother Saulius was born. He was taken to a crèche and she attended kindergarten while their parents worked extended hours and took them home on weekends. She acted, sang and danced in her new Russian language. Every morning, lined up across the room, children were given a tablespoon of whale oil. She hated the taste and scrunched her face after receiving the dose. Others did the same. Their teacher told them that fish oil was good for bones, and strong bones made them fit. Daily exercises involved stretching, running, jumping, gymnastics and playing with a ball throughout the day. "Only strong and healthy children can build communism," they were reminded over and over again. Lina asked her mother what it meant, but she just smiled and sent her away to play with her rag doll.

Ever since she had started school, Lina wanted to play the piano. She passed musical memory, rhythm and singing tests and was accepted into the piano class. As they didn't have a piano at home, she practised at school. Her mother picked her up after each lesson, forty-five minutes, twice a week. The teacher approved of Lina's longish fingers, hoping she'd become a pianist. But it was never meant to be. Her mother, adjusting her golden hair, shed some tears and told the teacher how she wanted to be a pianist herself but had not had the opportunity. Her fingers were short and stubby, with little cuts and burn marks from cooking.

From the age of eight, Lina didn't see her father much as he was on lengthy assignments, travelling as far as Karelia. When she did see him, he couldn't stand still and was fidgety with his hands. He practiced boxing and, while away, kept his boxing gloves under his bed. One night, knowing he was returning from Rostov, Lina's mother hid in the wardrobe. Oh, how she wanted to leave him for good one day! She even packed her suitcase and squeezed it between her legs, asking Lina to close the door from the outside. Zigmas entered the room with a friend. Lina announced that she didn't know where her mother was, even before being asked. The men sat at the table, opening a bottle of vodka. After gulping clear liquid, sniffing and then sharing pickled cucumber, Zigmas said "Oh, you ugly toad!" The other man added "G-o-o-d toad!"

Lina asked them why they called the vodka a toad. "It's only an expression," the guest said. She was curious why tears were coming from their eyes, and they responded by saying their drink was so tasty it caused them to cry of happiness. The men exchanged anecdotes and continued drinking. Saulius woke up and crawled under the table to play with his father's keys.

Wearing red lipstick and thick make-up, holding a suitcase in her hand, Regina eventually stepped out into the room in her high stilettos.

"It's rather hot tonight," she said, fanning herself with one hand, lightly twisting her ankle on the way to the kitchen. The men followed her with their mouths ajar before bursting into laughter. Returning to the table with a couple of slices of bread, it was clear Regina didn't think it was funny. With her cheeks blushing and her lined eyes focusing above Lina's head, she looked embarrassed. The men banged the table with their fists, glasses rattling and moving about. Saulius started crying.

When the visitor left, Lina's parents raised their voices. She was told to go outside. Through the shadows of the surrounding buildings, frightened and upset, she ran to the playground. She spotted her friends Julija and Margarita near the swings, and joined them. When Lina told them what happened, Margarita admitted to being outside for the same reason. Julija said her mother worked night shift and she could stay out as long as she wished.

The following morning Lina noticed her mother's bruised eye. She met her father's angry glance with fear and swallowed her two thinly buttered pieces of bread as soon as she could, leaving the table.

*

Lina was ten years old when the Soviet citizen Yuri Gagarin became the first man to travel to space. She remembered the citizens of Taganrog spilling onto the streets, dancing, cheering and hugging strangers. That day, her favourite sparkling mineral water with cherry syrup was available for free—one glass per person from a huge wooden barrel. She wondered why someone going to space made people cry and sing at the same time. Some years later, reading her deceased mother's diary, she hungrily followed her neat and clear handwriting, revealing so much about this memorable day.

> People glued to the radios or, those that had them, black and
> white television sets, listening for the unfolding events. The
> clear strong voice of the male reporter who kept repeating
> how on April 12, 1961, the first Russian cosmonaut travelled

to space. Loud speakers installed all over the town announced how he launched into orbit on the Vostok 3KA-3 spacecraft.

The newspaper cuttings, glued to the diary pages, revealed to Lina how the twenty-seven-year old Senior Lieutenant was chosen out of two hundred cosmonaut candidates to explore space. Her mother noted:

> So young, practically a child. Hope he can handle the pressure of fame. One out of so many—great achievement in itself.

Lina found another article, reading it with interest.

> The spacecraft reached the maximum height of three hundred and twenty-seven kilometres, staying in space for one hundred and eight minutes. By entering space, Yuri Gagarin became the first man to leave Earth's orbit and to circle once around the world!

The man must have had an enormous effect on her mother, Lina thought. She was obviously intrigued by Gagarin reentering Earth's atmosphere, battered by forces up to eight times the pull of gravity. Regina wrote how during the course of the day every new detail was reported, no matter how small. How factory workers, university professors, kindergarten teachers, pilots and surgeons spoke on radio and appeared on television, discussing the importance of the first Soviet man conquering space and stressing the greatness of being a Soviet citizen. The government assured the people that soon they'd be able to reach way beyond the stars.

On the following page of the diary, Regina's thoughts drifted to her own life.

> I only wish these things would come true but don't see how. My neighbour has no going out shoes and I have one pair.

I don't want to lend them to her and why should I? She is an alcoholic and would lose or ruin them at once. We share the kitchen among the three families but hide our potatoes and bread in our bedroom. That means when communism arrives, we'd have to share our savings for everyone to consume. How unfair! The manager of the restaurant where I work has a car but none of the workers do. Does that mean he'd be sharing his car with employees? I don't believe it. Communism sounds like a strange system, like an unreal dream against grim reality. I am stuck in a kitchen making sausages, cabbage rolls and soups. Nobody comes to thank me for a nice meal. They thank the manager and the waiters, but never me. I despise the communist future where we'd all blend in, earn the same wages and eat our meals at the communal kitchens ...

Lina never knew what her mother thought of the classless society and it came to her as a shock. Eagerly turning the diary pages, she became convinced Regina didn't love her father, with admiration for Gagarin spilling over the pages.

Thanks to his youth and strength, Yuri achieved his dream to become a cosmonaut. Apparently he wanted to be one since witnessing a Russian Yak fighter plane making an emergency landing near his home. He must've been overwhelmed.

I also want to feel special but have no identity. We, Soviet citizens, must act and think the same, but having no individuality suffocates me. Zigmas practising his boxing skills on me doesn't help. But I must be patient for the sake of my children. I'm not going to leave him until Lina and Saulius grow up. I know he'd kill me if I left him now, but one day I'll be free. I will!

With her suspicion confirmed, Lina made the people's hero largely responsible for her parents' split. After she and Saulius went to university, moving to hostel accommodation, their mother also left. Lina contemplated Regina's determination to leave at the right moment, when Zigmas wasn't home. She was finally free but five years later had died of a heart attack. Lost in her memories for a moment, Lina resumed reading about Gagarin being cheered in Red Square by a crowd of hundreds of thousands. How he travelled around the world to celebrate the historical Soviet achievement. How he became an international sensation. How the news about him kept pouring and pouring into the night, people gathering in large groups outside the multistorey flat buildings, discussing the future of the growing Soviet power.

Lina studied Gagarin's flawless face with his straight nose, wide inviting smile showing his even white teeth, bushy eyebrows and dark hair hidden under his hat. Wearing a uniform and a white scarf, smiling to photographers, he held an aura of absolute content, his eyes reflecting the brightest stars he'd seen up-close. Waving to Italians, Germans, Brazilians, Canadians, Japanese, Egyptians and Brits during his historic tour, he must've been regarded the most fortunate man in the world. The dream came true for the boy from the tiny village of Klushino in the Smolensk region!

Many years later Lina would discover how Gagarin, regarded a national treasure at the time, had to be ejected from the Vostok spacecraft as it didn't have engines to slow down and land safely. He didn't touch down with the spacecraft, instead parachuting about seven kilometres back to Earth. Imagine that?! Such news was considered so scandalous it took ten years to filter to the West, and even the Soviets weren't immediately aware of it. Deceived by glorified celebrations of the first Soviet man walking through space while the authorities carried such a dishonest secret, Lina wondered what would've happened if he had crashed during his landing?

*

As a ten-year-old, Lina remembered the news spreading quickly of a man walking in space. One evening the whole neighbourhood gathered in the courtyard surrounded by the four-storey government flats. Rumors circulated that soon Soviet citizens would be able to fly to an established lunar base for excursions. Robertas, a twelve-year-old boy that used to run away from home, ushered the children around him and told them to follow him up the stairs of Lina's building where he also lived on the third floor. She thought they were going to his flat but he passed his floor and climbed to the top. Lina joined the group, and they used the drop-down ladder to reach the roof through the fire escape. The roof was flat and easy to walk on. Some joyful, some apprehensive, the children scattered around. Those afraid of heights complained they felt dizzy from glancing down. Those unaffected enjoyed the view, comparing the appearance of the people, buses, trees and factories to a miniature town. Robertas shushed all present, talking loud and clear:

"If a man can go to space, so we can fly!"

"How?" "When?" "Where is the plane?" "Where are we flying?"— questions, coming from all directions, bounced off each other.

"Let's jump up and count to ten," Robertas suggested, making them join their hands. Jumping up together was fun. "See how easy it is?" he said, pulling the row of children towards the edge of the roof top. Breathless, some stopped, some disjoined their hands.

"I am afraid to fall!" said Julija.

"How would we jump up from the roof?" questioned Margarita.

"I want to pee." "Me too!"—two boys crossed their legs and held their hands between their thighs.

"I'll show you," said Robertas, spreading his arms out. He looked at them, smiled, and flapping his hands, disappeared from view. Curious children leaned over the edge watching Robertas' body swiftly falling to the ground. "How come he didn't fly to the sky?" Julija asked.

Margarita pulled Julija and Lina towards the emergency exit and they lined up to go down. The panic set in. Lina lost sight of her friends, passing her flat door on the second floor and running all the way down. Her short fringe was sticking to her sweating forehead and her skinny legs were shaking. Screaming children dispersed to their homes. Lina desperately wanted to see the fallen boy. She noticed women, fussing over him, taking off their scarves to cover him. She saw the fingers of his right hand sticking out from under a light scarf lifting in the wind, and huge tears filled her eyes. She wiped them with the back of her hand and kept staring at Robertas' limps, shuddering disobediently on the ground. Women were trying to bring them closer together but the left foot kept turning outwards, reminding her of her rag doll with wobbly legs that did the same. A man approached with an army blanket and covered the body. Lina heard him saying that Robertas' features were badly flattened because he had landed face down. She wanted Robertas to kick off the thick blanket, to stand up, to stretch his arms, and to say "I told you, if a man can go to space, so we can fly!" Instead he lay in the middle of the concreted pathway, lifeless. She saw the women wiping their tears with the corners of their scarfs they removed from under the blanket. She watched men running up and down, giving directions, organising help. Somebody said they felt sorry for the boy's mother who cared for him alone. Apparently she was at work, now on her way. The sharp ambulance siren made people open their windows and more came out to see what was happening. Lina heard her mother's voice calling her home.

She remembered her childhood with regret, eager to grow up. She often contemplated running away to the Azov Sea she saw while travelling with her father once. She thought living on the seashore would be great, and she could talk to the whales. She'd stopped taking their oil since going to school, but still wanted to apologise.

*

Lina's family returned to Lithuania in the summer of 1962, managing to exchange their dwelling in Taganrog for a separate one bedroom flat in the town of Kėdainiai. Luckily, the occupants were originally from Taganrog and, wanting to return to their hometown, were willing to swap places even though they were not equal. Their Lithuanian language, only used at home, had to be improved by hiring a tutor who helped Lina and Saulius with writing and building up vocabulary. They resumed their schooling in autumn and integrated well. In fact, living in Taganrog served them well, making them the best pupils of compulsory Russian language and literature classes. Others envied their excellent Russian command as most couldn't master pronunciation.

The Soviet Union had been preparing to fight the United States. Sitting with gas masks during the preparation for war lessons became compulsory practice. A tall, middle-aged General Alexandr Aleksandrovich Gavrilov, who spoke Russian only, taught boys how to be tough and girls compassionate. Playing soldiers, boys pretended to fight and the "injured" were attended by pretend girl nurses. Everyone had to learn how to dismantle Kalashnikovs. Lina was one of the fastest in pulling the gun apart, but the slowest in putting it back together—parts scattered in disorder around the table. Shooting lessons took place in the school basement with cement walls and low ceilings. The loud bangs of blank bullets disorientated her, but there were no earplugs. Constantly missing the targets, she was told she would never be a great Soviet soldier. Deep down, she was relieved but found it hard receiving low marks for not meeting the General's expectations. Regardless, most girls were called weak, and only good for administering First Aid. The gossip persisted that Americans were planning to attack the Soviet Union. They would escape to a new land, the General said, to calm them down.

"New land?" "Where is it?" pupils asked. The General told them he could not reveal the exact destination and advised them to keep the secret to themselves. Also, not to panic and to prepare for departure by packing dried and tinned food as well as minimum clothing: "It would be warm in summer. You'd be transported there in a huge aircraft," he assured them.

"Is it a big country?" the smartest pupil, Jonas, asked.

"It has no borders. It houses huge islands, and is very green."

Asked when they would return to Lithuania, he smiled and replied with confidence. "But you don't have to! Your new life is waiting for you there. You'd be living in moon-shaped flats with huge windows to absorb the sun, warm and cozy inside. You'd be building your own dwellings, side by side in long rows. That would take a long time."

"What about food?" Lina asked.

"Food would be delivered in capsules: chicken capsule, meat capsule, soup capsule, cake capsule, drink capsule. No need to cook! But remember, only the most obedient pupils will be chosen to go."

Lina told her parents about the General's promise to take them to the new land, and they mocked her until she couldn't stand it anymore and ran outside. She also learned that other children's families dismissed the General's stories as lies.

*

In 1995, Lina got a job as a Human Resource Officer at the Kėdainiai Hospital. One morning she was sitting outside during her lunch break, watching patients and visitors walking through the alley of trees. She saw a man trip over the root of a tall pine tree and quickly ran towards him, helping him to stand up. She watched his arthritic fingers trying to adjust his dressing gown. She supported him by his elbow. Holding the right side of his abdominal with his hand, he said he had an appendicitis operation and was recovering in hospital for a couple more days. They sat on a bench and continued to talk, Lina looking closely at him, and finally recognising him. It was the General Alexandr Alexandrovich Gavrilov! She recalled never seeing him without a hat. Today his hair was grey. She had never seen him out of uniform but now he was wearing pyjamas. She had never seen him without his polished boots. He was wearing slippers and no socks. His body had shrunk. The sharpness of his glance was gone and his small eyes were dim. She was curious about the new land and asked him if he recalled such conversations at school. His face lit up and he giggled.

"It was New Zealand."

"New Zealand?"

"Yes, novaija zelionajia zemlia—new green land! My friend was there on a special government assignment during the Second World War. Injured, he spent three months in a temporary hospital, surrounded by the blue mountain tops and giant moving clouds. He returned to Russia alive and passed his stories to me."

"I see."

70

"My job at school was to prepare you for war. It was tough, you know. So, to make it more interesting, I used snippets of these stories to keep you focused."

"You definitely made us focused!"

"It seems like yesterday we lived in the Soviet regime where even mentioning the West was forbidden. That's why I only spoke vaguely of a new land that could've been anywhere in Soviet Union."

"Very clever."

"I couldn't openly talk about tall black trees and strong waterfalls originating from moist and wet forests, cascading into the large green rivers. I couldn't talk about colonies of penguins and seals playing on the surface of the Pacific Ocean. I couldn't talk about hundreds of colourful birds and giant snails, as big as my fist."

"Oh, please tell me more."

"Well, New Zealand houses two islands that are famous for volcanos and glaciation. Surrounded by mountain vistas, breathtaking coastline and ancient forests, this secluded country is a wild as a no man's land."

"How interesting."

"The continent is lined by mountains and the Southern Alps buried in snow. When the snow melts, thick and long alpine buttercup roots rejuvenate and spread their bright yellow flowers around the rough and rocky mountain surface. During the summer nights, spiders lure insects into their symmetrically woven webs, and the insect's salivary secretions shine in the dark, lighting the forest floor with a white and silver glow."

"Ahh … it seems that I am in a fairytale."

"It was like that …" He stopped, suddenly realising he said too much.

"So, it was you on assignment to New Zealand, not your friend?"

"Yes."

"I thought so. Only a person who's been there could paint such a rich picture!"

"Sorry for deceiving you."

"I understand. You couldn't do it any other way."

"I couldn't."

As they conversed, they entered his room and, before parting, Lina mentioned she worked in the HR Office, promising to see him soon. Two days later she popped in to check on his recovery, but there was a new patient occupying the General's bed. Apparently he was discharged in the morning. The elderly man lying in his bed asked her if by any chance her name was Lina, and she nodded.

"He left something for you. Come closer," he encouraged. "He told me about how he taught a preparation to war subject at school, and how he was psychologically grooming the students for the resettlement in the archipelago in northern Russia."

"To the new land?"

"Yes, the same, to a land of nuclear testing."

"But why?"

"Communism had to be built all over the country!"

Disappointed with General's lies, Lina spotted a brochure, called Novaya Zemlya tourism attractions laying on a side table, and walked out the room.

Acting Animals

At the end of 1988, Renata was invited to provide New Year's Eve entertainment for a gathering of over two hundred people in a small village, twenty-five kilometres away from the port of Klaipėda. Since completing her theatre studies, she had been organising cultural events for seven years. She was tall and slim, had a good stage voice, and was lauded for her performances in excellent works of Chekhov's *Three Sisters* and *Uncle Vanya*, Žemaitė's *Marti*, and others. Being offered the role of host for the New Year's Eve celebration, she was worried as to whether she'd be able to engage her audience without the benefit of alcohol. Mikhail Gorbachev's policy of de-alcoholisation, still in place from 1985 in Soviet Lithuania, forbad consuming alcohol in public places or at business functions. The so-called "dry law" resulted in long queues at the bottle shops. Since homebrewed vodka had become a more attractive option, people experienced a great sugar shortage.

With this in mind, Renata hired a band with a soprano saxophone player, a guitarist and a drummer to help her along. While the saxophonist led with the popular *Pearl Fishers* tune by Bizet, she wiggled her body out of a huge Santa's bag. First came her fingers, hands, arms, followed by her seemingly boneless body swaying back and forth. She wore a crown, a long-sleeve silver top and a mini skirt that blended well with the silver threads woven into her black net stockings. After the haunting music stopped, she greeted her audience with some fun remarks. She said that she was inspired by the Chinese zodiac in materialising as a snake, a symbol of wisdom and prosperity. Those gathered for the evening applauded without enthusiasm.

During the supper, Renata was mentally preparing for her next number. She already regretted her commitment to the evening, but forty roubles for one night's work amounted to a quarter of her monthly wage. After the main course, she told a few jokes and an anecdote about how poorly people cope without alcohol. She saw some smiles and the applause sounded a touch louder ... maybe just to her? Afterwards, the band started drowning out the noise of the chattering. Doing invigorating snake movements, Renata encouraged people to step onto the dance floor. But her audience was unmoved. Watching them from behind her mask, she saw sober faces drawn with coldness and criticism while she used her acting tricks to engage them in her game. It was in vain. Worrying that the evening was becoming a flop, she eyed a slim man with charcoal hair approaching. He introduced himself as Vitas, an agricultural scientist specialising in soil fertility. He was nervous shaking her thin hand as if afraid to break it. His hand was sweaty. After their dance solo, he suggested she accompany him to see his office upstairs. She wondered if it was right to leave the party but, given how badly it was going, she decided to leave.

On their way to the third floor he talked about the village and its people. Vėžaičiai, with some one and a half thousand citizens, was famous for scientific testing. It was also home to fifteen scientists, collaborating with thirty lab technicians and agronomists who worked and lived there as part of the Lithuanian Agricultural Research Institute Branch. Local tractor drivers were hired to lend the required support. Chatting away, they reached Vitas' office and found a young man sitting on a sofa as they entered. Aidas introduced himself as scientific assistant. While shaking her hand he seemed unsure of himself, making Renata wonder why she was having such a strange effect on men that night. The coffee table was set with slices of cold meat and pieces of chicken, potatoes, cabbage, carrots, herrings, sweets, fruit and alcohol. Pointing to the bottle of vodka, she commented that they weren't supposed to drink at work. The men laughed and she did too. She wished the citizens could openly sip alcohol on New Year's Eve. Vitas popped a bottle of champagne and dropped a strawberry into her tall flute. She loved it. The men shared some vodka. Music from a loud record drowned out their conversation but she didn't care much for it anyway. The words they used were too technical for her. Then they danced around the table, clinking their glasses and wishing each other happiness and prosperity. She batted her eyelids at them from beneath her mask, which she had elected to keep on to preserve an aura of mystery.

A bulky, average-height man in his twenties entered the office, looking for Renata. As the theatre producer of the local Cultural Centre, Zenonas was wondering what happened to her. His handshake was strong and his busy eyes lingered on her. She noticed his friendly smile and his smooth face. He accepted a glass of vodka from Vitas who, taking a seat at his desk, began explaining how the Vėžaičiai Branch operated an experimental farm that researched fertilisation, and ran a mineralisation program investigating the effect of different chemicals on soil. For their research they tested a variety of crops like oats, maize, clover, barley, winter rye and potatoes. Vitas named some articles he had submitted with his colleagues to the national magazine of agriculture on agrochemistry and soil science, crop production, grassland husbandry and microbiology. Lifting his glass with an aura of confidence, he described how he'd successfully presented papers at conferences, competing with the scientists of older generations. Renata, slightly intoxicated after her third flute of champagne, looked at his round face with deep respect. His sultry gaze was following her every move, and she giggled with appreciation. He was a scientist and she was an actress. What could be more intriguing—listening to but not comprehending each other's words? Contemplative, she beat a strong-weak-weak, strong-weak-weak rhythm with her gloved hand on a corner of his desk. The record playing was the "Vienna Waltz." Zenonas had been listening to the conversation, looking as though he also did not understand. He interrupted Vitas, asking him to hold his thoughts. He brushed his fine fair hair from his forehead and then bowed down, summoning Renata to dance. He took her into his chubby arms, and spun her around the office. She was touched by his tender look. He was a great dancer, not once stepping on her toes.

Renata suddenly woke to the sound of voices and music coming from the hall downstairs. She lifted her head from the sofa and abruptly threw up on the floor. Walking unsteadily, she found a switch near the door and turned on the light. She immediately squinted, feeling an oncoming headache. Finding the ladies room at the end of the corridor, she took off her black ballet flats, then pulled up and straightened her stockings. Neatening her scrunched skirt with her hands, she observed herself in the mirror, wiping away smudges of her red lipstick from her perfectly shaped lips. She smoothed the cheek padding, invisible under her face mask, with her trembling fingers. The cotton wool made her nose look more proportionate. Her slightly bent nose provided an appropriate profile to play a witch, a swan or an ugly sister, but she favoured masks, completely covering her imperfection. She checked her make-up for stuck-together eyelashes—all was fine. The only problem was that she could hardly keep her diamond-shaped eyes open. Puzzled, she tried to remember how she ended up asleep on the sofa. She didn't have any pain in her body, sighing with relief that the men didn't touch her. Her head pulsed with a ¾ time rhythm. Involuntarily closing her eyes, she saw Zenonas lightly lifting her up in the air and sending her a kiss.

Renata never drank during rehearsals, functions, or performances. Tonight was different. She believed as an actress she had failed to move the crowd, and was thankful to Vitas and his companions for trying to cheer her up. She recalled all three of them kneeling in front of her, telling her how talented she was, and Vitas apologising for what he'd done to her. She couldn't ask what as they were all gone. Only the scratchy noise of the needle on the record player was real.

When she walked downstairs, her head was slightly spinning. An elderly couple, sitting outside the hall entry door, were selling homebrewed vodka—distilled samagon. People were willing to pay twelve roubles for a half litre bottle of unclear liquid, secured with a newspaper cork. Inside the venue, Renata observed previously stony faces bursting with joy—some singing along with the band, others drinking in small groups, those already intoxicated jumping on the dance floor. She decided to go back on to the stage. She saw Vitas dancing with a young woman in a midi blue dress, her honey-coloured hair gathered in a long ponytail, huge earrings swaying to and fro. Their bodies touched. His hands clasped her bottom. He waved to Renata, and soon joined her. Spotting his black eye, she jokingly asked whether his lady had punched him for leaving her alone on the dance floor. He didn't reply. Renata scanned the audience under her mask, very much disappointed that she could not see Zenonas anywhere. She hoped to wish him a Happy New Year.

Renata studied her program but Vitas told her not to worry about further engagement. He said they should count down from twelve as the snake year was rolling in already. She had missed three hours of the evening and it was nearly midnight. She took a microphone into her hand and counted the seconds. Midnight arrived and Vitas was the first to kiss her hand. Her New Year's Eve entertainment was finished. She sighed with relief. Vitas insisted they should try to catch up at the Café Pupelė in Klaipėda on Saturdays between 4 to 6 pm. She thought "bean" was a good name for a café and easy to remember.

*

The following summer, 1989, Renata found a suitable dress for a hunting weekend. More than one hundred hunters, mostly men, gathered in a forest near Telšiai in the Samogitian Region. Renata dressed as a fox and was part of the event. She walked through the open fields, holding the corner of her white ankle-length dress with one hand and carrying her ginger fluffy tail with the other. She wore a fox face mask. Her slender figure and rich contra alto voice attracted a lot of attention. Some men, instead of going hunting, followed Renata around. She received at least three invitations for a date. She never thought she was beautiful. On the contrary, her nose was a worry, but these men couldn't see beneath her mask. She dismissed the middle-aged Hunting Club Director's marriage proposal, suspecting most of these hunters were already wed.

During the evenings spent in her rented one bedroom flat, she thought about Zenonas and his mysterious disappearance. It was always the case—

good men were usually already taken and the rest were in jail or alcoholics. But which one was he? Her thoughts drifted to Vitas sitting at his desk and analysing the effects of manure spread on oats or winter rye, flies buzzing around. She imagined him walking in his rubber boots around the muddy fields with his measuring tape in his hand, calculating, writing down his findings, finally taking samples of soil to his lab for scientific research. She shook herself out of such boring images. The incident on the sofa in Vitas' office never left her, but no matter how hard she tried to recollect that night, she couldn't find an explanation for falling asleep. She wasn't planning to return to Vėžaičiai to seek her answers. She hoped to meet Vitas in Klaipėda where she lived. Occasionally she went to Café Pupelė but never saw him.

*

The following winter Renata decided to go to a disco with her friends. Her fox collar, wrapped around her neck, was secured with two shiny buttons imitating animal eyes. The tail hung down loosely. She met Vitas unexpectedly near the entry to the dance hall and they stared at each other, momentarily surprised. In the -25°C temperature people hurriedly passed them, pushing them aside, trying to get inside to the warm venue. Vitas' nose was red, and she covered hers with a scarf across her face. As they strolled through the city centre all she could think of was her nose, pulling her scarf over it, making sure it wouldn't protrude too much. They reached the bridge and paused in the middle of it, watching the partially frozen river Dangė. Two white swans graciously swam close to shore. Oh, how she wanted to have a faithful boyfriend. Vitas pulled his coat collar up to protect his ears from the increasing wind. Renata's fox tail flew off. She started to run after it but Vitas stopped her, taking her gloved hand into his.

"Let it fly. Your fox looks alright without the tail."

"Oh. It was a present from my grandmother. Now I've lost it."

"Don't worry. I'll get you another one."

"That would be nice." With the fox tail out of her sight, she contemplated what to tell her grandmother.

"My uncle is a member of a hunting club. I can get a new fox for you anytime."

"That's very generous of you. You hardly know me!"

"Seems you love to act like an animals. You are even becoming one," he teased as they continued their brisk walk through the Old Town.

"Wearing a fox fur does not make one become an animal!"

"Maybe it's time to stop acting and settle down?"

"Why?" she said, curiously looking into his round eyes.

"I've been thinking of you. I've been coming to Klaipėda every third Saturday but never met you in Pupelė."

"But I visit my grandmother every third Saturday of the month!"

"No wonder we couldn't meet. If not for your fox collar, I could've missed you tonight!" Vitas said, squeezing her gloved fingertips.

"I don't blame you. So much time has passed since we last met. You most probably forgot how I look."

"No, not that. When I saw the fox tail hanging from a woman's neck, I didn't look at her. I watched the tail moving in the wind, thinking of the sexy body of a snake I once met in my village."

She giggled.

"Do you always cover your face?" he asked, putting his hand around her waist. He drew her closer, gently moving her scarf from her face, kissing her on the lips. When she opened her eyes, she heard him say he found her nose interfered with kissing. He admitted being taken aback by such an unusual nose.

"I wish I was blind and didn't see it. Imagine our children walking around with Pinocchio noses?"

He continued as the tears swelled in her eyes slowly.

Seeing her crying, he apologised for his inappropriate remark. She changed the subject, wanting to know what actually happened to her on the sofa in his office. Avoiding eye-contact, he said how ironic it was that the alcohol restriction policy expired soon after she entertained the sober crowd in his village. She persisted with her question. He confessed to dissolving a quarter of a sleeping pill in her drink before giving it to her. Her body stiffened, the expression on her face hardened as she took a step back from him. He came closer, explaining how the plan was made to remove her from the venue. He assured her it was not her fault, but, invited to entertain the villagers without alcohol, she became an obstacle because everybody wanted to drink! Her role was to keep them sober. The local government officials, clinking their lemonade glasses with stony facial expression, were also invited to do the same. Once the Head of the Local Communist Party Branch left the venue with his apparatchiks, Vitas lured her into his office.

Listening to such unpleasant ramblings, Renata contemplated her next move. They were passing a bus stop with the last passenger getting on, and she jumped in just before the door closed. She watched Vitas running after the bus, shouting "I am sorry. I am so sorry." As he was left behind, she observed the pedestrians hurriedly walking the streets, steam coming from their mouths. She thought everybody had somewhere to go, except her. She had no close family. Her mother had died during her birth. Renata often studied her photo sitting on the coffee table. She had short hair, parted in the middle, dark eyes, and a proportionate nose. Renata never knew her father. She was convinced he had a long nose. As she got off at the next stop, she lifted her grey scarf from her face. "One day someone special will find me and fall in love with me. He'll love me for who I am," she said quietly, walking home in the opposite direction.

*

Five years later, Renata was invited to Klaipėda's Cultural Centre to entertain children. She was dressed as a big rat. She brought her two children with her—four-year-old son Rolandas and three-year-old daughter Laura. Rolandas wore a squirrel outfit and Laura was a snake. Inside their masks, cotton wool paddings were evenly spread around their cheeks. Everyone loved Renata's fairytale about a rat and her helpers, who kept fighting over a piece of cheese. Her husband, dressed as Santa, gave out presents. She spotted Vitas in the audience. A little girl with thick eye glasses was sitting on his knees. She noticed his intense look and was pleased that she was hidden behind her rat mask.

Vitas approached, greeting her with an embrace. Learning of his casual relationship with a blind woman whom he was forced to marry due to her unexpected pregnancy, she said she didn't want to know him. "There is a wise saying ... 'be careful what you wish for.' I remember you wanted to be blind so as not to see any ugliness."

"I was so stupid mocking you about your nose. You are so much fun to be with," he whispered, trying to grab her hand which she quickly hid behind her back.

"It's too late. I've married Santa!" she pointed to the center of the hall.

"Is he a good man?" Vitas asked, turning his head towards the Christmas tree.

"He is one hundred percent better than you. By the way, you know him."

Squinting his eyes, he stared at the white-bearded Santa, listening to his voice.

"The actor from my village?"

"Yes. Zenonas. He told me the whole story of the sofa incident!"

"But I explained what happened to you."

"You forgot to mention how Zenonas, discovering you had mixed a sleeping tablet in my champagne, gave you a black eye!" She watched Vitas' blushing face and laughed when he threw his hands in the air and walked away.

After the delightful afternoon came to an end, Renata watched Vitas helping his young wife stand up from her chair. Tightly holding her cane in one hand, she rested her other hand on his shoulder. Their daughter, wearing a white tutu, was walking in front of them. Renata stretched her long rat's tail and reclined on the stage, her children running around her. Santa joined them. He took a green army truck from his bag, and Rolandas started playing with his new toy. Laura, holding her new doll to her chest, crawled into Santa's bag. Still in her snake costume, she started wiggling her flexible body out of it.

Prince Charming

He was young and handsome. With a soft oval face and slightly turned-up nose, he exuded confidence. His honey curls, swaying in the wind, were something women would remember. His name was Vytenis. I often saw him passing the library where I worked, and my heart would beat faster until the sound of his steps could no longer be heard. I wasn't sure what he did for a living. Dressed in a tailored suit and carrying a black briefcase, he had the aura of a detective.

The library staff decided to facilitate a joint event with the Kretinga district Cultural House. Our Director suggested we should provide some entertainment for newlywed couples. One afternoon Vytenis walked in and introduced himself to the library staff. I watched him through a gap between the shelves, straining my almond-shaped eyes. I grabbed my handbag and rushed to the ladies. I had to steady myself before applying my burgundy lipstick onto my medium-size lips, then running fingers across my arched eyebrows. I messed my sandy hair with the tips of my fingers and, satisfied with my appearance, was now ready to meet him. As I approached the reading room, my body shook with anticipation. Deeply inhaling his woody aftershave, I said my name.

"Hello Ramune. Nice to meet you." He shook my hand, eyeing my knee-length linen dress, making me conscious of my chubby legs. He smiled at me and I interpreted his slightly open mouth as an invitation for a kiss. Embarrassed, I raised my gaze and hid my arms behind my back. My female colleagues were obviously enjoying his compliments. Dressed in a white shirt, grey slacks and matching shoes, he said he was a disc jockey. Vytenis took notes throughout the meeting regarding our joint event. The Director of the library appointed me to lead the evening with Vytenis.

Seeing disappointment in my colleagues' faces, I had no doubt I was the most experienced in running regular adult literature reading sessions and knew how to deal with people in the most diplomatic way. But I sensed they were more jealous about my time with the handsome man than the job itself!

Vytenis and I were left alone to work out the details. We thought it would be good to include some comedy to entertain the audience, and we decided that we would be the hosts. Vytenis cheekily suggested that we wear clothes of the opposite sex. The idea came from the wedding parties when the bride was "stolen", and a male imposter dressed as her. We started giggling and agreed to cross-dress. With a deep sigh of relief, he told me he felt comfortable with me because we were having so much fun in thinking of a public event with fresh eyes. I had no doubt it would work! He asked me whether I had some funky clothes in my closet that may fit him. I assured him I did, breaking into a sweat. We agreed to meet later that night at my flat. For the rest of the day I drifted in a pleasant daydream, fantasising about what would happen next.

*

When Vytenis knocked on the door, I had my dresses, tops and skirts spread on the bed. He picked out a deep-blue chiffon dress, complimenting it for its light weight. He put it on and turned around, admiring the wide sleeves and the sheer fabric woven of alternative S and Z twist crepe yarns. I was taken aback as he seemed to know more about women's clothing than I did. I hadn't noticed the intertwined twists before, nor could I spot them now. He said he'd never seen such an impressive dress, made from material sent by my aunty from Australia.

"It must be exciting living there," he suggested, and I shrugged my shoulders.

"The letters we receive from my mother's sister aren't that exciting. She doesn't write about such an exotic continent. She was separated during the Second World War from her family. She gives us weather reports, complaining that it's either too hot or too cold for her, that she has bronchitis, stiffness in her joints and so on."

"How could that be? She has the oceans at her feet and she is still not happy?!"

"I don't know. At least she is kind to us. In the last ten years we've received a couple of parcels from her."

Lifting his straight eyebrows, Vytenis wondered why my aunty sent so little.

"She is probably poor," I said, and he laughed, not convinced westerners could be poor.

Swinging his hips in a figure eight, he made me take notice of how the oversized dress moved. He opened the bag he brought along and took out a cream-coloured brimmed hat, white shirt and black pants. His hat perfectly suited my narrow face and Nordic nose. The pants and shirt sleeves were too long but I rolled them up to suit the length of my legs and arms. He passed on his shoes. Luckily they weren't too big. I said I'd stuff some newspaper inside and they should be fine. He didn't even attempt to try on my pearly-blue pumps that would've perfectly matched the dress. He said he'd ask his mother for a pair, as she had big feet. We agreed that we'd be the funniest couple ever seen in public!

When we sipped leaf tea in my tiny kitchen, I purposely touched his knee with mine. I don't think he noticed. I thought there was plenty of time to seduce him while we worked on the newlywed evening together for the next two months.

*

We rehearsed our program in the library reading room. As the day approached, Vytenis gathered the necessary equipment and set up the microphones in the ballroom of the Cultural House. The staff helped by hanging balloons and stretching streamers from wall to wall. More than a hundred couples started to fill the allocated seats. At 5 pm Vytenis and I entered the stage. Pretending that we had been married for a long time, we shared some wisdom on how to make a marriage last. We were changing our roles for tonight, we said, to try to understand the needs of the opposite sex. Vytenis assured the men that he loves me for my manly strength, and I told women I love him for his feminine flourish. We introduced a beauty therapist who talked about skin types and various treatments to prolong natural beauty. A psychologist spoke of how to attempt to resolve marital problems. Both guest speakers did well in holding people's attention, receiving loud applause. In a deep, pleasant voice Vytenis entertained with marital jokes, and those gathered were rolling with laugher. When the music started, everybody spilled onto the dance floor.

The following morning Vytenis and I were called to the office of the local Communist Party Leader Juozas Augaitis. Not only were we scolded for our low morals in cross-dressing, but also for excluding the Communist Party agenda from the event. We forgot to talk about Marxist-Leninist ideals. We should've done that instead of planting bourgeois ideas into the heads of young families and entertaining them with western music. Overwhelmed with these accusations, neither Vytenis nor I could utter a word. I had never seen him with such a serious face. I jumped as the Party Leader slammed his strong fist on the table.

"What has beauty therapy and psychology to do with building a classless society?!"

Observing Augaitis' bushy eyebrows, massive chin and wide-set eyes staring at me, I sank in my chair. More so, his aggressive tone rang in my ears, making me dizzy. Augaitis criticised Vytenis for not being masculine, making him even more upset as he spoke of a useful person in society bearing children.

"You should've encouraged women to produce at least five children each instead," we were told before being ordered out.

After leaving the Communist Party Committee building with its heavy walls and cold corridors, we wished each other luck and went back to work our separate ways. As soon as I reached the library I was asked to sign my letter of resignation. It was already written by my Director. A couple of days later I met Vytenis near the Post Office, learning that he was also dismissed. Ignorant passers-by, walking on the yellow and red carpet of fallen autumn leaves, provided no comfort to us. We were outcasts who weren't pulling our weight in building a flawless society.

*

I found a job in the House of Pioneers in Klaipėda, leading a variety of events. As part of my duties I organised bus tours around famous attractions such as the Old Town and the statue of Lenin in the heart of the city. The young children were encouraged to recite poems about him and were rewarded with chocolates after repeating "Lenin is our father" and "Russia is our mother". During one of the outings to the statue of Lenin, I gathered them around and read some Soviet fairytales. I lifted my head from the page and spotted Vytenis approaching. Dressed in a checked shirt and well-pressed trousers, with one hand in his pocket and a leather jacket over his shoulder, he greeted me from afar. I hadn't heard from him for a year and learned that he worked as a disc jockey at the International Hotel Klaipėda. We laughed about our experience in our previous job and were surprised that straying from the goals of communism didn't prevent us from being employed. We decided to meet again on Saturday.

Vytenis brought me flowers and we lunched at a restaurant. He told me about his mother who worked in a Klaipėda bakery and his father who was a surgeon, both bitterly regretting having nothing in common. He rented a flat in his hometown which he shared with his male friend. His older sister lived in Vilnius. I told him that my parents were farmers from the region of Gargždai, and that I studied librarianship at the University of Vilnius for five years. Also, that I was still living in the same flat in Kretinga where we tried our clothes before the newlywed event. We chatted for hours until it was time for him to go to work. He invited me to his school friend's wedding in six weeks' time. It was rather unexpected. I raised my eyebrows, pretending to be thinking about it, burning with desire to join him. When I agreed to accompany him, he said Rolandas and Nemyra would be delighted that he'd finally found a partner. Smiling, he gave me a kiss on a cheek, leaving me with a promise in his heavy-lidded eyes.

Each time we met I yearned for his embrace but he never held my hand or kissed me. At the movies, while other couples sat close together, whispering and cuddling, we sat erect. Once we watched *Romeo and Juliet*. I cried at the end, feeling sorry for both lovers lying dead side by side. Trying to find comfort in the darkness of the cinema theatre, I touched his hand, but he kept staring at the screen.

*

Six weeks later, Vytenis picked me up in his grey car. At the beach resort of Palanga, Vytenis and I joined the bridal party at the Wedding Bureau. I watched the flower girl and the ring bearer. Slowly walking in front of Rolandas and Nemyra, both were dressed in exact miniature copies of the bride and groom's wedding outfits. I was jealous seeing Vytenis' friends exchanging their vows by pledging themselves one to another until death parted them. I glimpsed at Vytenis but he seemed far away with his thoughts. At the conclusion of the ceremony the bride and groom placed wedding rings on each other's fingers and the marriage was sealed with a kiss. Walking towards the exit of the ceremonial hall, Rolandas grabbed Nemyra by her elbow when she tripped on the hem of her long white dress. On their way out the newly-married couple was showered with sprays of water and grain. The water meant approaching challenges while grain symbolised future harvests—wealth, children and longevity of marriage. They were then wrapped in furs to ensure that their life together would be successful.

When four white Volgas and Vytenis' Moskvitch—the most popular cars at the time—drove through the main dusty street of the village of Girkaliai, seven kilometres outside Palanga, people came out of their dwellings with little gifts and flowers. Children surrounded the newlyweds' car, trying to catch lollies thrown at them by the official male and female matchmakers, called piršlys and piršlienė. At the door of the groom's house, Rolandas and Nemyra were met by family and friends. The bridal party of ten couples, including Vytenis and me, lined up behind them. Men wore black suits and women long, pink, open-necked dresses. I was pleased with my well-fitting dress, elongating my plump body. I admired Rolandas, with his medium build dressed in his dark blue suit, holding Nemyra in his strong embrace. Her veil lifted in the air, revealing ash-blond hair falling all the way to her waist. They held hands as they thanked everybody for their best wishes. Rolandas lifted Nemyra up but was stopped from entering the house. Following the ancient tradition, the couple had to taste bread dipped in salt, and drink red wine given by both parents. Piršlys told them that bread, salt and wine were symbols of married life, representing joy, tears, and the hard work needed to keep loving each other. Ah, how I wanted to be a bride! How I wanted Vytenis to take me to the alter! I tried to catch his gaze by squeezing his hand. He responded with a faint smile, gazing back over my head.

The jokes, dances, the "stealing of the bride" and ceremonial "hanging" of piršlys as punishment for his loose tongue continued into the morning. After the wedding cake was cut, and the last chord of the live band music faded into the stillness of the countryside, the guests dispersed to allocated places to rest. Vytenis stayed behind chatting with a drummer. I found myself on a floor with a mattress for a base, two pillows and a blanket for a bed, the sofa and a single bed already having been taken by two other couples. Exhausted after a lengthy day, I fell asleep.

When I woke up, I could hear a rooster outside clearing his throat. I noticed a half-naked Vytenis, with a towel around his waist standing in front of a full-size mirror. Fascinated with his slender body and straight legs, I was taken aback in observing what he was doing. I'd never seen a man spreading cream on his face. I watched his long fingers gently circling around his low forehead, cheeks and lean neck. He used invigorating fingertip movements to plump his lips, skillfully applying Vaseline over the top and the bottom lip, then patting them with his fingers and finally wiping the excess with a hanky. After combing and parting his curls, he packed his things in his overnight bag. I couldn't take my eyes of his proportionate body with slightly rounded shoulders and his hairless chest. I half-shut my eyes, observing him pulling his pants on, buttoning up his shirt, pulling his socks on, slipping his feet into his shoes and eventually leaving the room. After hearing the noise of the squeaking door hinges, I lifted my head to see if others witnessed what I did but the two couples seemed asleep.

The wedding celebration continued all of Sunday and we left Girkaliai at about 9 pm. On the way to Kretinga we went over the details of the wedding, recalling the most enjoyable moments. I slipped in a question as to why he used cream and Vaseline, as I'd never seen a man put such effort and time to complete his morning ritual. His hands, lightly braced against the wheel, started to shake. After an uncomfortable silence, he admitted he always cared about his looks and had no interest in the opposite sex. I was truly shocked when he uttered he was gay, as I had never heard of gay people before. I replied that I'd heard of the word "pervert", used to describe a man who would hide behind the multistorey building or in the laneway, waiting for women to pass. Exposing his penis he frightened them and made them scream. Some, seeing him playing with his penis, spat at him. Vytenis explained that he'd never do such a thing—he simply preferred to have a man as a close friend. I sensed disappointment in his voice and his facial expression looked worried.

"Why did you ask me to attend the wedding then?"

He gave me one of his playful looks and concentrated on the road for a while before replying.

"Ramune, I value you as my dear friend and invited you to keep me company out of my good heart. Can you imagine me turning up at the wedding with my male friend?"

"No. Not really."

"See! Besides, you just told me about how disgusted people felt about the pervert in the alleyway. Unfortunately they seem to feel the same way about gay people."

I lowered my head, feeling ashamed of my words.

We parted hastily, wishing each other good night. Watching his car driving off, I was choking with tears. How could Vytenis be so desirable and yet feel nothing for me? I cried myself to sleep, wishing he was different, regretting that I'd fallen in love with an outcast of Soviet society.

I didn't see or hear from him for three years. One morning while reading the newspaper, I spotted a picture of him on a page holding his parents' photo. My knees bent involuntarily and I grabbed the back of a chair so as not to fall down on the floor. I learned how on the 20th of November 1983, Paulius and Valė Sasnauskai were found dead on their property. Their bodies hung in the air for six hours before their son Vytenis discovered them. No suicide note was found. Maybe he removed it? Maybe they decided to end their lives due to them having nothing in common with each other? Maybe they were ashamed of their son's sexuality? I thought about Vytenis, wondering how he was coping, wanting to visit him but I didn't know his address.

Two months later I discovered how he gassed himself in his parents' garage by lying in front of the exhaust pipe of his running car. The second tragedy, happening so soon after the first, numbed me. I was confined to bed due to strong pains in my chest. The following morning, waiting in a queue to see a doctor, I recognised Nemyra sitting close by. She was here to check the progress of her pregnancy. I congratulated her on her wonderful news. We spoke about Vytenis' family tragedy, embracing each other in grief and wiping our tears. Nemyra gave me Vytenis' home address. I wished I'd met her in time for his parents' funeral as I would've wanted to attend, only hoping I wasn't too late this time.

Despite my heart problem, I went to Vytenis' family house where small fir branches, spread on the pavement, led inside. Vytenis' open coffin, still available for viewing before the funeral, seemed to contain a porcelain doll whose long lashes covered closed eyes. His intertwined fingers rested on his chest with no visible veins or freckles. He was dressed in his tailored suit and a crisp white shirt. His look-alike sister, sitting at the head of the coffin, kept adjusting the underlay around his body. Her eyes were badly swollen. I saw a young man in a corner of the room. He was Vytenis' age, smartly dressed, angrily wiping away his running tears. He wore a gold bracelet, identical to the one I used to see on Vytenis' hand. I was tempted to approach him but his blank expression stopped me from doing so. I stood there, listening to the murmur of elderly women, moving their rosary beads between their fingers and praying for his soul.

A few weeks after the funeral, I visited the places where Vytenis and I met, including the library. The chair where he used to sit during our rehearsals stood empty. I braced it, reminiscing how much fun we had preparing for the newlywed evening. I now regretted that it didn't occur to me to place my chiffon dress he adored in his coffin. I'll always remember him as a man who had so much joy to spread around. A carefree youth that had women melting in his presence, he lived his life to the full and died young. After his passing, more than ever, I wanted him to remain my Prince Charming.

My Soviet Passport

Inga Plečkytė and Kęstas Lingys were selected for the Mayakovsky poetry reading competition, set to take place in Moscow. The Director of the Stasys Šimkus Higher Music School of Klaipėda announced the panel's decision in May 1977. Inga, studying to become a singer, and Kęstas, the school's best male percussionist, were pleased to be chosen as finalists from the thirty candidates at their school. They were both promising musicians and loved poetry. Both in their early twenties, Inga had been writing poems since she was fifteen and Kęstas had read poems during school functions and events. That very evening, sitting on the steps of the school entrance, they shared their concerns about competing with participants from all over the Soviet Union. They discussed at length their excitement at how they'd be travelling to Moscow, settling into a hotel, enjoying the sightseeing and daily meals—all costs covered by the school administration!

Before their first weekly rehearsal with a Soviet literature teacher, Inga kept repeating "Oh, I can hardly breathe! I cannot believe we are going to Moscow!" In reply, Kęstas whistled a catchy tune while drumming on the lid of the grand piano. Then they began to review their readings. Standing on a stage of a spacious concert hall Inga recited a few lines from her chosen poem, "My Soviet Passport":

> *For one kind of passport—smiling lips part*
> *For others—an attitude scornful.*

Kęstas took great pleasure in saying two particular lines from "Our March":

Our god is the god of speed,
Our heart—our battle drum.

Interrupting him with her critique "All you think of is drumming!",
Inga blurted out her favourite verse:

The porter's eyes
Give a significant flick
(I'll carry your baggage
For nix, mon ami ...)

They were soon joined by their female teacher, Janina Stonytė. Each
repeated their poem, and Janina gave suggestions on how to effectively
change intonation, which lines to join, how to emphasise certain words, or
to pause in prolonging a purposeful silence.

*

The following week, Inga chose to sing her verses. She put on a tape of
George Bizet's "Habanera" evoking the sensual and passionate opera, and
sank her childish fingers into her straight, black hair, exposing her high
forehead and her oblong face. Then she mimicked placid movements of
Carmen, adding her own punctuations to each line:

I'd tear like a wolf, at bureau-cracy.
For ma-andates, my respect's but the slightest.
To the devil himself, I'd chuck,
With-oout mercy every red-taped paper!

When Inga paused, Kęstas applauded, enjoying the unexpected
entertainment. Patting the cover of a book of Mayakovsky's poems, Janina
spoke at length about the purpose of the event.

"You are going to read the poetry in front of hundreds of people and
the responsibility to do your best rests on your shoulders. Just imagine

young Mayakovsky in love with his country's ideals. Imagine him writing on behalf of all Soviet citizens. Imagine the pride and joy seeping through his words. His poetry begs to be read with all possible nuances to reveal the core meaning."

Listening to Janina's words, the two of them watched her expression grow harsh. Composed, Inga continued to recite her lines with a serious facial expression. Digging her fingernails into the palms of her hands, she lamented,

> *Down the long front of coupés and cabins*
> *File the officials politely.*
> *They gather up passports and I give in*
> *My own vermilion booklet.*

Janina complimented her on the emotional and physical transformation. Kęstas also had another attempt in reading his poem slower, trying to delve deeper into the meaning:

> *Beat the squares with the tramp of rebels!*
> *Higher, rangers of haughty heads!*
> *We'll wash the world with a second deluge,*
> *Now's the hour whose coming it dreads.*

When he paused, the teacher urged him to continue. Inga whispered, "Here he comes to his favourite part!" He raised his high-pitched voice, stressing the last word of each line.

> *Too slow, the wagon of years,*
> *The oxen of days—too glum.*
> *Our god is the god of speed!*

Scrunching the sides of his pants with his thick fingers, he completed the last line in haste,

Our heart—our battle drum!

After the rehearsal, the trio sat on the edge of the stage. Janina appreciated their attempts to impress her with their readings but advised them not to overdo it. She raised her eyebrows, and, before speaking, licked her lips. "The key to success is sincerity. Every syllable should reveal a special message, encoded in letters, long dashes and exclamation marks. But to achieve this you don't need to use force. You must drift into the flow of words as if you were swimming in the sea that swells and eventually calms down. Alternating between naturally augmented fortissimo and diminished pianissimo would keep the audience interested."

Before leaving the concert hall, she returned their exercise books with her comments. Inga and Kęstas remained seated, sharing their notes. When they left the building, Kęstas looked up, noticing a couple of faces watching them from the second-floor window.

*

The following month, Inga and Kęstas travelled by bus to the capital. Kęstas either slept or exercised his drumming on his thighs. Inga recorded her observations in her diary. Having a window seat, she enjoyed looking at the fir trees lining the sides of the road. She saw black and white cows grazing on the lush, green grass. She counted white horses, unsuccessfully trying to spot one hundred for good luck. When they stopped in the town of Raseiniai, she observed the oak trees listening to the rustling of their symmetrically trimmed leaves. She was drawn to the flapping of bird wings above the tops of the swaying birch tree branches. Inga and Kęstas had a three-course meal for ninety kopeks, equivalent to ninety cents, in the canteen, where people seemed preoccupied with their daily matters. Some complained about the meat shortage and standing in line for hours to get a chicken, others about small wages. Getting the same wage as those who did little seemed unfair. It didn't surprise Inga that they spoke of the poor-quality Lithuanian-made shoes. Stiff and out of required sizes, the shortages left many with little to chose from. Walking in footwear that was too small or too tight caused all sorts of problems. Inga's mother had sizeable bunions below her big toes and found it painful to walk. Inga considered herself lucky having a pair of leather sandals. She also had a pair of lacy underwear, purchased at the black market for five rubles. Kęstas, lost in his thoughts, ate his lunch with a great appetite, oblivious to the conversations taking place around him.

Upon their arrival in Vilnius, the two companions boarded the Moscow train. A male attendant confirmed there was no one else sharing their sleeper on the way to Moscow. The news pleased them. After the middle-aged attendant returned with tea, served in glasses with metal holders, they paid five kopeks—five cents—each. Kęstas opened his carrying bag and started to look through the contents. He was surprised what he found there, embarrassed that his mother packed so much food. He took out four boiled eggs, four pieces of buttered bread and a couple of apples. Lastly, he put a tin of canned meat on the table. Inga placed a small homebaked cake, some cheese, a fresh cucumber and an identical tin next to his. They giggled, comparing their tins, realising they were produced at the same place—the Conserve Factory of Klaipėda. They discovered that both of their parents worked there. Kęstas confessed to how his father, one of the night guards at the factory, would steal the tins and throw them over the high brick fence. Inga burst out with laughter, saying that her parents were among those patiently waiting for magic tins to fall from the sky!

"They pay beforehand, do they?" asked Kęstas.

"They certainly do. Apparently, the guards pair-up with the shift workers and do a thriving business," she said.

"No wonder goods move to the black market—my father said it's impossible to get tins through security screening gates," said Kęstas, and Inga agreed, thinking of her own lacy underwear she would've never purchased in the women's clothing shop.

"But there is no other way," she said, carefully removing her leather sandals, making herself comfortable by placing a pillow under her seat. He changed his black shoes to slippers and reclined against the thin wall.

They ate in silence for a while and then Inga talked about herself, revealing a stubborn streak that couldn't forgive and forget. Kęstas swallowed a piece of cake and asked why. She told him how she had a fallout with her best friends Sofija and Silvija because they walked out during a concert where she was performing.

"Maybe they had another engagement?" he said, prompting her to put her tea holder on the table, and to wave her hand in front of her as if trying to get rid of an irritating mosquito.

"I wouldn't get upset about such an insignificant matter," he said, slowly wiping around his lips with his white hankie.

"But that's not all! I know they talk about me behind my back," she continued.

"Great. When we die, nobody will," he said jokingly, but she protested, thinking herself different from others and would rather stay alone than put up with disrespect.

"But there is a pinch of truth in any gossip, and gossip stimulates people's imagination."

"You are right. Only sometimes, it results in adding extra details to make a story more intriguing. You know, I've heard vocalists gossiping about the two of us."

"So what?" Kęstas said, drumming on the side of his wooden bunk, recalling curious faces watching them leaving the school.

"You don't take life seriously," Inga admonished him, simultaneously admiring his long eyelashes when he winked at her.

"And you take it too seriously and may miss the best bits! I see you are prickly as a stem of a budding rose," he said, gently glancing at her as she blushed.

They finished their meal and tidied up the table. Then chatted and gazed through the window at the dark sky and the shadows of the passing fields, shrubbery and small country houses sparingly spread apart from each other. The stillness of the summer night was soothing, making it easy to converse. They talked about the advantage of living with their parents, feeling sorry for those boarding in the hostel. While Inga and Kęstas each spent their monthly stipends of forty rubles on themselves, others struggled. Inga shared a story about a piano student who would buy a dress or a skirt that cost just under forty rubles and then live on bread and water until the next pay day. Kęstas asked if her name was Dalia.

"Do you know her?" Inga asked.

"Yes, male students often speak of her beauty."

"But she turned into a skeleton!"

Kęstas was not bothered with details and firmly supported Dalia's choice. Inga argued that it was the wrong way to win male attention, feeling disappointed he didn't agree.

They sat quietly for a while until she suggested they should go to sleep. They helped each other to put their bags in the trunks inside their bunks. When he stepped out, she undressed and lay down under the army blanket. He did the same upon his return, first taking off his clothes, socks and slippers in the dark. They soon fell asleep to the monotonous beat of grinding train wheels.

*

Following their overnight journey, Inga and Kęstas joined other students who were met by the members of the Organisational Committee and taken to different hotels by buses. Upon their arrival at hotel Sputnik, Inga and Kęstas were told they would be staying in one of the best hotels of the Russian capital. Their guide proudly explained that Sputnik, located in the south-west of Moscow on Leninsky Prospekt, was built in 1968 and offered accommodation to members of the All-Union Central Council of Trade Unions. Mayakovsky's poetry competitors warmly welcomed each other. The delegation of over one hundred Soviet citizens had been conveniently placed roughly five kilometres from the Kremlin and Red Square, which they were scheduled to visit during their stay.

Soon after dispersing to their rooms, Inga and Kęstas met again at the front reception and took a lift to the fourteenth floor to enjoy panoramic views, dominated by the Moscow State University building in the Sparrow Hills and the Luzhniki Central Stadium. An elderly couple, standing close by, pointed out that the Bolshoi Theatre was a walking distance from the Red Square. Excited with the news but also conscious of the great pressure to know their poems by heart, Inga and Kęstas returned to their rooms for more practice.

In the morning, they found their way to a spacious Kremlin Conference Hall with huge windows and polished floorboards. Some three hundred people were ushered to comfortable red velvet seats. Inga later recalled walking onto the high stage in her ankle length denim skirt and a white, long sleeved blouse revealing her delicate waist. Folding her hands in front of her tiny chest, she put her feet apart, posing as a proud Soviet citizen, repeating the thoughts written by Mayakovsky in 1929. She imagined holding her red passport in her hand, its cover decorated with a golden star as well as a hammer and sickle, bound by the wheat wreath. She listened to her voice echoing among the long, wide rows of people with curious looks. Raising her voice with a colourful tune, she recited…

> *I'd tear like a wolf at bureaucracy.*
> *For mandates, my respect's but the slightest.*
> *To the devil himself I'd chuck without mercy*
> *Every red-taped paper.*

Towards the end of the poem she paused, glancing at the five judges sitting in the first row hastily scribbling notes. Taking a deep breath, she put her right foot forward, announcing,

> *But this … I pull out*
> *Of my wide trouser-pockets*

Hearing an unexpected wave of laughter, she stopped, focusing her hard gaze above the audience and stood with her left hand stretched out. As the laughter subsided, she continued with arousal,

> *Duplicate of a priceless cargo.*

In complete silence, she concluded:

You now: read this and envy,
I'm a citizen of the Soviet Socialist Union!

The applause deafened her, and she ran off the stage forgetting to curtsy. Her legs entangled in the folds of her skirt. Kęstas, who read his poem before her, caught her from falling back stage. In his arms, the sense of safety and security overwhelmed her.

"You did very well," he said, squeezing her fingers with one hand and pushing back his light-brown hair from his sweating forehead with the other.

"It was a disaster," said Inga, trying to regain her composure.

"You don't get the joke, do you?" he said, giving her a penetrating look. As he held her hand, a sudden rush of blood through his body made his limbs weak. Oh, how he wanted to hug her, to spin her around, and kiss her upon returning her to her feet.

"What joke?" she said, removing her hand from his, covering her cheeks with her shaking fingers.

"They loved it!"

"I don't believe you. All I heard was people laughing at me. Maybe it was my Lithuanian accent?"

"No. They laughed at the lines about the wide trouser-pockets but you were wearing a skirt! That was hilarious."

"But I don't wear trousers!" she raised her voice, making her way through the backstage door to the hall.

"Doesn't matter!" he replied, following her. "You, standing there, not laughing with the rest, had a comical effect! You'll see, you'll win the competition."

She dismissed his idea and listened to "At the Top of My Voice", "To All and Everything", "To His Own Beloved Self", and other poems, names of which she'd never heard before. To her surprise, the most common poem was "My Soviet Passport" and she envied the male readers for portraying the image of a Soviet citizen better than she. At the end of the day, Inga and Kęstas watched gold, silver and bronze medals hung on the winners' necks and monetary prizes distributed among thirty-five participants. When Inga's name was called, she accepted her Certificate of Appreciation for female interpretation of a manly poem with pride. Kęstas, like the rest, received just a Certificate of Participation in the event.

*

The following day they returned to the Kremlin. War veterans, prominent politicians, actors, musicians and sportsmen joined the competitors. Inga wore a V-necked hibiscus dress, tightly hugging her figure and revealing her long legs. Kęstas wore his dark blue suit and a white shirt with a matching tie. They enjoyed the photo session and afterwards went on a tour of Lenin's Mausoleum. The line of at least two hundred people along the Kremlin, patiently waiting to get in, was patrolled by soldiers. The poetry participants were rushed through with their special passes. They were instructed to enter the funeral chamber quietly and pause at the coffin for exactly three seconds. Inga saw Lenin before Kęstas. Taken aback by the glass coffin, covering his short body, she sighed but was immediately shushed by a guard. She observed Lenin's face with curiosity, trying to take mental note of as many details as she could. He had a big nose, thick lips, wide ginger eyebrows, a moustache and a neatly trimmed beard. His yellowish hands rested on his thighs. He was dressed in a black suit, white shirt, the collar of which completely covered his neck, and a dark tie. Once they reunited outside, Kęstas spoke of feeling threatened by the stern looks of the guards, standing at each corner of the coffin with Kalashnikov rifles hanging from their shoulders. Inga nodded her head. She tried to describe Lenin's features, teasing out snippets quoted about the founder of the Soviet Union from the poem "Conversation with Comrade Lenin":

> His stubble slides upward above his lip
> As his mouth jerks open in speech.

The tense creases of brow hold thought in their grip,
Immense brow matched by thought immense.

Kęstas asked Inga whether she noticed how the sun peering through the chamber windows made Lenin look like a stuffed dummy. She scrunched her face with disgust, and said the gloomy atmosphere of the place would never make her come back. Afterwards, walking over the smooth, cobbled stones of the Red Square with their group, they couldn't relax. Each time they turned their heads towards the Mausoleum, they thought about the decaying "Father of the Revolution".

A group of poetry competitors, including Inga and Kęstas, was met by a tour guide in his early forties. He waived his hand, welcoming all. The group, consisting of students from Ukraine, Murmansk, Georgia, Kazakhstan, and the Baltic States among others, surrounded the dark-haired guide who cleared his throat each time he spoke. He welcomed them to Moscow and in reply some clapped, some nodded their heads, and others stood erect in anticipation of what else he had to say. He praised the Red Square parameters, stretching over three hundred metres in length and seventy metres wide. He named the date of November 7, 1941, when the first parade in the Red Square took place and the young cadets marched from the square to the frontline, not even fifty kilometres away from where they stood. He talked about the Russian victory over the Germans, spilling over into the military parade of June 24, 1945. He continued, revealing how on that day two hundred Nazi flags and banners, thrown in front of the Mausoleum, were trampled by mounted Soviet commanders.

Then the guide asked if anyone knew the original colour of the passport. A Georgian youth replied that when first introduced in 1932, it was dark grey and remained grey until 1974. The guide was pleased, adding how since 1953, Soviet citizens followed the USSR Council of Ministers decree of the new Passport Statute. The Statute made it compulsory to have a passport from the age of sixteen, and in getting the passport, one had to have a proof of propiska—permanent address. He assured the tourists that this system helps authorities to protect citizens from the negative influences of the West. When he said they should be proud of their Soviet passports, Inga and Kęstas exchanged warm glances.

Following a break to immerse themselves in their surroundings, the group once again gathered around their guide. Lifting up his black umbrella with a tiny red flag attached to the end of it, he led them back towards the wall of the Mausoleum. Kęstas' thin lips tightened, turning down at the ends. Glancing at him often, she noticed his expression and rolled her eyes to amuse him. Approaching the Mausoleum, the high-spirited guide went on to explain how Lenin died in 1924, but the Mausoleum, designed by the architect Alexey Shchusev, was only built the following year. He pointed towards the granite platforms, added some ten years later on the sides of the Mausoleum, where the government and the military heads continue to stand during important speeches.

Soon the excursion was over, delegates thanking the guide, saying goodbye to each other and dispersing around the Red Square. On their way to the hotel, Inga took a quick look at Kęstas' face. Oh, how she wanted to touch his deep dimples. By now she'd adjusted to his finger drumming. Kęstas, looking at her alluring lips, gave her a gap-toothed grin. He didn't mind her assertive and bubbly personality. When he reached for her hand, he stopped himself from bringing it to his lips, gently embracing it with two of his fingers instead. The thought of spending their lengthy journey back to their home, hopefully alone again in their sleeper, stirred them with romantic anticipation.

Dancing Figurines

Elena started dancing at the age of four, like her grandmother Valda—a prominent ballerina of the Kaunas National Opera and Ballet Theatre in Soviet Lithuania. Elena was told how, in the early 1930s, Valda was paired with famous ballet stars such as Vera Nemtchinova and Anatoly Obukhov, who emigrated from Russia to Lithuania. How Valda performed in all three of Tchaikovsky's ballets, and in other famous works like *Gisselle*, *Sylvie* and *Grand Couture*. How she died in 1949 in Italy on her way to Australia. Apparently, while she and other migrants endured the long wait for transport to their new home, she went mountain climbing. Being petite and accustomed to stilettoes, she tripped, broke her heel and fell many metres down. Nobody could reach her and thus she was left behind, buried in the rubble of rocks. She was thirty-three years old. Her son Julius, aged sixteen upon arrival to Australia, married a Lithuanian woman Gertrūda, and their daughter Elena was born in 1964.

Elena would always wear her long pale blond hair tied up in a bun that revealed her slender neck. Her hourglass figure turned people's heads. She danced from an early age, developing a classical ballet posture that distinguished her from the other pupils at school, standing tall with feet turned outwards. She joined the Australian Ballet School in her native Melbourne, winning a scholarship to the Royal Ballet School in London when she turned sixteen. Returning to Australia as a prima ballerina, she wished her scholarship could continue! She had been having so much fun with her daily practices and regular performances, consumed with her career as a ballerina. Mingling with Margot Fonteyn and Rudolf Nureyev at the Royal Opera House in Covent Garden and seeing the Paris Ballet Company had shaped her as an aspiring dancer.

She had more curvy lines than her grandmother, she was told. Constantly on a diet, she did well in London. But upon her return to Melbourne, even putting on a couple of hundred grams made her male partners struggle to keep her in the air. Every morning before her dance rehearsals she practised her five barre exercises to warm up different body parts and to strengthen legs, ankles and feet. She continued en pointe, standing on the tips of her toes, conducting her warm-up at the Ballet School, located in Kavanagh Street, Southbank. Having greatly improved her technique since her return, she expected to dance solos. Sometimes her artistic director Dame Peggy van Praagh would try to adjust her expectations, reminding her that even the best ballerinas don't get the major parts all the time. Elena's narrowed eyes would show how she didn't appreciate hearing such answers.

*

One night, returning from rehearsal, Elena slowly opened the front door and overheard her parents discussing Valda and how she struggled to survive. "We should send her another parcel," her father said, and her mother suggested asking other family members if they wished to contribute. Confused, Elena walked into the kitchen and questioned their conversation. Hadn't Valda passed away on the cliffs in Italy? Surprised by her early return, her parents looked at one other before looking back at her, assuring her they meant another person.

Elena started listening more intensely for unexpected conversations, and began looking for clues about Valda. The following Sunday when her parents were attending Church, she noticed a piece of paper sticking from under her father's pillow. It was from Novosibirsk, Russia with a neatly written name and return address in blue pen. Valda's surname, Songailaitė, revealed a single woman's status. Her letter dated 15 April 1979 didn't say much. She missed her son. She missed Lithuanian forests sprinkled with mushrooms, berries and field flowers. She missed sitting around the school campfire, watching the falling stars, singing. She regretted life going past so quickly, erasing the names of her friends, neighbours and work colleagues. The beautifully written letter, saturated with loss, made Elena want to immediately compose her own reply. She wanted to know more about Valda's youth, her dancing career and the reason she lived away from her homeland. She dropped her aerogramme into a green postage box at the end of their street before her parents' return.

The reply from Valda arrived in six months. Elena found it sitting on her dressing table. Even though the envelope had been opened and resealed, she didn't care. She read the letter hastily as if dying of thirst, finding only a brief response. Later that day, her parents sat her down to explain why she wasn't told the truth about Valda. They said, being born and bred in the West, Elena wasn't able to comprehend how people had lived behind the Iron Curtain. They weren't free over there. Those that had land, property or both were forced to share with the less fortunate. Communist government propaganda lauded the equality of Soviet citizens, causing neighbours and strangers alike to turn against each other with a literal interpretation of the message: "What's yours is mine." Her grandmother was regarded as an outcast for owning a family house. Nobody considered how much losing the land and private property, passed from generation to generation, affected the rightful owners. During and after the German-Russian war, even servants had a right to occupy their owners' dwellings, use their china, furniture, clothing, linen and sleep in their beds.

Picturing herself living in the Soviet Union under such conditions, Elena felt foolish to be writing to her grandmother without consulting her parents. She now knew why Valda's reply didn't reveal much. She wrote about being happy in Novosibirsk where she taught ballet. She also mentioned her daughter Diana, aged thirty-three, who lived with her.

"And that's why you told me she had a fatal accident in Italy?" Elena whispered.

"Yes. Until Stalin died in 1953, Valda had no right to return to her homeland. After he died, she discovered her family house had been occupied by strangers.

"Why was she away? Where?"

"She was deported to Siberia for two reasons: for belonging to intellectual society, and for being a bourgeois element. That is, for having a house in Kaunas," her father said, making Elena cringe.

"Luckily", Julius continued, "while in exile an elderly Russian General fell in love with her, protecting her from rapists, bullies, thieves, making her time in the camp more bearable." Trapped in a concentration camp, in comparison to others, she was treated well. Vasilij loved her so much. In 1946 they had a daughter together.

"Did Valda love him? Didn't you say he was old?" asked Elena.

"Yes, he was, but love was probably the last thing on her mind. She needed care, protection, basic necessities to survive."

Elena learned how thousands of farmers, students, intellectuals and others were deported to weaken the core of the Lithuanian nation. Valda was pulled off the stage during her performance, where, together with randomly selected members of the audience she was pushed into an open truck. They were taken to a train station, cramped into cattle wagons and taken away.

That night Elena dreamt of Valda dancing in a field of cornflowers, with blood seeping under her feet. Trying not to dirty her satin dance shoes, she kept herself suspended in the air as long as she could until falling down, ripping her white see-through dress, hitting her head on a rock and losing consciousness. Elena saw the heads of the huge sunflowers turning into the distorted faces of the prisoners, pleading for help, crawling around like dung beetles. In the morning, shaken by her dream, she anticipated meeting the woman whose steps she followed as a dancer. She wanted to get to know the woman who experienced great fame and a great fall.

*

Elena had been made aware of a Russian diplomat who followed Australian ballet with great interest, sitting in the front row at her performances. Her friend Belinda, also a ballerina, had met Mikhail Zverev at the Russian Embassy in Melbourne. He was hosting a VIP party which she attended with her parents. Listening to Belinda, Elena eagerly analysed the photos her friend was carrying in her handbag. Oh, how handsome he was, apparently in his early thirties. At the party, to his guests' surprise, he admitted he'd dreamt of being a dancer but became a diplomat instead. His confession caused a stir of giggles. Both ballerinas also agreed how incompatible these two professions were! Curious, Elena wanted to get acquainted with this Russian diplomat and Belinda promised to help.

During the next performance, Elena tried her hardest to spot him, but as usual the blinding stage lights prevented her from seeing anyone in the audience. All the same, she danced with speed and passion, exemplifying brilliant technique, enjoying very loud "bravos" coming from the front.

One night, after performing *Swan Lake*, Belinda brought Mikhail backstage to meet Elena, leaving them alone. Still in her black swan tutu dress, Elena stood up to greet him and raised her fair eyebrows. Admiring his Roman nose and styled black hair, she watched the gallant Mikhail unexpectedly lower himself on one knee. The gesture made her heart jump. Overwhelmed by the wild thought he might propose, she tried to withdraw her small fingers from his smooth hands. Holding her tight, he feverishly pressed his hot lips to the top of her hand. He told her how Tchaikovsky's music took him back to his homeland, and how her portrayal of the black swan made his heart beat out of control. Intrigued by his healthy-looking oblong face while taking in his kind words, she thought her body would explode from the pressure building inside her. Until now, she had dedicated her life to dancing, leaving no room for courting. Watching Mikhail standing in front of her, so tall, so persistent, she knew her prince had arrived. She couldn't help glancing at his moustache that tickled her skin when he planted his moist kiss on her pale hand. His majestic stance and his large, glassy eyes mesmerised her.

Bringing her small gifts backstage before each show, and flowers afterwards, Mikhail continued to sit in the front row during the ballets. After her last bow, as tired as she was, she repeated the moves she wasn't happy with during the performance. Positioning her feet en pointe, she lifted her arms in the air, working on different parts of her body or repeated pirouettes, perfecting them again and again. As she took her time to snap out of her stage-role, she curiously watched Mikhail from the corner of her eye. Whether it took half an hour or an hour, he waited for her, reading the paper with his legs crossed in a corner of the rehearsal room with its shining floorboards. The reflection of his erect body followed her like a sunbeam, bouncing from the mirrored walls. During their outings, Elena opened up about her relatives living in Siberia. In reply, he said there were millions of innocent people affected by Stalin's regime who were killed, perished or died of starvation there. He blamed the German-Russian war that resulted in forced deportations and the enormous loss of Soviet citizens who managed to escape from their homelands. She wondered how he knew so much, given his young age!

Since she was little, she had envied her parents, her uncle and two aunties coming to Australia on the army ship. She was convinced they came here just as British migrants, to enjoy sunny Melbourne weather and spacious Australian land. British children at her school called their new country paradise on earth, with flowers and bushes as tall as giants. Julius and Gertrūda were actively involved in the Lithuanian community but Elena hated travelling to North Melbourne to listen to long, tearful speeches in a stuffy hall. Those around her spoke Lithuanian and she felt conscious of mispronouncing or putting wrong endings on her words. Being scolded by an elderly woman for speaking bad Lithuanian, she cried until her parents promised her she didn't have to go with them anymore. Now, remembering the unsettled atmosphere at the Hall, she felt guilty at not showing any interest in the Lithuanian culture or trying to find out the meaning behind the sorrowful gatherings.

*

After a year of courtship, Elena and Mikhail became engaged. In preparation for their wedding the following summer, she wondered what kind of bridal outfit she should choose to wear. There was also a problem of religion. She—a Roman Catholic and he—a non-practising Orthodox Christian, were not allowed to marry in church. As neither of them were willing to change their faith, they chose to marry at the Registry Office in Melbourne. Elena wore her ballet shoes, Coppélia's dress with modest cleavage, and a face-covering veil. To her surprise, Mikhail turned up dressed in white tights, a white shirt and a long white jacket with matching bowtie. He joked that while he'd never make it to Nureyev's standards, this was the least he could do! This gesture made Elena proud of him. Witnessed by their friends Belinda and Misha, the couple were married on a cloudy day of 15 December 1984. After posing for professional photos, Mr and Mrs Zverev travelled in a hired Mercedes to Elena's family home in Coburg for celebrations.

While purchasing tickets well in advance for their overseas trip, Elena and Mikhail also applied for four-week visas for Europe. In addition she received a two-week visa to stay in Moscow. During their honeymoon, they visited London, France, Italy, Norway and Sweden. The highlight of their journey was seeing *Swan Lake* in Paris, choreographed by Nureyev. With Scandinavian weather reaching -27°C, Mikhail bought Elena a white sable coat with a generous hood, admiring how it sat on her gracious body. Since she wore a full-length coat, he called her moya prekrasnaja Snegurochka—my beautiful Snow Maiden. She'd never heard of Snegurochka before, and learned that the character originated in the nineteenth century as part of Slavic pagan myths and folktales. Snegurochka, a daughter of Mother Spring and Father Frost, materialised at the home of a childless couple as a winter blessing. Loving and caring for her, and not realising she wasn't human, they wondered why she never left the house. But one day, overcome by curiosity, she ventured outdoors and met a boy. Impressed by the way Mikhail told the legend, Elena embraced him on the street.

"As much as I enjoy your attention, I must relay the ending," he said. "Once Snegurochka fell in love, she melted."

"How nice to be human," Elena said as they walked on the slippery street, holding hands for support.

Before their last destination, sitting in a café in Stockholm, Mikhail asked her to tell him whether she noticed any difference between people of their visited countries. Looking around, she remarked that people in Paris, Rome and Stockholm seemed as happy and hospitable as in Australia, while in London they seemed quiet and reserved. He took her hands into his, beginning a grave conversation as to how things in Russia would be different. He revealed he was afraid for her safety due to the possibility she might be followed. Taken aback, she withdrew her hands and sat still to listen, feeling more and more uneasy.

"You must know, my darling, visitors from Australia on personal business are confined to certain places," he said. "Soviet authorities aren't pleasant when dealing with those caught doing illegal things."

"Such as what?"

"Such as visiting forbidden places. Places outside Moscow, without permission."

"So, Lithuania is out of the question?" she asked, receiving his disappointed nod.

"How about Novosibirsk?"

"Hm. Maybe. I'll see what I can do," he said. "By the way, it would be good if we spoke Russian while we are in my homeland. It would be easier for those who don't understand English and less questions will be asked."

She noted how quickly things had changed. Here they were, conversing in English up till now, suddenly needing to switch to Russian! To shake herself of her uncertainty, she tried to maintain her spirits by thanking God for providing her with a second opportunity to be in Europe, pushing Mikhail's words of warning from her thoughts. She was looking forward to sitting in a balcony of the Bolshoi Theatre, to admire Nadia Pavlova, Nina Ananiashvili and Boris Akimov—the dancers Mikhail kept talking about.

At Moscow airport, they were met by Mikhail's family and representatives of the Russian diplomatic services. On their way to his parents' place, Elena immersed herself in her new surroundings. The women were stunning, wearing black winter boots and dark coats—some with hats, others with fur around their hoods, most with heavy make-up on. Good-looking men in bulky clothing with over-pressed, dark trousers hurried up the street. Most had withdrawn faces. It seemed that winter, with fluffy snow, didn't bring joy to the lives of the Muscovites. Even children in identical coats and uniforms, carrying books in cases, resembled robots as they made their way to school. Elena saw a truck, loaded with snow, wondering why the workers used shovels to spread it on the road. Mikhail giggled at her observation, explaining that in fact they were spreading salt. It muddied the streets and ruined shoes, but salt made the ice under the snow melt. She took note to be careful how she walked around in her new white boots. Even though it was winter in Europe, vehicles and buildings there were extravagant in comparison to worn Russian-made cars or rusty truck trailers, billowing black smoke from their exhaust pipes that covered multistorey buildings with fumes.

Listening to Mikhail speaking with his father as they drove, Elena was lulled by the pleasant voices of her in-laws. She recalled Mikhail mentioning his mother worked at the University of Moscow, and his father as a diplomat. Irina spoke very clear Russian, which seemed apt to Elena given she taught Russian linguistics. Her husband Boris spoke at length about the countries in which he'd worked: Spain, the US and the UK. Curious, Elena checked the years of his stay in London, discovering he was there when she danced her way to prima ballerina on her scholarship! She relaxed in a company of Mikhail's parents, and now knew his good looks came from his mother and his diplomatic skills and sense of humour from his father. Hearing about Elena and Mikhail's wedding outfits, his parents couldn't stop laughing, Boris running through a red light in his new Lada. They thought it sounded surreal, something only possible in a fairytale, and soon Elena understood why—for their union to become legitimate in Russia, they were expected to marry again!

Upon entering Zverev's two bedroom flat, Elena smiled at seeing a row of slippers near the door for everyone to change into as they took their shoes off. What a great way to keep the place clean! The floors were covered by colourful carpet. After being wined and dined by her in-laws in their spacious lounge, Mikhail took Elena to his own dwelling by taxi. On the way she reflected that his parents seemed well off. The walls of the lounge room were covered with paintings. The overflowing bookshelves housed many souvenirs, obviously brought from different countries. Using gold-plated utensils, they ate from expensive china.

When Mikhail unlocked the door of his flat and put the light on, there were about ten people waiting for them with a table spread with caviar, torte and alcohol. The surprised couple soon learned that Mikhail's parents had organised the gathering to congratulate the newlyweds.

Over the next couple of days, Elena found her head spinning from speaking Russian and drinking alcohol. She couldn't understand how the seemingly unhappy people from the streets of Moscow transformed into affectionate and highly-spirited individuals in the privacy of their homes. Maybe it was because there was so much alcohol that it led to dancing and endless hours of stimulating conversations. Maybe their other, not so happy faces that masked the struggles of their daily lives, dropped off for her. Maybe in like-minded company, they solved the problems of their supposedly utopian lives.

*

Elena and Mikhail arrived at the Central Moscow Registry Office, followed by his parents, relatives and friends. With other couples and their bridal parties lining the long corridors, Elena was told that nobody here would marry in a church after the official ceremony, unless they did it in secret. The couple behind them looked serious, as if doubting their decision to join their lives together. Some members of the bridal parties were more cheerful than others. Most stuck to allocated places, obediently waiting their turn. Holding a small bunch of hyacinths to her chest, Elena was pleased not to outshine any bride. They were all dressed more extravagantly than her! She wore a long white dress with matching veil, Australian opal necklace and earrings complementing the colour of her nail polish. She found the male registrar stiff and icy, not even attempting to smile throughout the ceremony. She felt self-conscious, receiving Mikhail's prolonged kiss in front of him and her in-laws. She wished the official part was over.

Disappointed that nobody threw streamers, glitter or rice upon their exit outside, as apparently this was not a Russian tradition, she soon found herself in Mikhail's arms, carried over a bridge. The elegant fir trees blew gently in the breeze. Hearing the car drivers beeping their horns for good-luck, and passers-by wishing them a long-lasting marriage, Elena began to relax. She was taken aback to see how her wedding affected people, as if waking them up from a long sleep and reminding them of new beginnings. She enjoyed the tradition of a new husband carrying his wife over seven bridges, and was proud of Mikhail for not getting puffed even once! The newlyweds were transported to the reception in a white Volga, hired for the occasion.

Their second wedding celebration was attended by more than a hundred guests. Elena found the Russians highly entertaining, sharing jokes and anecdotes, spilling onto the dance floor after official speeches. Elena joined in, smiling and laughing, relaxing amongst the complete strangers. She noticed Mikhail's mother wearing flashy jewellery and a fox tail hanging over her cream evening gown, decorated with glittering diamonds. Her short, black hair neatly sat around her flawless face. Boris, standing next to her, kept scrunching his thick eyebrows in response to whatever she had to say. He appeared older than Irina, greyish steaks of hair visible around his temples. Elena sensed that intellectual Zverev's family was highly regarded by Moscow's upper class. She observed women dressed in long frocks, hats and gloves, men in suits, ties or bowties. The party took place in a huge hall. Crystal chandeliers hung from the ceilings with strands of sparkling jewels draped across their frames. Long tables, stretched from one end of the venue to the other, plentiful with food and drinks. Elena, in the same, white tulle dress, and Mikhail in a black dinner suit, waltzed to Strauss' "Blue Danube" to the clapping and cheering of those standing in a circle around them. She was also asked to dance solo, and when she did, Mikhail's parents congratulated her for being an excellent ballerina, now their dear daughter in-law. The ballroom music, played by a live orchestra, entertained all night. In comparison to her Australian wedding ceremony at the Registry Office with a small gathering of family, this was a grand performance with all the actors playing their parts to perfection.

During the week, Elena and Mikhail visited the Red Square. Learning they would have to wait in the freezing cold to see Lenin's embalmed body in the Mausoleum, Elena decided to miss the viewing. The following night, they saw *Esmeralda*, at the Moscow Ballet Theatre. The faces and bodies of principal dancers Nina Sorokina and Yuri Vladimirov, a husband and wife in real life, were very expressive. Nina's electrifying presence and technique, and Yuri's masculinity added to the joy of the performance. The cast of the Bolshoi Theatre, the costumes, decorations and atmosphere left her short of breath. She couldn't wait for the red plush curtain to lift before each act, watching de corps dancers practically flying from one corner of the stage to the other. All of the same height and physical features, they moved together with absolute precision. Watching the principal dancer Nina with envy, Elena worried that she was already out of practice. During her honeymoon she had been gaining weight—a big no for a prima ballerina! After getting married, she decided dancing was not something she wanted to do for the rest of her life. Most of all she hated the fierce competition from other ballerinas. Besides, she wanted to have children and move to teaching.

During the first interval, Elena recognised faces from her wedding, some seated in the audience and others walking around the hallway as if to show off their fancy attire. A small group of Mikhail's acquaintances came forward to greet them, ushering them towards the overcrowded bar. Splashing money on champagne and clinking their glasses, they wished Elena and Mikhail endless happiness.

Elena gently broached the subject of wanting to go to Novosibirsk to see her grandmother, giving Mikhail time to plan around his work commitments. It took three days to obtain special government permission to allow her to travel to Siberia. Seeing Mikhail's frustrated expression, she began to doubt whether she'd get an opportunity to see her relatives. Her Moscow visa was expiring in a week's time! In his opinion, the delay was caused by the Soviet authorities and their hesitation to let an Australian tourist snoop around Novosibirsk. "They think your visit may compromise their image. What rubbish! I've never met a more apolitical person than you in my whole life!" Finally the authorities relented and, holding her pass to her chest, she felt privileged to be married to someone who cared and could afford to take her anywhere! Sitting next to her, Mikhail took her in his arms, passionately kissing her lips, face and neck.

*

The newly-married couple boarded the Aeroflot plane Tu-104 to Novosibirsk. Keeping Mikhail's warning of being followed in mind, she wasn't surprised to find stewards meeting them with ready-to-drink champagne. Elena and Mikhail drowned their flutes hastily, well aware of other passengers wanting to pass at the entry. Once again, she noted many stiff bodies walking towards their seats as if they were programmed. Even Mikhail carried himself with authority, totally removed from the person she knew—as if he forgot how to joke and laugh. Looking out the small window, partially covered by snow, she felt overcome with the anticipation of meeting her grandmother. Suspiciously glancing towards the ground, she imagined the window transforming into a peep hole. Her body stiffened from the thought of someone watching her with binoculars from the outside or listening to her conversation inside.

Taking off her new coat, she stood up, purposely facing two young men sitting in the next row. She smiled, but they didn't acknowledge her, staring in front of them straight-faced. She was convinced they were going to Novosibirsk to follow her. She pretended to sleep nearly all the way, afraid a listening device might be planted under her seat. When she spoke with Mikhail, she took care not to mention how pleased she was to hear Valda's and Diana's voices over the phone upon their arrival in Moscow. She didn't want to talk about Australia, mention her parents nor her work, providing no clues to an invisible recorder, allowing gently-snoring spies to relax.

The distance from Novosibirsk to Moscow was three thousand kilometres. Reaching the Karakansky forest, the plane flew above the Ob River and made a smooth landing at the Tolmachevo Airport. Valda and Diana, both the same height, wearing thick, dark coats, hats, boots and mittens, met them with tears and embraces. They took a taxi to the Southern district, some sixteen kilometres from the airport. Elena glanced out the back window but didn't see the suspicious men from the plane.

The blocks of the multistorey buildings mirrored each other around the industrial town. Valda and Diana lived in one of the flats. When they stepped inside, their suitcase had to be pushed aside to fit all of them taking off and hanging their warm clothing, then changing their shoes to slippers. Only now Elena noticed Valda's dark hair, pleated and curled around her head. Diana's shoulder-length hair was of the same colour. Their small, clear amber eyes, moved from Elena to Mikhail and back. Elena had no doubt they wondered what a Russian diplomat, probably a KGB spy, was doing in this farthest corner of the world, in -40°C.

Valda turned on a self-boiling metal container with a tap near the bottom of it where she poured hot water into a teapot with strong tea-leaf concentrate. Elena had never seen a samovar before and was fascinated by it. A cheerful Diana served cabbage rolls for dinner, a crumble pie for desert, followed by Soviet champagne to celebrate their reunion. Valda told them how she enjoyed living among Ukrainians, Uzbeks, Tatars, Germans and Tajiks. "But we also have Belarusians, Yezidis, Jews, Georgians, Armenians, Azerbaijanis, Kazakhs, Kyrgyz, Chinese, Koreans," she said. "I can't recall the names of over a hundred nationalities!"

Mikhail speculated the reason for such a mix of nationalities. "It must be due to the industrial expansion here."

Nodding her head, Valda told of how in the fifties the Soviet government ordered the construction of a hydroelectric power station on the shore of the Ob River.

"Was it completed?" Elena asked.

"Yes. In 1961," said Valda. "Not to mention the Scientific Research Centre."

"When was it built?" Elena wanted to know.

"In the late fifties," Mikhail said. "There's also the Academic Town of Novosibirsk, stretching thirty kilometres south of the city!"

Valda agreed, explaining that the Academic Town—Akademgorodok was widely spread and host to about thirty-five research institutes and universities.

"I work there," Diana added. "At the lab, experimenting with mice."

Only now did Elena spot how similar Diana's small hands were to her own, with thin fingers obviously suitable for microscopic experiments!

"How fascinating," Mikhail said. "And what about you, Valda? You're most probably enjoying a well-deserved retirement."

"Believe me, I still consult classical dance teachers in Novosibirsk State Conservatorium from time to time," said Valda. "They call me when they need help."

Elena envied this tiny woman for her inner strength, unable to take her eyes off her thin face. Touching her own face, Elena turned to Diana, observing hers, and exclaiming loudly "All three of us have the same facial features!" When she sat next to Valda and Diana, Mikhail couldn't agree more. "You look like sisters," he said. "Long lost and found sisters."

*

Elena and Mikhail checked into their hotel, searching their room for bugging devices under their bed, window seals, lamps and behind the toilet seat. Not finding anything suspicious they were soon asleep, exhausted after a long flight and emotional reunion.

The following morning they returned to say goodbye to the two women. The pleasant aroma of a freshly-baked apple pie filled the flat. The samovar was already boiling and Diana filled everybody's cups with tea. Elena wanted to know more about the city. Mikhail—a walking encyclopaedia—recalled the greatest Soviet undertaking in building the Novosibirsk metro transit system in 1979.

"It'll be up and running soon, apparently in a couple of years," said Diana. "With over a million citizens, and more constantly arriving from all over the Soviet Union, we have great capacity in achieving the deadlines!"

"A million! That's a lot," Elena said.

"With some seven hundred thousand in the fifties, the city keeps growing and growing," Valda said.

"Were you in Novosibirsk in the fifties?" Elena asked, suddenly pausing to cover her blushing face with both hands.

"Don't worry darling," Valda said, strongly embracing her, assuring her they could converse freely in the flat. "Even though Vasilij is not present, his spirit is out there to protect me. Besides, my daughter—the daughter of the General—acts as a deterrent to those that may try to ask any questions about our past."

Elena, sitting close to her husband, listened intensely to Valda's somber voice.

"Since my exile from Lithuania in 1944, I lived in the outskirts of Tomsk, a couple of hundred kilometres west from Novosibirsk. I moved here in 1953."

"And what happened to the General who loved you so much?" Elena asked.

"Ach. He had to return home to his family in Tomsk. Believe me, we were both heartbroken. But being a decent man, Vasilij couldn't divorce his first wife. In the camp, he cared for me and made sure I could survive by assigning me to work in the kitchen. There I could feed myself and help others by passing around stolen vegetables or feeding scraps from his parties. Everybody was hungry, cold and angry, but only the sound-minded refused to eat dead men's flesh. Those that dared, died soon afterwards from corpse diseases."

"How terrible," said Elena and Mikhail in one voice.

"Yes. It was. I've seen too much ... Vasilij never punished me for helping adult prisoners and undernourished children. He had a good heart, being a father of two grown-up children. Feeling sorry for me constantly talking about my past life as a famous ballerina, he improvised an exercise bar from a long round wooden plank. It was in vain. How could I practise my ballet steps in such an environment? My swollen ankles, stiffened-up legs, blemished, bruised, blistered and reddened hands were not fit for such pleasure. Previously I loved my body, worshiped by huge audiences. Now, in exile, I hated it! It completely lost its shape."

"Mother, don't get stressed please," said Diana, placing her finger on Valda's wrist, soon becoming content her pulse was normal. Patting her daughter's back, Valda revealed how since Diana's birth, Vasilij remained hidden in her heart, glowing like a crystal, showing her the way.

"What a story. Sort of grown-up Romeo and Juliet," Elena said, absorbing what she'd just learned.

Mikhail asked what Diana recalled from her time in exile but she knew nothing. After her birth she was taken to Tomsk to live with her father's sister.

"Aunty Anuska was a spinster. When I was growing up, I thought her thick glasses with black frames and her puffed, fizzy hair made her look like a witch. But she was very kind to me. My father visited us occasionally, assuring me that my mother would come for me after completing her assignment.

"When I was older, I kept questioning him and Anuska about why Valda's assignment was taking so long. But he would leave in silence, and she would pat my neatly-plaited hair with white bows, with tears running down her wrinkled cheeks."

"You would've died if you stayed in the camp," said Valda, confessing that she and Vasilij didn't plan to have a baby. But, surrounded by the hopelessness of their useless existence, they yearned for warmth and affection. After her infant was taken to Tomsk, she couldn't wait to be reunited.

"And finally you came! I think I was seven at the time."

"That's right, seven years, two months and five days! My poor girl, cuddling Anuska and me, calling us her mothers, wanting to take Anuska with us ..."

Thinking of Valda's words, Elena discreetly looked around the humble flat, equivalent to a one-bedroom dwelling in Australia. It comprised of a hallway, a small kitchen, a lounge room, a bedroom, a bathroom and a toilet. The lounge room was furnished with a sofa-bed, a square table and four chairs, and a side cabinet containing a dinner set, cups and glasses. The rug hanging on a wall portrayed a Kazak on a horse, galloping through the red steppe in his high narrow hat.

"So, you spent fifteen years in exile?" Mikhail asked.

"No, only nine. The rest of my time in Siberia became sort of voluntarily exile. We could've resettled anywhere, apart from my homeland. If we went home, we would've endured hostility and abuse by people living in our own house … there was no point. We would've still lived under Russians."

Probably trying to ease the charged emotions in the air, Mikhail complemented the hosts on their excellent command of Russian. Elena couldn't write or read Russian, but could speak quite well. Luckily she understood everything as she grew up conversing with her Russian neighbours, living at the end of their street. Elena played with Sara and Aron, the grandchildren of the Russian-Jewish refugees, remaining good friends to this day. Only now, sitting in her grandmother's flat, did she learn more details about the German-Russian war, the extermination of Jews and the exile of the Baltic people from their homes. Also, how the Soviet authorities regarded those who escaped in 1944 from the Soviet Union as traitors of the state. Only now she realised her family members were amongst them, living with fear, not trusting even their closest neighbours. Only now she understood why none of the invited members of the Lithuanian community attended her wedding—she was marrying a Russian—definitely a KGB spy! Observing him, so removed from the authoritarian image of a foreign diplomat, she didn't know what to think. Even if he was a spy, she loved him and didn't care.

Valda got up from the table and excused herself. She returned in a long dress with a huge colourful scarf around her shoulders. Before she entered the room, Diana put a gypsy record on. Like a gust of light wind Valda flew past them, tapping the floor with her bare foot and vigorously shaking her shoulders. Her swollen fingers, holding the scarf corners, would point to the ceiling with each lift of her chin. Elena looked at her grandmother with pride, soon jumping to her feet and improvising some steps, while Mikhail clapped to the rhythm of the dance. Diana joined them too, doing splits in the middle of the lounge room. The trio, aged seventy three, thirty eight and twenty stretched their hands across each other's shoulders, moving to the right and to the left in perfect synchronisation. Mikhail began circling around them. Once the music stopped, he asked all to remain standing and took photos of the three women enjoying themselves in their reunion. Valda in her long, floral dress with loose sleeves, Diana in her grey slacks and matching V-neck jumper, and Elena in a body-hugging burgundy suit and pink, frilled blouse. While Mikhail clicked his camera, they kept changing poses, improvising different dance steps. Then they embraced for the last photo, crying and laughing at the same time. From the distance, Valda appeared rather girlish, but from close-up her unhealthy, greyish face revealed deep wrinkles and puffiness under her tired eyes. She reminded Elena of a butterfly. As she twisted and turned her skin-and-bone body around, Elena could see how this woman had captivated audiences with her dancing, with a determined and fiery presence. Sadly, the tips of her butterfly wings had been long frozen by harsh Siberian winters.

*

Elena gave birth to a son, Rudolf, who was her first ballet student at the dance school she opened in 1990. Many of her pupils entered the Australian Ballet Company, becoming international stars. During the following years, Elena and Mikhail made various attempts to invite Valda and Diana for a visit but their applications were rejected by Moscow. Even Mikhail's connections with the Australian Embassy there couldn't help. Then the letter from Novosibirsk arrived with news of Valda dying on the 26th of December 1991, on the day of the disintegration of the USSR. Diana decided not to relocate to Australia, and continued to live in Novosibirsk where her mother was buried.

When Elena thought of the two women who meant so much to her, she would dust the dancing figurines sitting on a shelf above the fireplace. They were made of bronze, custom made from Mikhail's photos taken in Novosibirsk. Valda was in the middle, with Elena with Diana on each side—their hands curved in the shape of tulips. Valda's and Diana's faces revealed their unfulfilled lives, and Elena's—glowing with happiness. Looking at them, Elena reflected on how meeting them, had changed her life. She felt a gratitude to them for showing her how to be grateful for what she had. She wanted to carry on their traditions and to do what they could not. She wanted Rudolf to grow up as a sensitive and honest man, and to reconnect with his roots by teaching ballet in Novosibirsk. She wanted Rudolf to learn his family stories without a single lie.

One Night in Ossetia

I'm packing my clothes and necessities for my trip to Ossetia. It's the end of July and my train from Vilnius to Moscow departs today. I'm travelling alone but will be joining the rest of the group in Georgia. My mother adds some pears, apples, half a loaf of bread and a couple of tomatoes to my food bag. My father gives me twenty-five rubles for unexpected expenses. I've also saved forty-five rubles for the trip. When my mother and I are chatting in the bedroom, she tip-toes to the door and gently closes it. She begs me not to give into any men's advances. She whispers that if a man is serious, he'd never touch me but would instead follow me all the way to Lithuania. I smile, embrace her and kiss her on the forehead, promising not to get tangled in any love affairs. I think she is being overcautious. What can happen to me? I don't want my parents to go with me to the station as I hate goodbyes. When I leave the flat, I see them glued to our second-floor window. With a mixture of sadness and excitement about my new adventure, I wave to them and they wave back to me.

The train to Moscow is overcrowded with travellers returning from the Baltic coast. I find my place in an open-plan cabin with bunk-style beds, called platskart. Each cabin consists of two parts: two lower and two upper bunks on one side and one each on the other, separated by a narrow walkway. The night train, crowded with tanned bodies, speeds on. Chatty children eventually settle down and smooth conversations tune into the rhythm of motion. I line up in the queue for the toilet at the end of the carriage. The queue hardly moves but ten minutes later I enter through the narrow door. The water runs in a weak stream and the sign on the wall advices to use it sparingly—a good wash is out of the question. I brush my teeth and decide to leave on my make-up. I try to prolong the return to my bunk by crossing into the almost empty restaurant carriage and sitting down. A young waiter of medium height approaches my table and I order a glass of mineral water. He soon returns with a bottle and two glasses. He greets me with a smile and fills my glass to the top. I'm thirsty and empty it quickly, admiring his thick chestnut hair and straight nose. He introduces himself as Atsamaz from Ossetia and sits in front of me, pouring some water into the second glass.

"Zita from Lithuania," I say, extremely pleased I am still wearing my mascara. When I ask for the meaning of his name, he tells me that according to legend Atsamaz was a singer, a musician and the winner of the golden flute. He purposely lowers the corners of his well-shaped lips, expressing his regret at not being able to play any instrument. His deep and pleasant voice takes me to the Caucasus, to the lands that legend had populated with gods and supernatural beings. The Ossetian gods, often identified with Christian saints, gave birth to legends of semi-divine heroes. Atsamaz is convinced that his name has much in common with a so-called hero in the epic *Nart*. He uses the Abkhazian version of the myth, in which Narts—war bandits—fought with local heroes. One of the legends features the one hundred sons of the mythological figure Satanaya, the mother of the Narts. I comment that being a bandit is not very nice and he assures me it wasn't always the case, recounting snippets of the Ossetian myth version depicting the Nartic tribe of the bravest Æxsærtægkatæ clan. I try to repeat the name Æxsærtægkatæ after him, and he is amused with my Lithuanian pronunciation. He whispers to me that I must keep his stories to myself. "There is no room for *our* ancient myths in the Soviet history," he says. Only now I realise I don't know any ancient Lithuanian myths.

While I'm taking in his words, Atsamaz changes the subject and tells me that he spends his summer holidays working in train restaurants. This summer he has been lucky to get a job on the Vilnius–Moscow train as it allows him to visit his uncle Ruslan in Vilnius. In turn, I share with him the details of my trip from Georgia to Ossetia. He listens, warmly looking at me with his lively eyes. His skin is tanned and his wavy hair suits his sculpted face. He leaves me for a minute, swiftly returning with some sweets. Mesmerised by the enormous moon we see outside, we share dried figs, apricots and some chocolate. At about three in the morning, he takes me back to my carriage. We part with a gentle kiss. I stare in front of me, but can't distinguish my fellow passengers' faces in the dark. The only face in my mind is the face of Atsamaz. I observe the full moon, trembling slightly while counting the falling stars. I see the lights flickering from the distant country houses filled with people who probably can't sleep.

The train arrives in Moscow at 6 am. Passengers look sleepy, some children are crying and others resist being carried out. The passage is full of bags and suitcases. The attendant encourages passengers to disembark in an orderly fashion. I'm disappointed not to see Atsamaz, but that's what travel is about. In an unplanned moment, people meet by accident, sharing their lives, going so far as to reveal their deepest secrets to a complete stranger. That's because they are most certain they'll never meet again. For me, during that special time, a stranger suddenly becomes a best friend who understands me, who cries and laughs with me, who tells me stories I never forget. That kind of experience enriches me and changes me for good.

*

Securing my luggage in a station locker, I explore Moscow. After finding a canteen I get a bowl of porridge, a cup of tea and a sweet bun from the service counter. I pay thirty-five kopeks—thirty-five cents—and sit near the window. With a ray of sunshine touching my table, I feel as though I can sense the eyes of Atsamaz on my back but when I turn around he is not there. All I can think of is the unmistakable attraction between us. He didn't want to let my hand go after he took me back to my carriage. But then again, I may have imagined there was something in his strong embrace. Maybe our youth made us behave as we did instinctively. Maybe, both in our twenties, we were too careful to assume that the summer night conversation was more than a pleasant encounter. Trying to find the answer to justify my growing fondness of a complete stranger, I recall my trip to Murmansk in 1981, just two years before. We had arrived there in the evening, wandering around the town. It was close to midnight, but the streets and buildings were fully lit up. The white night was as bright as day. Sitting on the park benches, people read newspapers and books. The next morning we toured the central library. Among the book descriptions, the librarian Svetlana inserted her personal story of her holiday romance, instantly becoming the object of discussion. I'd never forget how she also travelled with a tourist group to Murmansk where she met her future husband. They fell in love during her trip and, after their wedding, she relocated here from Moscow. Some women congratulated her on having such good luck while men nodded or stood in silence.

Svetlana showed us around the huge library, pointing to publications by Tolstoy, Lenin, Dzerzhinsky and Pushkin as well as to Russian translations of Dumas' and Stendhal's novels, and Anderson's fairytales. Suddenly she stopped talking and excused herself, hiding behind one of the shelves. Browsing through the books, some of us secretly observed her speaking with a young man. His thick eyebrows added to his angry facial expression. She stretched her neck as if trying to be taller. They talked in haste. He stormed out. When Svetlana rejoined us she apologised for leaving us, then sighed and said unfortunately things were not going well with her husband and, given a second chance, she wouldn't have uprooted herself from her family as she did.

My thoughts return to the canteen in Moscow where I'm still savouring my tea and a half of a bun. I finish my meal and my table is immediately cleaned by a polite dishwasher. She says I can remain here as long as I want, as there are plenty of empty seats. I order another cup of tea, scribbling a couple of sentences to my parents on a postcard with an image of the Red Square, purchased at the station. The letters during my travels are always positive, like this one—everything is great, the August summer morning is perfect for the last leg of my journey that is just about to take place. I don't mention Atsamaz, trying to shake away my sense of disappointment at what seemed so real. Oh, how real he still is, making my heartbeat increase with the hope that, any minute, he'll tap me on a shoulder. While wandering the streets of Moscow, I'm angry with myself for thinking about him, for being so naïve in dismissing my mother's warning of a man's charms. Noticing that I'm still carrying the card in my hand, I find a post office and wait for the unfriendly face behind the counter to stamp it.

After hours of window shopping, sitting on a bench in a park, eating ice-cream, and reading my book, I return to the station. The Moscow–Tbilisi train sits on the platform with its windows covered by the faded shutters. Taking a seat in the platskart carriage, I study my map, following a line along the shores of the Black Sea that passes through Abkhazia. I read the names of notable Tbilisi tourist destinations that include Rike Park, the VDNKh Exhibition Complex and Tbilisi Botanical Garden. Soon a family of five spread themselves around, filling in the remaining places of my cabin. In comparison to the twelve-hour journey from Vilnius to Moscow, this one will take twenty-four hours and is nearly two thousand kilometres in length. I put my jumper under my hard seat, every so often walking up and down the carriage so as not to stiffen up. With passengers talking, eating and moving around, time passes as fast as our speeding train. When we reach Abkhazia's capital Sukhumi, I move amongst the passengers disembarking and getting on, to jump onto the platform. Picking up a brochure from the station, I learn that today the local population is more than two hundred and fifty thousand and Abkhazia's territory stretches eight thousand six hundred square kilometres. I read how, during the summer months, some families relax in their holiday dwellings, called dachas. Being afraid to miss the train's departure, I hurry back to my carriage. Once the train moves, I see a stretch of disorderly sheds rather than dachas, built close to each other, the land separated by crushed stones and narrow passages between fences. Two hours later we arrive in Tbilisi with its one and a half million inhabitants.

*

By the time I reach the tourist base in 30°C heat, I'm tired and my rucksack is pressing on my back, saturating my top with sweat. I find people gathering around the reception lobby with their luggage. I spot a young couple who are here on their honeymoon. Their names are Tania and Volodia from Belarus. Next to them stands Gunnar from Tallinn, Inese from Riga and Dmytro from Ukraine. Our instructor Murat asks for everybody's attention and the induction into our tour begins. We'll be travelling on foot for twenty days, carrying shared food, cutlery, tents, sleeping bags plus our personal belongings. Because we are going on an extensive walking trip, each of us needs to have our blood pressure and heart checked. Noisily we line up near the doctor's room for a one-on-one examination. I smile with relief that my health is perfect.

After supper, we travel to Rike Park for a musical water show. The singing and dancing fountain is huge, full of differently sized streams which rise and fall to the sound of music. With each emerging wave, the changing colours, shapes and direction of the water makes the fountain a great spectacle. We scream, especially when the music reaches its peak and the multiple streams of water formations shoot into the sky, refreshing us with a cool, moist breeze. We return to the hostel just before midnight.

The following morning the chartered bus takes us on an excursion around the town. Murat sits near the driver and talks into a microphone. He points to Stalinist architecture, explaining that this term is associated with the Social Realism School of Art and architecture since the leadership of Joseph Stalin. We pass Rustaveli's cinema and the Stalin Museum of Gori, apparently both exhibiting authentic Soviet era relics that due to our limited time we are unable to explore.

Murat shows us samples of Modernist architecture that emerged after the Second World War, based upon new technologies of construction made of glass, steel and concrete. We discover how, since 1955, building in the whole Soviet Union became non-decorative due to Nikita Khrushchev passing a resolution about minimising construction expenses. The curved wooden balconies, flower ornaments and detailed exteriors were replaced by strict and simple forms. The only decorations left were mosaics and bas-reliefs, celebrating Soviet cosmonaut achievements. Murat points to the VDNKh Exhibition Complex, a modernist building built in 1961, the same year Yuri Gagarin went to space. We leave the bus in front of the Exhibition Building at Tsereteli Avenue. Walking around the pavilion, we view a mosaic on the wall that was inspired with visions of space, portraying a cosmonaut, a hard-working male and female worker against a background of a flying spaceship and sputnik.

We have one hour of the tour left to visit the Tbilisi Botanical Garden with one hundred and one hectares and a collection of over four and a half thousand plant groups. A botanist guide talks non-stop, and my head is hurting from information overload. We discover that the Garden is located at the foothills of Narikala Castle, bursting with blossoming flowers, old trees, and new seedlings. We learn the origins of the Garden's collection, containing flora from the Caucasus region, the Himalayas, Siberia and Japan. Given a few minutes to rest, we listen to the chirping birds while admiring rock formations as well as thick vegetation alongside the Tsavkisistskali River. The concrete bridge connects the Garden with the waterfall. The botanist encourages us to use observation decks, made from natural materials and reachable by stairs, to gauge the vastness of our surroundings. The views of the Garden from the decks are as spectacular as from the bridge. Due to the bow-shaped structure beneath it, the bridge appears even more majestic from afar.

On our way to the base, Murat praises the Georgian capital, lying on the banks of the Kura River, some one and a half thousand kilometres long. The river, overflowing with dams and channels, drains into the Caspian Sea. He explains how, starting in north-eastern Turkey, it flows through Turkey to Georgia, then to Azerbaijan where it joins with the river Aras and enters the Caspian Sea. At the conclusion of our tour, we return to our hostel to quickly freshen up before supper is served in the ground floor canteen.

*

Our group, made up of thirty tourists calling each other narod— comrades from all over the Soviet Union—travels to the South Ossetian border by bus and disembark. Everyone lines up, side by side at arm's length, receiving equal portions of condensed milk, fish and meat tins, a loaf of bread each and a sleeping bag. Our guide, Murat, distributes pots, pans, cups and parts of the tents. Those who brought too many personal belongings complain their rucksacks are too heavy. Murat gives us instructions on making sure we are carrying our load correctly. He walks around, checking, pulling, stretching and tightening our gear. He notes that each of us should be loaded with thirty kilograms and, if we have more, our own belongings should stay on the bus to be collected at our last destination. He reassures us that the extra load will get easier with each passing day. Persuaded, none of us move. As we take our places behind each other, the early morning sun is already warming the air. The climbing of the five thousand and sixty square metre Caucasus Mountain begins. We rest every hour. I have a sip from my water bottle, but just a small sip as it has to last until we reach our first camp, hopefully at 5 pm. I have been preparing for this trip by running every morning for the past six months and exercising on weekends. I rush upwards without running out of breath, admiring the view.

After three hours or so, it's clear some of the narod are well behind. We are stretched like an accordion bellows to its limit. Murat descends to the bottom of the line to investigate what has happened. The news echoes back up the line—the newlyweds are struggling with the climb. We hear that Murat kneels down to assess Tania's breathing. She sits on a stone, leaning onto her husband, looking as though she needs to throw up. No more is said, but we later discover she has admitted to being pregnant. Murat gives us a signal, we continue to ascend without him. He stays close to Tania while Volodia now carries both of their rucksacks.

About 6 pm, we reach the flat surface where we break for our camp. Everyone helps to erect three army tents, fitting ten people each. It takes nearly an hour to stretch them by evenly pulling the corners in all four directions, then attaching strong ropes to the brackets and using stones to secure them below the ground. We are instructed to use the bushes for our toilet needs and wash in a small creek.

The next morning, I get up early and descend to a nearby creek. Quickly dipping into the knee-deep water, I gasp for air as the water is shockingly cold. While I'm drying myself others begin to arrive, making me pleased I had my wash in privacy. We eat, pack our rucksacks, collapse our tents, tidy the area and prepare to ascend.

*

A week later, Natasha lets me in on a secret. At the start of the trip, she had found herself in Murat's tent. And, she had stayed, and had spent each night with him since. She complains that she has lost one of her contact lenses—she asks me to follow her into Murat's tent to look for it. She unzips one sleeping bag and feels her way through with her fingers. I turn another sleeping bag inside out and thoroughly examine it. Then we both search every corner of the tent. Again and again, she checks inside her bra. She adores manly Murat, who could easily lift her up with one hand. And why not, I think to myself, the twenty-three-year-old daughter of the Professor of Philology is short and thin. As if to rebel against this intellectual upbringing, during the climb she revels in messing up her dark hair, draping a huge-tussled scarf around her shoulders and reading our palm lines. After checking the tent for the missing lens, we sit outside to contemplate the next move. Irina, Inese and Tania walk past curious as to what we're doing. Natasha tells them the truth. On their knees, the trio inspects the surrounding territory, combing the grass in vain with their fingers.

From now on, Natasha walks close to Murat, needing his guidance to keep her balance. Soon the rest of the group know about their relationship. We envy Natasha when Murat places five of her tins into his rucksack. But the other women are still rather pleased with his attention. Every time we meet, he greets me with a grin, making me wonder if he favours me. The way he looks at Vera's big chest or at Olia's and Inese's bodies while they sunbathe flatter them, because he is not vulgar. His dark hair highlights the intensity of his eyes. His hawk nose, strong jaw and thick moustache "transforms him" into a brave Nart. The bulkiness of his body is complemented by well-rounded muscles. There is no doubt he must be strong at all times—physically and mentally—in leading a sizeable group who are dealing with daily challenges.

The greatest challenge is measuring the rationing of food against the reluctance to carry too much. We are only halfway through our journey, and already some walk easy, having eaten shared resources themselves.

The following morning, Viktor from Charkov joins me on the way up. He is approximately one hundred and seventy centimetres tall, has a bulky nose and workman's hands. Taking a reasonable break with our rucksacks off and reclining on a grassy patch, we watch the mountain valley coloured with purple, pink and yellow flowers. He gazes at me with his clear amber eyes. The wind messes his hair, exposing his longish face. When he speaks, his shy smile partially reveals his uneven teeth. Squinting against the bright sun, he wants to know my name.

"You have a lovely accent, Rūta. Where do you come from?"

"Soviet Lithuania," I reply, adding that I work as a primary school teacher. We're pleased to be able to communicate in Russian as we don't know each other's native tongue.

"As a factory worker, I'm nervous speaking to a well-educated lady from the Baltic States. Ach, I wish we could live as well as you do there!"

"Do you mean the Baltic people from the 'West of the East?'"

"Precisely. You've got everything! Your meat and milk products are of the highest quality. You have toilet paper while we still use newspapers. The Baltic Sea is literally licking your feet."

I don't want to spoil the moment by telling him that we also use newspapers and pages of exercise books in the toilet …

"You dress nicely, you have a sense of fashion," he continues.

I don't want to reveal how women in Lithuania make their own clothing from colourful materials purchased at the black market. They know how to neatly attach the Chanel or Wranglers labels to the garments, making them identical to the clothes in western magazines smuggled to the port of Klaipėda by Soviet fishing liners.

Viktor lightly pulls on my long plait, admitting it's difficult for him to tear himself from my unusual eyes speckled with gold and brown rays. He thinks my lips are desirable and my neck is as gracious as that of a swan. After such compliments, I'm glad to have his company. From now on we walk together. In an hour or so, part of the group is dragging behind. Some find it difficult to breathe. Some, afraid to look down or fall over, stop all together. Faster ones, including Viktor and me, are advised to wait for the rest to catch up. After the initial struggle, we manage to evenly line up, moving again, Murat shouting *vperiod*—forward!

We stop at about 6 pm and this time we stay in the prepared accommodation of a run-down dwelling. Years ago it used to be a school, but children grew-up and moved with their families elsewhere. Today the bad weather is making the stone structure disintegrate. Luckily it's dry inside. We organise ourselves into two groups—women on one side of the room, and men on the other, with the exception of our newlyweds who stretch their sleeping bags on the women's side. Murat checks that we haven't lost anyone, counting twenty females and ten males, aged between eighteen and thirty-five, gathered from seven Soviet Union republics: Belarus, Ukraine, Moldavia, Lithuania, Latvia, Estonia, and Russia. We clap and shout *ura*! Murat drops his things on the men's side, and urges us to make preparation for supper.

We gather twigs and wood for the fire place outside and soon tinned soup is boiling in a pot with a round metal handle secured by the wooden poles. The search through our rucksacks for bread and potatoes, buried among our personal belongings, is followed by distribution of aluminium cutlery around the fire. The soup is ready. It's hot, watery, but it's just what we need for our empty stomachs. Then we wait till the flames subside, placing potatoes on top of hot embers. Leaving the blackened jackets on, we scoop the insides of potatoes, sharing each between two people. Dmytro is humming the tune of the universal song "My address", and we sing along

> *My address is not a street or a house,*
> *My address is the entire Soviet Union!*

Sitting around the fire in a tight circle makes the catchy melody special, complemented by drumming of the spoons, pans and pots. One by one, the travellers make their way to bed. Soon only Murat, Natasha, Viktor and I linger near the fire. Sitting close to Natasha, Murat caresses her long hair, scrutinising our faces, finally announcing we are alright.

"Do you mean you trust us?" Viktor and I say in unison, and our quartet has a good laugh. Murat nods and begins telling us a Georgian fairytale about a boy who has a dream that his feet stand on two different sides of Western Georgia. In the dream, the sun shines on one side, and the moon on the other. His stepmother and the King of Western Georgia interpret the dream as a bad omen. The King demands the boy to "give" his dream to him as a gift. When the boy, called Dreamer, refuses, he is thrown into a dungeon. The daughter of the King persuades him to use the boy's wisdom to exert pressure over Eastern Georgia. The unfairly punished boy is released. Not only does he become the people's hero but also marries the King's daughter, all living happily ever after.

Coming from a mixed marriage, a son of a Georgian father and Ossetian mother, Murat knows many myths. He tells us a Nart saga that shapes the essence of the Caucasus mythology. The main character of the story is the temptress Satanaya who is capable of being a figure of fertility and wisdom at the same time. Satanya is unaware of a shepherd, watching her bathing. Her presence ignites his passion. To express his feelings, he shoots a "bolt of lust" into the distance which hits a rock, and gives birth to the Achilles-like Sawseruquo. The heat of the sparkling fire flames, shooting into the air, seep through my body as a reminder of how much I miss my secret storyteller, who knows how to make the memory of his stories last. It must have been Atsamaz's soothing voice that sowed the seeds of love for the Nart legends in me. I listen to Murat feeling tense, not warming up to his husky voice which makes the Nart legends dry and impersonal. We finally go to sleep, leaving the embers to extinguish themselves.

It takes three long days before we reach the peak, finding ourselves walking among the seemingly close clouds. But when we try to touch them, they keep lifting up. Most of us tie hankies, socks, ribbons and other bits and pieces around the pole with a red flag, signifying we've reached the summit. Then we congratulate each other on having made it. We learn from Murat that some of his groups never conquer the peak with its constantly changing weather. Just two hours back we had been sunbathing in the extreme heat, and now our faces are red, lips blue, our bodies shivering all over. At the first sign of the snowflakes, we pull our warmest clothes from the rucksacks.

We descend in twelve days. Going down is much easier as we are aware of more difficult paths in advance. This makes our landing more enjoyable. In the distance, we see our driver standing near the familiar bus, waving to us. Viktor and I are chatting about our adventures while he keeps squeezing my hand. A freshly-made wreath is sitting on my head. Viktor assures me I was a princess in my other life, making me go along with his words that I might've been a daughter of the King of Western Georgia. He shakes his head when I ask him whether he knows any Ukrainian legends or myths. He is honest and kind, but there is no chemistry for me—I see him only as a friend. Afraid he may have other ideas, I decide to tell him about this tonight.

*

When we reach the tourist base in Tskhinvali, we receive keys for our shared accommodations—four same sex travellers per room. We have six hours to prepare for our final evening together. Inese, Natasha, Olia and I share a narrow room with double bunks. We unpack, separating our dirty clothes from clean, trying to find what to wear. Inese lends us her tiny portable iron and each of us use it to press our outfits. As the weather is warm, I select a light-blue dotted dress, Natasha puts on a white see-through blouse and a grey skirt while Inese covers her bare shoulders with a pink jacket, and is the only one wearing shorts. Sitting on her bunk with all her clothing spread around her, Olia is still undecided as to how to mesmerise Gunar. She confides in us that they've fallen in love. We offer her pieces of our wardrobe, finally making her look pretty in my orange top and Inese's white skirt. Then we use the shared facilities at the end of the long corridor to wash our hair and put on make-up in front of the cracked mirror.

The hall is decorated with travelling gear: aluminium cups, saucers, pans and spoons, stretched on a rope above our heads. At the bottom of the stage, the white tablecloth covers a lengthy table with food and drinks. I take some grapes, cheese, a slice of bread into one hand and a glass of wine into the other, and find an available seat. Viktor soon joins me with a piece of dried fish, some garlic bread and beer. During the evening Murat makes his goodbye speech. He congratulates us on travelling close to forty kilometres per day and thus achieving our goal of reaching the peak. He is certain most of us will continue with our travels as "Once one learns how to fly, one will always yearn for the sky!"

Soon the lights are dimmed, and the dance floor is packed. Natasha, dressed in her gypsy clothes, puts her hand around Murat's waist to drag him to the middle of the floor. Viktor invites me to waltz. I watch his serious face and want to tell him that our relationship has no future. He beats me to it by whispering into my ear that he loves me. I'm just about to reply, but at that very moment someone taps me on the shoulder. I turn around to see Atsamaz with a red rose in his hand. He asks Viktor's permission to dance with me. Surprised and shocked at the same time, I accept the rose, instantly finding myself in his strong embrace. I can hardly breathe. Closing and opening my eyes, I keep reassuring myself that I'm dancing with Atsamaz. As I turn my head from side to side, holding the rose in my hand, resting on his shoulder, everything is a blur. The hanging pieces of travelling gear, every item and every person, including Viktor's unhappy face seem to spin around me. Atsamaz admits it was his fault we didn't see each other at the arrival platform of the Vilnius–Moscow train. He'd fallen asleep and nobody woke him up after the train stopped. Luckily, listening to the description of my Georgian-Ossetian trip, he remembered the dates and location of this hostel. Hushing his cracked lips with my finger, I say I've never heard a more convincing story!

Atsamaz's father works in a restaurant not far away and we ask Murat's permission to go there. Murat teasingly warns that our hostel closes at midnight and he expects me to be back by then. We check our watches. It's 8 pm, plenty of time! Atsamaz takes me in the delivery truck to introduce me to his family. His father meets us at the door of a sand-coloured restaurant with open arms. His hair and moustache are black, and his face is youthful. His wife is also here for the occasion. I'm treated as a guest of honour and soon our table is set with a traditional South Ossetian meat pie, chicken with sour cream, beer and wine. Atsamaz's parents seem well-informed about us. We watch gracefully moving performers on a low, fully lit stage, with four young men dancing on tip toes, not taking their eyes off their female partners. The traditional long-sleeved clothing prevents dancers from touching hands. Following the steps of the dancers, everyone claps to the music. I do the same. The hours pass too quickly and it's time to leave. On the way back to the hostel, Atsamaz asks me if I could stay with him a bit longer and I say yes. Fifteen minutes later, we stop at the door of his friend's flat. The friend is away for the whole summer and Atsamaz is minding it for him.

The one-bedroom flat is tiny and clean. Atsamaz sits me on a sofa and fills our glasses with wine. We slowly sip it, talk, and kiss until he takes me into his arms to the bedroom. He removes my sandals, leaving me to undress under the silk blanket. After a while I hear his approaching steps. He walks in and holding the vase with my rose in it, gently places it on my bedside table. Then he lies down next to me fully dressed. I anticipate he'll switch off the light, take me into his arms and, after passionate kissing, make love to me. My body aches from his closeness but instead we talk about ourselves. He says he does ten-hour shifts at the restaurant where his father works as he wants to save for his future. I'm impressed with his determination. When it's my turn to speak, I admit how much I love Vilnius and my teaching job. I don't remember when I fall asleep.

The bright light is shining inside, making me jump out of bed. As I enter the kitchen, Atsamaz greets me with "Salam" in Iranian—I know that it means "How are you?", and I reply "Fine, thank you", checking the time. It's 7 am—only three hours to the departure of the Tskhinvali–Moscow train! He calms me down, explaining how this morning he went to my hostel, how my roommates packed my things and how Murat wished me a good journey. Atsamaz is taking me to the station. Only now I spot my rucksack sitting under his feet and shake my head in disbelief. Then we kiss and giggle. We eat boiled eggs, some Khachapuri pie, finishing our breakfast with strong coffee. Afterwards I excuse myself, taking my rucksack into the bathroom. I have a shower, put on a t-shirt and long pants, then brush my overgrown fringe back and pull most of it into a ponytail. After spreading pink lipstick over my thin lips, I return to the kitchen where, from the sound of the crockery Atsamaz is tidying up.

We lock the flat and drive towards the restaurant. Both Atsamaz's parents are already there. His mother eagerly welcomes me. She is kind and friendly. Looking at her, I realise Atsamaz has his mother's hair, and her electric eyes—his eyes follow me wherever I turn. She tells me that her cousin Ruslan lives in Vilnius. Even though she's never been to Lithuania, her son visits him regularly. Her husband kisses my hand, wishing me a pleasant journey home, then whispers into my ear how much he'd hoped I could stay for good. I'm taken aback by such words, touched by this family's hospitality. I begin to regret that one night in Ossetia might never repeat itself.

When we reach the station, my train is already at the platform. Atsamaz gazes at me, promising to be in touch. We exchange our addresses. Before we part, he takes a gold bracelet from his pocket and asks if he could put it around my wrist. I don't want his gift and let him know that no gold can replace his presence, tucking the bracelet back into his pocket. Then we kiss, saying our goodbyes, and I tearfully watch as his slight figure blends into the crowd.

*

The autumn and winter pass joined by my weekly letters to Atsamaz and his monthly calls. When I tell my parents about him, they're pleased but feel sorry for me that he lives some three thousand kilometres away. In the spring a telegram arrives that he is coming to Vilnius. My mother lends me her most treasured leather jacket to meet him in at the station. When I spot him jumping out of his carriage, I rush passing between some grumbling people, reluctantly parting to let me through. We stand close to each other for some time, looking into one another's eyes, hug and kiss, then walk towards the exit. Atsamaz is staying with his uncle who lives in the Old

Town, which is conveniently reachable by electric tram. When we arrive at his door, Ruslan and I greet each other in Lithuanian but quickly switch to Russian, making sure Atsamaz understands our conversation. I soon discover that Ruslan is single, living in his flat for more than sixty-five years. His Ossetian parents were also born and bred in the capital, and his grandparents settled in Lithuania after being displaced by the First World War. Over the meal, Ruslan shares with us his decision to relocate to Ossetia. Atsamaz wants him to stay with the family, and Ruslan pats him on his broad shoulder. He admits having an ancestral calling running through his veins. His words make me emotional, imagining how difficult it would be starting everything anew. I ponder Svetlana's words, said in the Murmansk's library, on how hard is to remove yourself from one's family. But it's different for Ruslan who may have deeply rooted himself in Vilnius but no longer has family here. It's time for me to go. Atsamaz waits for my Justiniškiai tram and sees me off. We agree to meet the following weekend to explore the city. I think about him from morning to night.

On Saturday, Atsamaz and I browse through the cobbled streets of the Old Town, packed with tiny houses with small windows and sun-bleached shutters. Some curtains are open, allowing us to take a quick look inside the dwellings with chipped walls and humble furnishings. Walking away from the narrow streets, we find ourselves in front of a huge cathedral. It's the Museum of Fine Arts, with paintings on the walls that we enjoy viewing. Afterwards, we walk around the Bell Tower in front of the cathedral. Lifting our heads up, we see the huge clock on the top of the tower. But the clock has only one handle. A passer-by confirms that it's been purposely left off! Even though missing the minute handle, it shows precise time, making the bell sound every fifteen minutes. We later find how the fifty-two-metre tower is visible from different angles of the main city streets. I show Atsamaz an exclusive tile on the pavement. It has magic powers. I say that if, standing on top of the tile, each of us turns around three times, our wish will come true. He is game to try. I can't guess what he is thinking as each time he turns around, his face is secretive and stern. When it's my turn to turn on the tile, I wish that Atsamaz never leaves.

We order our meal in the Café Literatų Svetainė, across the road from the majestic cathedral and the Bell Tower. While we wait for traditional cepelinai—potato dumplings with meat—to arrive, I'm taken aback with the news that Atsamaz's uncle decided to pass his flat to him! I bombard him with questions: "What did you say? How did you react? What are you planning to do with it?" He composes himself before speaking while I want to caress his face. He keeps me in suspense until we finish our meal and order black coffee. Then he reveals that having his own flat in Vilnius makes all the difference. That now he'll be able to see me more often. I'm sad we wouldn't see each other for the coming week: I live and work on the other side of town and he has legal business to attend to.

*

On Sunday, my father, pacing in the kitchen, dressed in his only suit, notices a taxi stopping under our windows and calls me to confirm whether it is Atsamaz. My breath rushes as I recognise him below. My tall father, hunching from his height opens the door and shakes hands with Atsamaz. Atsamaz gives my mother a huge bunch of roses. She is wearing her best dress, and her hair has been in curlers all night. Blushing, she goes looking for a vase while I usher our guest into the lounge room. With flowers sitting in the middle of the table, we share drinks and sweets. We suggest Atsamaz try a piece of šakotis—a tree-like cake with protruding tiny pyramids. My mother explains the reason šakotis looks bright yellow is that it's made of eggs, butter and cream, but also needs flour, sugar and is baked on a rotating spit. He's amazed by the horn-like pastry sticking out in all directions, and the hole in the center of the cake, shaped in a well. He seems pleased that we purchased a medium-height šakotis in his honour and even more pleased to learn that such a treat is a part of every traditional Lithuanian wedding. He giggles on discovering that the well is made for placing good wishes inside. He suggests we should also think of some. We cut pieces of paper in different shapes to make sure each of us can reveal our wishes to others, and drop them inside the well. Eating and drinking some precious alcoholic beverages, we relax ... except my father who starts pacing up and down the room, fidgeting with his fingers, pressing down his hair to the right side of his worried face, buttoning and unbuttoning his jacket. Then he sits down to talk about his vegetable garden outside Vilnius and a shed built with his own hands on government land. Atsamaz asks whether our shed is similar to a dacha, and I agree, making an observation how, due to the size of our dacha, it's only suitable for keeping tools and work gear. My mother, sitting across the table, keeps pulling her loosened curls from her face. Now it's her turn to tell Atsamaz how much she loves the fruits of the forest and how she collects berries in summer and mushrooms during the autumn months. She is very keen to share her butter-fried boletus secret.

We taste balandėliai—cabbage rolls with hot potatoes. After lunch, we return to picking the horns of šakotis and taking folded pieces of paper out of the well. My father wants to own a car, my mother wishes all of us good health while I dream of travelling. Before unfolding his wish, Atsamaz stands up and looking at both of my parents, says he wishes to marry me. While I'm hardly breathing, he turns to my father and asks for my hand. When he hears yes, he lowers himself on one knee in front of me. Before he has a chance to say anything, I whisper yes. We embrace, kissing each other on the lips. Then he places a gold bracelet around my wrist admitting to all how much he wanted me to have it when he first gave it to me. He knew before I boarded the Tskhinvali–Moscow train that I was the only one fit to wear his grandmother's bracelet. My parents keep wiping joyful tears from their faces. My mother's words that if a man is serious, he'd follow me all the way to Lithuania turned out to be true.

I Want to Be Like Simas

When she received the telegram from her boyfriend, Asta didn't read it straight away. She could see typed letters stretched across the inside of a thin card. The letters had been glued directly on the card using narrow strips of paper. She knew that the message would be meaningful, as always. She put the kettle on and waited for it to boil, a bunch of flowers greeting her from the cover of the telegram. She washed an apple, slowly chewing it while sipping some Ceylon leaf tea. Afterwards she wiped her small hands with a tea towel, curiously opened the folded card and began to read: "Best wishes for International Women's Day from the Mediterranean. Back in May. Love. Gintaras."

No envelope. The postman who delivered it to her door seemed excited for her.

"Well. Getting a message from over the sea! How romantic."

She knew some of Gintaras' friends and acquaintances were undertaking their Maritime studies at technical school in basic sailing methods and techniques, and being trained in how to catch, gut, process and can fish while aboard refrigerator trawlers. Most importantly, the monetary return was much greater than working on shore.

Asta brought the telegram close to her narrow face to kiss it before gazing at it from arm's length, and imagined Gintaras watching her through the tips of the ink carnations, his broad face and tired eyes absorbing her into the picture. Asta lowered the flimsy telegram into her lap, fiddling with its corner. Oh, how she longed to be in his arms. How she yearned for the closeness of his strong, solid body. She imagined him smiling, his lips shaping into a round cherry before kissing her.

They had been going out for two years, and she hoped that he might propose soon. She'd wished to be his wife since they met at the beach of Nida resort, forty-six kilometres from the Port of Klaipėda. Nida, separated by the Curonian Lagoon, was easily accessed by ferry. On that fateful sunny afternoon, sitting on the fine, white sand close to the shoreline, she had been sketching a ship barely visible in the distance. As she worked her pencil, she enjoyed glancing at the children building sandcastles, running back and forth, splashing water into holidaymakers' faces. Smiling at the parental reprimands, she hoped to have a boy and a girl of her own some day.

As she enjoyed the waves coming up to her feet to greet her, she heard a new greeting from behind.

"I am sorry to disturb you, but I noticed your exceptional eye for detail."

A young man with reddish-brown locks was gazing from over her shoulder, and introduced himself as Gintaras.

She trembled on hearing his rough voice.

"I'm Asta."

"Nice to meet you, Asta."

"I appreciate your words, but I must admit it's hard to work out the features of a distant ship." She found it funny seeing him struggle to cross his bare feet in front of him because his legs were too long, but he finally managed to sit down. She warned him against ruining his white, well-pressed trousers. His loud, clear laugh interrupted the screeches of a passing seagulls. Watching them fly in the cloudless sky, he remarked, "All that matters is freedom. Look at their white bellies and easy gliding bodies, just look at them." He continued to point at the birds swooping over the waves, and her gaze followed his hand. "Free and happy like Simas."

Asta pursed her thick, curvy lips. "Who is Simas?"

"May I?" she heard him say, taking her pencil into his strong sturdy hands to adjust the stern, expand the wavy sails and elongate the silhouette of the ship. She was impressed with the way he worked with a pencil, the confident strokes he made, contrasting darker and lighter shades to enhance the ship's features. The measurement technique he employed while glancing into the distance and back to the page, and the way he curved the letters in Algerian font in the middle of the Spanish-built Maryana ship's hull made it obvious he was an artist. He smiled at this observation, revealing the reason he knew so much about Maryana—he had been on her deck before. Asta decided that he must be a sailor, unable to take her flirtatious eyes off his tanned face. Reworking her sketch, Gintaras admitted to being able to draw from memory. He used his skills to create detailed maps. And there was more—he was the Vice-Captain of a ship, but not of the one hovering in the distance. He said he had just returned from the Atlantic Ocean, sailing for three months on a fishing trawler, steering the way and noting newly-discovered fishing locations.

After completing the sketch, they signed their names side by side on the bottom right corner with a date of 5 July 1985. She'd had the Maryana hanging in her lounge room ever since.

*

Asta came to Klaipėda after completion of her studies at the Pedagogy Institute of Vilnius. The two years since she met Gintaras had been marked by memorable events—settling into her job as a secondary school teacher, trying a new hairstyle by layering her shoulder-length hair, learning how to apply lipstick, and treating herself to a manicure and pedicure. She wished to resemble a model from the magazine Gintaras had brought from his last trip. He smuggled in the fashion magazine, risking being caught by the Soviet authorities. But seeing his stunning girlfriend upon his return to Klaipėda, he said it was more than worth it. In his opinion, women in the West didn't care about themselves as much as Lithuanian women were. He worshiped her for her sense of fashion. Being able to read English, Asta discovered how to use a new tube of mascara without sticking her eyelashes together. She glided the brush over a hankie to remove any excess formula, and, spreading mascara over her lower lashes, moved to the upper ones. She learned how to wear a ribbon or light scarf in her hair, highlighting her hairline or using a special holder to gather all her hair into a looped ponytail.

She was twenty-five, six years younger than Gintaras. He'd begun his seaman's career at the bottom of the ladder. First, by finishing his course that lead to practising sailor's skills on various fishing liners, then by continuing with tertiary studies to progress his way to the top. After completing his studies at the Admiral Makarov State Maritime Academy in Leningrad, he was assigned to the Vice-Captain's position on the merchant fleet. One step from being a captain was considered a most honourable and respectable position, and Gintaras himself could hardly believe he had reached it.

With him now on shore, they spent every possible minute together. They discussed marriage and children but he worried Asta wouldn't enjoy the life of a seaman's wife. She told him she'd already learned to be patient and to look forward to each of his returns, treating them as special moments. Having him in her life made her content. She resided in a rented one bedroom flat in a multistorey building not far from the food market, fifteen minutes away on foot from the main bus and train terminal. She taught at a school close to her dwelling, walking to work in her new heels. She was petite, wearing silk stockings and form fitting dresses, always complemented by the same colour lipstick and nail polish. Men openly eyed her when she hurried past, but she looked straight ahead, thinking of Gintaras. She stood out from the crowd, with Gintaras providing her with so-called 'deficit' items; hard to get, thoughtfully brought gifts including designer jeans, bright fashionable clothes, perfume, wool, silk underwear, runners, coats or leather jackets. She was extremely grateful to her boyfriend who would pay her rent, amounting to ninety rubles for six months. Before leaving, he would encourage her to sell any of his gifts if she ran into trouble, making sure she wasn't in need. She helped her parents instead by selling extra pairs of jeans, jackets, make-up kits and some of her jewellery. Her parents lived in the country, milking collective cows for their living. Both aged fifty-one, they were to retire in four years. Putting money aside for the time when they would no longer working was important.

Gintaras hated his life in the Soviet Union. He hated the concept of Communism. He couldn't imagine Soviet citizens being equal in a future classless society. He doubted people could be content eating in communal kitchens, equally sharing everything, working according to their ability and getting paid according to their needs. He wished Soviet citizens didn't have to work multiple jobs to make ends meet, and wished they had something to smile about. There was a mysterious name Gintaras continued to bring up in conversation: Simas. One time he said: "Just consider, Asta, S – for svoboda, laisvė or freedom, I – for aš or independence, M – for mama or mother, A – for artimieji or family, and finally, S – for sėkmė or success. What do you think?"

Asta shrugged her shoulders, remarking that invented words sounded great, but she'd never heard such an interpretation of a common name. He moved on to fantasising about a future where Soviet citizens could travel the world and had all they needed, just like westerners. Asta couldn't imagine anything of the sort. Teaching, correcting homework and afterschool activities took up all her time, making her too tired to think about the future. Her weekends were preoccupied with going to the movies, theatres, concerts or visiting friends and parents. But deep down she wanted to be the westerner Gintaras talked and talked about. She wanted to have a house, a car, to have an extended selection of clothing, good quality shoes, to buy meat without waiting in lengthy queues and, most importantly, study arts. After completing her teacher's degree, she couldn't further her studies. She wanted to, but she was given a job and needed to take it. She also wanted to see, to touch and to feel the colourful world he used to bring with him. He became a messenger of new ideas and possibilities awaiting somewhere out there. He became an elastic band, stretching further and further into a non-Soviet world.

Gintaras dreaded to be apart from Asta for long periods of time, he said, worried she may not wait for him. While waiting for partners to return from fishing at sea, some women couldn't cope by themselves. Some, nicely dressed and having American dollars to spend at the duty-free shops, were enjoying their luxury lives. Sailing through the frightful storms made men share stories of their lonely or unfaithful marriages. A young sailor had a heart attack in the middle of the ocean after learning that his wife had left him. A respectable captain, returning from sea unannounced, found his wife in bed with their dog.

Asta crossed each day on a calendar using a fountain pen, each "X" shortening her wait for Gintaras, each "X" bringing him closer and closer to her. At night, unable to sleep, she recalled his stories about sailors passing time, stuck in the middle of the ocean. She imagined the crew of the trawler, exhausted after a day's work, trying to think of an untold anecdote or a joke, hiding their tiredness and depression. She imagined the off-duty seamen forming a tight circle on the top deck, facing each other, some sharing cigarettes, others watching narrow streams of smoke floating up into the still sky, all inhaling the same mixture of salty fresh air. She drew a mental picture of sad-faced men reminiscing of good times they had on shore, lethargically staring at the horizon. She imagined the water licking the sides of the trawler with intensity, splashing her temporary residents with a force that made them lose their footing. She recalled her boyfriend talking about the huge metal trawler structure with its noisily-vibrating engine, reminding everyone of their vulnerable presence in strong currents, of loose items rattling, and dinner plates sliding from side to side. But then there were sunsets that made men forget about being trapped in the trawler with the bloody fish. The unusual stripes of turquoise, complemented by colours of lemon and cornflower, set the background for a bright red sun sinking deeper and deeper into the ocean. She imagined sailors watching the breath-taking picture of the sunset, wishing it would never fade into the night.

*

Not hearing from Gintaras for a few days after the return of his trawler, Asta went to see his friend Rokas. His curious, middle-aged mother opened the door and gave her a surprised look, remarking that she was the third woman turning up at the door this week. While red-faced Asta stood speechless,

Rokas emerged from behind his mother, inviting her in. His longish dark hair and deeply-set eyes made him extremely attractive, but even more striking was his frame, with his jeans tightly stretched over his solid legs, and his blue jumper, sitting on his midriff, accentuating his muscular figure.

"Asta? How nice to see you," he said flirtatiously, his welcome only increasing her anxiety. He led her into the kitchen, and with his mother following, asked her to make them some coffee. Asta sat on a chair in front of him, not taking her eyes from his asymmetrical lips. She wanted to hear about Gintaras. He pointed his head towards his mother and put his finger to his lips. Standing with her back to them, cleaning the stove knobs while boiling the kettle, she finally turned around, filling their cups with instant coffee. When she left, Rokas suggested they should go out to talk, watching his mother's shadow moving behind the frosted glass.

They walked toward the bridge over the river Danė, Asta shivering with the anticipation of finding out what happened to Gintaras. Rokas greeted a young, bottle-blonde woman passing them on their way. Her face lit up when he introduced Asta as his friend's girlfriend. He wanted to see Olia that very night, inviting her to the Restaurant Vėtrungė at 8pm. When they parted, he turned around, commenting on her curvy body and tried to elaborate on his other liaisons, but Asta stopped him. The way he behaved gave her the impression he didn't care about her matter. She blamed herself for seeking him out. After returning from sea, Gintaras used to bring Rokas to her place to celebrate their reunion. As the whisky filled their glasses, the two friends whistled, breaking into a song. The lyrics related to a group of sailors looking forward to meeting a young woman on shore, who reminded them of a seagull. Listening to their harmonious duo, she used to stretch her arms and flap them as imaginary wings to emphasise their certain words:

> Man **menas** lig šiolei tie **saulėti** toliai
> Kai **grįžta** iš jūros laivai.
> **Jūreiviai** merginą **žuvėdra** vadina,
> Nes **primena** paukštę jinai.

Listening to their harmonious duo, she used to stretch her arms and flap them as imaginary wings to emphasise their words. They had so much fun. Rokas was full of phrases for her, but today he must've decided to be indifferent. When they reached the popular Café Pupelė she hesitated at the entry, but Rokas pulled her in and ordered coffee and cake for two. While waiting for their order, Rokas said he had no news of Gintaras. She insisted on hearing the truth, even if her boyfriend was back but no longer wanted to see her. Mixing three spoons of sugar into his coffee, Rokas repeated there was no news from his best friend. Instead he was curious as to whether she had noticed anything unusual about him before he left. She hadn't. She was thirsty but couldn't bring her shaking fingers, holding her cup, to her lips. She was hungry but hadn't touched her cake. Opening her mouth, she heard her weak voice. "Well. He loved the phrase 'I want to be like Simas' but never told me why."

"Don't you know?"

"Know what?"

"Ach."

"It's strange how he joked about Simas," she continued, repeating Gintaras' words S – for freedom, I – for independence, M – for mother, A – for close ones, and S – for success. Reclining into his chair, Rokas grinned, noting how clever his friend was by speaking in coded language. "Don't you see he used the double meaning to tell you he was contemplating his escape? Don't you see he wanted to protect you, to make sure no harm would ever come to you? But the problem is, you don't know how to interpret his words!"

Tensing all over, Asta admitted to never considering the meaning of each letter. Looking at his mysterious expression, she waited to be reassured that everything would fall into place. Giving her a piercing glance, Rokas leaned forward and relayed a story of a Soviet Lithuanian radio operator named Simas Kudirka, who defected from a Soviet Lithuanian trawler by jumping to an American Coast Guard cutter. The Vigilant, anchored off Martha's Vineyard, side by side with Sovietskaya Litva, was there for the purpose of future territorial fishing negotiations. Asta became teary-eyed, listening to how he was returned to his trawler by force, beaten, taken back to shore and jailed for six months before being tried for treason and sentenced to ten years in a strict regime camp somewhere in remote Russia. His wife and children were threatened by KGB agents turning up to confiscate Simas' possessions, praying to God these horrible men would leave them in the government flat given to her husband just a few months earlier. Spies took things, removed pieces of furniture, returning to bang on their door again and again in the night.

Asta wept, unable to comprehend why Gintaras yearned for Simas' life.

"I sense how sheltered you are from the events of the seventies," said Rokas, and she urged him to explain.

"What I mean is that Simas tried to defect. 13 November 1970 to be exact. But later there was a turn of events."

"What events? It's hard to comprehend learning all of this in 1987!" Asta said.

"After spending four years in hard labour camps, Simas was freed. The friends and relatives of the Kudirka family in the USA helped to discover how at the start of the past century, his grandparents, wanting to escape the Tsarist regime, lived in America for nine years. Their children were born in New York. Simas' mother was one of them, meaning that her son was legally an American citizen."

"And the Soviet government released him?"

"Yes. Not only from the camp. Simas, his mother, his wife and their children were allowed to leave and migrate to America!"

"At least all ended well for him."

"Simas Kudirka was like a breath of fresh air to Gintaras, and a symbol of a man who showed strength and determination for personal freedom. It's not a secret that, while at sea, we enjoyed browsing in different ports, wishing to stay on. He knew who the informers were on each ship and had to be vigilant not to talk out of line, warning others to do the same."

Maybe someone from the crew reported on him. Maybe the spies caught him and put him in jail. Lost in her thoughts she felt rough fingers touching her cheek. It was Rokas, worried by her shaken look. She stood up, brushing his hand away. Before parting outside, he promised to visit her with any news from Gintaras.

When she returned home, Asta found two men on her doorstep. They were KGB officers with a warrant to search her flat. Trying to unlock it, she found the key didn't fit, finally realising she was using the wrong one in her consternation. Once they entered the lounge, one of them stood next to her while the other searched the premises. He didn't find her fashion magazine as she'd lent it to her friend, but he removed the drawing of Maryana and placed it in his briefcase. He assured her it would be returned to her after examination. Then she was asked to hand over Gintaras' correspondence. She took all she had from the kitchen drawer and passed on to them. Parting with her boyfriend's letters and telegrams made her feel naked. She imagined these straight-faced men returning to their KGB quarters, reading, examining, analysing the content, their mouths drooping with saliva over the sweet love letters. After they left, she couldn't sleep all night.

The following morning Asta was called to her school Principal's Office. Mr Laurinaitis assured her that she was one of the best teachers but he wouldn't want to deal with KGB agents again. It took him by surprise to be told she was associated with anti-Soviet elements. She didn't utter a word, counting his unsteady steps, one-two-three one way, one-two-three the other. Hearing him suggest voluntarily resignation, she tried to swallow the rising lump in her throat. Before completing the letter, she asked where she should go and what she should do now. Quickly removing her signed letter from the table and putting it in a drawer, the Principal showed her the door.

On her way home, she tried to breathe from the bottom of her lungs, convincing herself there was nothing to worry about. Her rent was not due for another two months, she had some savings, could sell more things, and while doing that, look for another job.

Within a month, with the help of her friends, she managed to secure a teacher's position in Dreverna, Klaipėda's County, in a tiny village in the Curonian Lagoon. Asta bumped into Rokas on the way to the bus terminal. He helped her to carry her suitcase, curious as to where she was going. After learning what happened, he expressed his regrets and apologised on behalf of his friend. He admitted being questioned by the KGB agents himself. He was told that Gintaras defected from his trawler and sought political asylum in Madrid. Asta stopped him carrying her suitcase and sat on it.

"Defected to Spain? Why Spain? Why?"

"How should I know? As it was, during questioning, they wanted to know his ideas, thoughts and aspirations. They wanted to hear from me that he planned his escape all along."

"What did you say?"

"I said I only knew him as a disciplined sailor and we had never discussed anything but whisky and women." She listened to his quietly-spoken words, wondering what the real reason behind Gintaras' decision was. Did he finally realise his dream to live in the West or was he afraid to come back and propose marriage? White-faced and stiff, Asta boarded her bus, crying all the way to her destination.

*

On the 5th of July 1990, Asta went to Klaipėda to spend a couple of days with her friend. The next morning they caught a ferry to Nida. The calmness of the summer day and the brightness of the blue sky reminded her of her first encounter with Gintaras. Birutė knew what happened five years ago, finding the twists and turns of Asta's story incredible. Still, in her opinion, regardless of the hurtful past, she should've moved on, found herself a boyfriend and ventured out more. Birutė's words were true but for some reason Asta couldn't let the memory of him go. When she returned home that night, she found a note in her door handle. *I am back. Just turn around and you'll see me.* Slowly she turned around. Wearing jeans and a t-shirt, Gintaras was walking towards her. When he gave her a bunch of white daisies, she pressed it to her heart. He took her in his arms and held her to his chest. His tight embrace made the daisies lose their yellow heads and white petals. They sat in her tiny rental flat looking at each other for a long time, Asta speechless, Gintaras explaining how he managed to find her through Rokas. With some grey hair visible on his temples, he looked drawn out and aged. His face was burnt by the sun, enhancing the fairness of his locks. She soon learned how after getting his political asylum in Spain, he eventually was allowed to resettle in Florida. There he lived with Monika, a single Lithuanian mother of two. He recalled his experiences, spanning from his defection, when he left his trawler in Spain, all the way to him finally reaching America. He confessed to Asta that he had lost his seafaring skills along the way.

Trying to cheer him up, she said she now knew who Simas Kudirka was. Gintaras smiled, kissed her on the cheek, keen to share more stories. During their visit to New York, he and Monika discovered that Simas had lived there from 1975 to 1982. Millions of ordinary Americans found out about his ordeal after he and Larry Eichel published a book *To Those Still at Sea: The Defection of a Lithuanian Sailor*. Then the movie "The Defection of Simas Kudirka" was made. The radio operator's story brought him fame. He was constantly approached by journalists, repeating how fortunate he was to be spared from another six years in a hard-labour camp. He kept bringing up the subject of suppression of human rights and the atrocities of the Soviet system. During his media interviews he spoke with excitement of his great life in America, working as a caretaker of the Brooklyn Lithuanian Cultural Centre with his wife. Simas proudly repeated that as long as he was free, he didn't mind cleaning toilets and painting houses to supplement their income.

Gintaras recalled going with Monika to the Brooklyn Lithuanian Cultural Centre where they joined some Lithuanian nationals for lunch. To his great surprise, he spotted Simas Kudirka. Together with his wife and his children, he was at the front of a queue lined up for cabbage rolls and potato dumplings. Gintaras left Monika to hold his place and used the opportunity to introduce himself to Simas. Simas' high forehead with several deep, horizontal lines, was quite distinguishable. After assessing the ex-Vice-Captain with his eyes hidden behind spectacles, his harsh rectangular face lit up. Learning of his fate, the legendary radio operator wanted to talk in private and they decided to meet after eating their meals. Gintaras reminisced on how for a split second their eyes locked in securing trust without words. At that very moment he thought Simas had a familiar facial expression, the look of a man who never feels comfortable on his feet on land.

After purchasing a traditional meal of potato dumplings stuffed with mincemeat and garnished with pieces of fried onion, bacon and cream, Gintaras and Monika sat next to an elderly Lithuanian man. Pointing towards Simas sitting at another table, he spoke with regret that their community should've done more to support the Kudirka family of five. He sounded upset about some organisations fighting over Simas. A friendly couple from New Jersey sitting across the table were bursting with the joy of personally knowing him. They had met during a picnic, and after having a great conversation with the Kudirka family, invited them to their house. Because of the spontaneous decision to do so, they were worried they may not have enough food or variety, but the guests truly enjoyed spending time together.

Watching Simas surrounded by admirers, people at Gintaras' table praised those who had made it possible to bring the Kudirka family to the USA. Gintaras learned how Simas, his mother, wife and two children initially settled in the city of Elizabeth, New Jersey. How since arriving, he became active in the American-Lithuanian Communities in New York, and later Santa Monica, California where he relocated in the early 1980s. Other diners joined in with their stories of Simas being a great supporter of different events such as the Commemoration of Deportations to Siberia Day, Lithuanian Independence Day, scout ceremonies and community picnics. He generously provided monetary support to fund Lithuanian activities. He voiced his relief to be let out of Soviet prison and wished Lithuania to regain independence from the Soviet rule. Gintaras clinked his whisky glass with those around the table, sharing their admiration for this strong, brave man risking his life!

Asta sat by Gintaras as he told his story late into the night. After he finished his last word, she wanted to know what he and Simas talked about on the day they met. Looking at the wall clock turning midnight, he seemed uncertain.

"No. I couldn't get to him. Apparently he wasn't in Brooklyn for long, so there was a lot of interest in his presence. Soon after lunch he was taken away by the VIP delegation and journalists who surrounded him with their cameras and microphones. He waved walking past my table, departing with a smile."

"Are you sure you weren't disappointed that you didn't get to spend more time with him?"

"That's life. Sometimes things one anticipates don't materialise."

"I agree. I didn't think you and I would reunite!"

"Me either. I expected to find you married with at least three children."

"But I only want two."

The couple hardly slept at all that night; there was still so much to be said. But the most important thing for Gintaras was to contact Monika, to explain how he found his lost girlfriend. She knew about Asta. She helped him through the grieving process of leaving his homeland and loved ones behind. He was confident she would let him go. After all, living as a couple, they weren't married and had no children together. He plucked up his courage to call her. The cheerfulness in Monika's voice confirmed how pleased she was for the both of them. Soon afterwards they received a congratulatory wedding card wishing them long lasting happiness.

*

Gintaras and Asta married in the Civil Registry Office. The next day they applied for her visa to the United States. Not having recovered full refund his Vilnius–Florida return ticket, Gintaras decided to fly there and come back as soon as Asta's visa was granted. Each time he called, he couldn't stop talking, making her suspicious he was very lonely. Monika temporarily moved out of her house to stay with her mother until Gintaras could find alternative accommodation. He ended up washing and cooking for himself. He was busy with repairing cars, cleaning gutters or painting houses inside and out. Working fourteen hours a day, he was proud to be saving every dollar for their future. Learning the truth of her husband's life in America, Asta was concerned about reliance on his cash-in-hand jobs. She worried that with no place of their own and no relatives or friends to turn to, they might have a difficult stay there.

While she waited, Asta's family received a letter from their relative in Australia. Asta never knew that her father's sister Zosė had been living there since 1949. In 1991, when Lithuania regained its independence from the Soviet Union, Zosė wanted her family to come for a visit. She explained how she'd been afraid to contact them during the years of Soviet occupation, but now she was overjoyed to freely write and call. Realising that her brother and his wife felt they couldn't take such a long journey, she was happy to see any family member. Asta talked the matter over with Gintaras, persuading him to go to Australia with her. When the official invitation arrived, she had to suspend her American visa process and rush to the Australian Embassy in Vilnius. Gintaras, still in Florida, applied for a two-year Australian working visa.

*

Four months later, the two of them arrived in Melbourne. They settled in with her aunt in the suburb of Coburg. Initially Gintaras worked at the Port of Melbourne, loading and unloading ships, but soon found an opening in the maintenance department where his skills became highly valued. They lived with Zosė for a couple of years and, after saving enough for a deposit, bought their own house in the same area to allow Asta to care for her ageing relative. The individual size and style of dwellings astonished her. After experiencing the benefits of living on a property that was hers, Asta no longer wanted to live in a Soviet style government flat again. The thought of the identical flat buildings, dirty, noisy and exposed to constant gossip, made her feel uneasy. Only now, away from her homeland, she understood that for most Soviet citizens, the only window to the outside world was their own window to the street.

While waiting for her husband to return from work, Asta did the housework and gardening. She loved going shopping, amazed at the size of the shopping centres and what they had to offer without the need to look for items in the black market. The shelves were jam-packed with shoes, underwear and designer clothing. She envied so many women driving. She enjoyed being in her relaxing surroundings, and the thought that she could leave her passport at home overwhelmed her. She loved to see people of different nationalities smiling at her, and as a proud owner of her Australian passport, she smiled back. Nobody cared who she was. Nobody came to search her house and confiscate her precious personal belongings. Standing in the middle of Princes Bridge in the heart of the city, watching the ripples in the Yarra River and listening to the playful ding-ding-ding sounds of the passing trams, she regretted that her parents couldn't be there to share it either!

Asta borrowed the book *To Those Still at Sea* from the Lithuanian library in North Melbourne, and after reading it studied Simas' photo on the back cover. Later she told Gintaras how she couldn't get the image out of her mind.

"He had looked like a man who has seen the worst."

"And he has," Gintaras said. "You know now what kind of 'royal treatment' he used to receive—beating, interrogations, deprivation of human rights and starvation."

"I cried when I read it."

"It left him scarred. I could see it in his eyes. He always seemed haunted, never at ease."

Joining Asta in bed, Gintaras shared how Prince Sadruddin Aga Khan, High Commissioner for Refugees of the United Nations, condemned the whole Sovietskya Litva-Vigilant incident at the time, blaming both sides for the way they treated an innocent sailor. Gintaras said he sometimes wondered what would have happened if Price made Simas and his family as guests of honour and gave them a place to live in his native France.

Then shook his head. They both agreed that such gesture would've been a western style fairytale the Soviet government wouldn't have wanted to hear.

"Well. You see, my darling," said Asta, placing Gintaras' hand on her growing belly. "It seems to me that even though Simas beat the Soviet system in achieving his lifelong goal to live in the West, he had to endure many obstacles."

"Ach. I can't even imagine."

Asta revealed how visiting the Lithuanian library she discovered that in 1980, Simas came on an official visit to Australia, travelling to the main cities and mingling with his fellow expatriates. Gintaras raised his eyebrows, gently patting her full belly.

"When our twins are born, let's call them Simas and Sima," she said, and he gave her a loving and appreciative hug.

Dreaming of Sweden

As a child, Gitana used to wait on the shore for her father to return from fishing. One evening when she was about twelve years old, she sat on the white beach and drew a circle around herself in the sand, scribbling with her index finger—mother, father, home, boat, oars, sun, clouds, seagulls. To pass the time, she drew a little picture next to each word. After stepping out of the circle, she used a thick tree branch to write six letters—SWEDEN. As the evening approached, there was no sign of the fishing boat so she started to contemplate going home. It was only with one last look at the sea that she finally spotted moving dots in the distance. Her father Tomas and uncle Rimas were rowing back to shore. She ran further and further into the water to meet them. The increasing wind agitated the waves, washing the sand from under her feet. She heard both men shouting "We are back!" and waved to them.

As her father and uncle came closer to the shore in their boat, the beach patrol truck and a tractor lined up next to the boat, helping first to pull Gitana out of the water. Men transferred fish into boxes and the truck drove off with Tomas on board. Gitana knew that as a member of the Soviet Fishing Association of Šventoji—a tourist resort, situated ten kilometres away from their village of Kunigiškės—her father had to take his catch there first. She stayed with the boat, listening to the roaring of the truck driving away along the coast. Her uncle soon returned with his three sons. She watched the men carrying the wooden boat towards the shed while a wide rake, attached to the back of the tractor, covered their steps.

It wasn't long before Tomas returned with the patrol soldiers, bringing a box of fish to the house. She often wondered why he always returned with so little. Still, there was plenty of cod and sprat, but mostly herrings—no less than fifty, some still alive and gasping for air! The helpers stayed for supper, waiting for the fish to be scaled and cooked. A bottle of vodka was brought to the table to celebrate their success. Everybody listened to stories of the stormy sea that nearly swallowed Tomas' boat, of the ripped nets left in Šventoji, requiring mending once again, of a huge, grapefruit coloured sun bouncing light over the green waves. Soon her mother Ina was serving the fish soup with potatoes and adding cream into their bowls while Gitana sliced the bread. After the plentiful meal, the men shared Soviet Prima cigarettes and then the patrol truck drove off.

While in bed, Gitana listened to her parents' conversation about Tomas and his brother seeing a Swedish ship passing by, with the sailors throwing a heavy-duty plastic bag with forbidden goods into the water for them to collect.

"We quickly fished the bag out, hid the goods, pleased at not being seen by anyone. But after an hour or so, the Baltic Coast Patrol Ship appeared out of nowhere."

"What did they say? What did you do?"

"What do you think? First they checked our fishing licences, comparing our names to those in the passports letter by letter. Not satisfied, they shined their torches on our faces, also exhaustively scanning inside the boat, loaded with fish."

"And what?"

"I tell you what! One of the officers seemed particularly agitated, asking whether we had any contact with the Swedish ship passing here earlier. But we swore she passed at a considerable distance. If only you knew how scared I was, how scared we both were," Tomas said. "I thought this time I wouldn't get away."

"It must've been horrible for you."

"Of course it was. Rimas and I were shocked to see new patrol staff and not the usual Russian soldiers, who were never rough with us."

"Maybe you should stop it?" said Ina.

"Hmm. Maybe. But tomorrow I'll take the cigarettes to Klaipėda's black market," he said. "You know yourself how much the American cigarettes are in demand."

"Yes."

"And dirty magazines."

"How many this time?"

"Five."

"That would be good if they sell."

"They always sell."

"I know."

Gitana, hardly breathing so as not to miss a word, wondered how it was possible to sell such magazines at all.

*

After completing her accountancy studies as a young woman, Gitana was employed by a tourist resort in Palanga. One evening, returning from work, she saw the front door of their two-storey house wide open and as she entered the hallway heard her uncle Rimas talking to her father.

"You must go on, brother. It's not your fault her car veered off the road."

"But I loved her so much!"

"Well. Stasė was very charming, but she wasn't free, was she? She was never fully yours."

Gitana removed her shoes, trying not to make any noise. Peering through the gap in the partially closed kitchen door, she saw her father sitting at the table with his head down, his ash-blond hair thinly drooping over his forehead.

"I wish she was in my arms now," he said, lifting his watery eyes to the ceiling.

"Maybe a bird or a small animal was crossing the road and she had to break," said Rimas.

"May-be," Gitana heard Tomas say in his trembling voice. Only now did she notice a bottle of vodka on the table.

"Something must've happened for her to hit the tree," said Rimas.

"Must've," repeated Tomas mechanically, tightly squeezing his fists.

She watched his rectangular face turning white. "I don't want to live anymore."

"Are you mad? You're not even fifty-five yet."

"What's the point in continuing with such a useless existence?"

"Well. You know what I think?"

"What?"

"If you were happy once, you will find happiness again. That's what I think, and let's drink to that!"

"Į sveikatą!" said Tomas, clinking his glass with his brother's. Gulping his drink down, he jumped to his feet. "Who is there?" As he walked towards the door, Gitana pretended to be removing her shoe. With her pulse strongly beating in her temples, she briskly greeted the brothers and passed them, running upstairs.

After that night, there were many angry exchanges of words between her parents, followed by prolonged hours of bickering until they stopped talking to each other. Before the house became a place of silence, Gitana understood that her father had had an affair with a much younger woman, who had died in a car accident. Ina, six years older than Tomas, accused him of heartlessness and betrayal. In turn, he admitted marrying her for her witty and caring personality, but not for love. He said he had been unfaithful to her for the last eight years ...

*

Day-by-day, Gitana noticed the change in her parents. Since his lover died, Tomas' hair turned white. His once average-sized frame seemed to shrink. He now looked the same age as Ina who had greyed years ago, not making any effort to colour her wiry hair. Her high cheek-boned face kept showing new wrinkles. Drinking became a norm for each of them—she drank secretly, hiding her bottle in a washing machine, while he drank openly. They turned into ghosts, passing each other with a slight nod of acknowledgement, spending their time in different corners of the house or outdoors. After reconciling, they slept in the same bed again—Ina knitting, Tomas writing, both watching TV, playing cards, and napping during the day. Due to their refusal to see a doctor, their health deteriorated—Tomas had sore kidneys and Ina heart issues. Every attempt Gitana made to persuade them to seek professional help was met with stubborn refusal. Eventually, at the age of thirty-five, she had to leave her job to look after them. As her parents found it too difficult to walk upstairs, they decided to relocate downstairs by converting their lounge room into a bedroom. Now their double bed was replaced with two single ones, separated by a hanging sheet. Lying on his back for extended periods of time aggravated Tomas' kidney problems. Ina, who used to look after their house and garden, soon stiffened up from the lack of mobility. While she ate raw garlic to soothe her chest pains, he dealt with the pain by sipping alcohol from his flask. Previously, they used to rise early, showering, then eating breakfast in the kitchen. Now they depended on their daughter for their care.

Alerted by the sounds of dogs barking, Gitana strained her eyes to see who might be opening the front gate. Realising visitors were entering, she quickly tried to tidy the light blanket covering her mother and pushed the chamber pot further under her father's bed. She greeted her parents' childhood friend Julė and her daughter Dalė at the door, letting them into the kitchen. Her face, extended by a double chin, broke into a sweat which moistened her dishevelled, frizzy hair. Moving between the table and the stove, she became aware of Julė asking about Tomas and Ina.

"They are asleep but look and feel the same since you saw them last."

"We can stay for two hours today," said Julė, checking her wristwatch. "The Palanga-Kunigiškės bus will stop outside your gate. A friendly driver promised to pick us up from your place."

"Lucky you," said Gitana, preoccupied with looking for a tablecloth.

"You know it's too far to walk to the actual stop," added Dalė, fanning her red face with both hands.

"Sure do."

Untucking her white blouse from her cargo pants, Dalė kept glancing in the mirror hanging on the wall in front of her. She caressed her over-dyed, egg yolk coloured hair with her fingers, while her mother gently patted her wrinkled mouth and thin nose with a hankie. Gitana watched Julė seemingly trying to keep her hands busy by picking the seam of her skirt or readjusting the pins in her thick brown hair, twisted in a bun. After stretching a white tablecloth around the square table, Gitana brought a pot of tea, made from fresh chamomile and thyme. The herbs, recently collected from her garden, released a sweet, minty aroma. She giggled at her guests as they eagerly helped themselves to stale biscuits from a large, red tin. When she began to apologise for having nothing else to offer, Dalė waved her finger in the air as if to say she didn't care what she ate. Julė softened her biscuits by dipping them into her drink. Eager to see her old friends, she finished her tea first.

Stepping into the converted bedroom, she looked at Tomas.

"Are you still fishing?" she asked him.

When he raised his eyebrows, she spoke of the time he lost an oar and how, thanks to a strong wind, managed to steer his boat to shore with only one. Tomas wondered aloud why she remembered more than he did. Julė, smug from the complement, encouraged him to show her his boat. Lifting himself up on his elbows, he tried to get out of bed. Squeezing the rail with his thin hands, he swayed to and fro, unable to straighten himself up.

Julė turned away from him to chat to Ina.

"Why are you laying here? Did you forget you were such a great dancer?"

"Really?"

"Nobody could dance as long as you! Remember how you won the dance competition by managing to stay on the dance floor all night?"

"Nonsense," Ina said, exposing her bad teeth as she giggled.

Julė, moving her hips and feet to the sound of her voice, ushered Tomas and Ina to join her. Neither of them did, leaving her humming the tune of a waltz in the middle of the room while turning and gliding around their beds.

"I envied you so much—young handsome men lining up to dance with you," Julė sighed, still holding her imaginary partner with her outstretched hands. "You were tall and pretty. I was a plump, country girl."

"And you still are," Gitana whispered under her breath, pointing at her watch, reminding her guests it was time to leave.

Gitana grew up not knowing the secrets hidden in her parents' cellar. Now that they had submitted to the inevitability of dying, she wanted to know the whereabouts of the key. Tomas sent her to the shed where she found the key, hanging on a ring with other keys—completely rusted. He warned her that everything in the cellar was damaged by damp and poor ventilation. When she entered, the stink of raw fish was such that it overpowered the dank smell of damp. Taking some time to explore, Gitana discovered the journals and magazines stacked on two large shelves. They were about Sweden. She selected a few and brought them with her inside the house. Night after night she flicked through the pages of water-damaged fashion magazines. She imagined being one of the glamour models, dressed in a striped dress wearing summer sandals, heavy mascara, nail polish and lipstick, hiding her eyes under the wide brimmed hat. People's faces were glowing with happiness. Not accustomed to smiling, Gitana lifted a round mirror from her side table and tried. But she wasn't satisfied with her forced smile, stretching across her face, giving her an unnatural look. Her mother never smiled. While going shopping, she wore her ordinary clothing, slouching heavily while carrying bags of groceries home. She didn't use lipstick on her dry lips, nor nail polish on her chipped fingernails.

One night, Gitana found a history journal and was surprised to discover that Sweden was a monarchy. She couldn't take her eyes off the picture of Charles XIV John, King of Sweden and Norway, who reigned in the first half of the nineteenth century. She admired his black curly locks, partially covering his low forehead, wearing his smart uniform with medals and a sword hanging from a golden sash. It made her regret that she wasn't born a Swedish princess. The photo of a three-year-old princess Victoria, taken in 1980, made Gitana fantasise about having her long face, narrow lips, and almond-shaped eyes. Victoria's hair was brown, resembling the colour of her eyes. Gitana took a deep breath, holding back her tears. Since she started caring for her parents, she'd become a Cinderella, preoccupied with household duties from morning till night. She didn't go out anymore as she didn't have the right size outfit, nor was she able to leave her bedridden parents by themselves. And then there was the problem of the six kittens their Siamese cat Murkė had given birth to after fighting with stray cats. Finding homes for the litter proved to be difficult given that they were not pure bred. Hidden in the overgrown garden bed, Murkė nurtured her blind kittens while Gitana weeded vegetables and strawberries.

Another responsibility was looking after holiday makers from Moscow, Kharkov and Tashkent while accommodating them in the spare rooms in their home. The same married couples—at first without, then with newly-born children and, in later years, with grandchildren, kept coming back to enjoy the Baltic Sea. From June to September, she looked after the three upstairs rooms, housing ten people. The summer rentals brought considerable income, helping the family of three to get by.

*

Gitana's parents passed away in 1987, one day apart from each other—Tomas, aged sixty, died from kidney failure and Ina, sixty-six, had a heart attack. Gitana folded their mattresses without taking off the sheets and hid them in the wardrobe. The beds needed to be prepared for the viewing. Her uncle and his family helped to wash and dress the bodies, and to lift them into coffins on the bed frames for people to pay their last respects. Standing at the head of each coffin, a group of elderly women chanted their prayers, interrupted by the sobs of friends, relatives and complete strangers. The sound of the monotonous rosary reminded Gitana of her parents' failed will to live.

After the funeral, while gathering the tucked away bed linen, Gitana discovered a small hole in her father's mattress which hid the cellar key, fastened to a safety pin. He had taken it away from her when she'd started asking questions about Sweden. Intrigued, she opened his diary she found in a pillowcase. She knew he'd been writing in bed. She started reading it, forgetting her initial task, forgetting to eat, drink or go to bed. She didn't realise her father, a member of the Communist Party, had justified his decision to join because of the privileges. For instance, he'd received permission from the Soviet Lithuanian government to keep his boat at home. His own father had fished all his life, and was quite prominent in the

Party ranks. He groomed his son Tomas for Party membership, and Tomas joined it after completing his university degree. They were pleased, being able to keep their family boat at home while other fishermen had to leave theirs in a designated place in the bay of Šventoji. Additionally, working at his second job as the Director of the Lifesavers Station in Palanga, Tomas could keep it in his shed, and use the boat in rescue operations.

In his diary, Tomas detailed how a few men tried to escape to Sweden. Their footprints, left on the sand leading to the water's edge, were a perfect give away. They were caught, tortured, tried and jailed for treason. How naïve she was believing the shoreline was raked to prevent drunken people drowning in the sea after dark! The more Gitana read his stories, the more she wished she could've had the opportunity to confront her parents just once more and tell them how hurt she was by not knowing so much. How foolish she felt going through her life proudly wearing her red Pioneer scarf around her neck, and then becoming a member of Komsomol. Because non-members found it difficult to gain entry to university, she hadn't hesitated to join. She pressed her hands against her heart until the tightness in her chest subsided.

The next diary entry was written for her.

"Gitana, when our homeland is no longer occupied, you will know what to do." The words made her jump from her seat, asking aloud, "Occupied? By whom?" Confused, she went outside to check on Murkė's kittens, patting and playing with three remaining fluffy balls of grey and white. Taking in the tranquillity of the evening, she wondered who the occupier Tomas had referred to was.

Re-establishing herself in a new accountant's role at the Restaurant Vasara in Palanga, Gitana hid her father's diary from her view. She hoped those questions his diary raised might leave her thoughts. She hoped that moving on from reading his memories might help her to cope with living in the empty house, which required major renovation and repairs. After five years of being withdrawn from the outside world, she hoped to improve her low self-esteem. She lost weight, bought new clothes and started to nurture her interrupted friendships. Pleasant conversations over a cup of coffee with her girlfriends filled her evenings with purpose. Dressed no less impressive than the Swedish models, they went to restaurants and discos hoping to meet their future husbands.

*

In early August 1989, Gitana learned that the citizens of Palanga were to demonstrate against the Soviet system, and particularly against Brezhnev's Villa and all it represented. Situated on the main street, Vytautas, it was protected by barbed wire and patrolled twenty-four hours a day. Standing at the front of the iron gates, Gitana was handed a leaflet, outlining how the Villa and its twenty-two hectares of park land was regarded as a prestigious residence of the leaders of the Soviet Union, Leonid Brezhnev and later Mikhail Gorbachev; how the famous Villa contained marble fire places, retro style furniture, tennis courts and the only heated salt water pool in the whole country! While most Soviet citizens were experiencing economic shortages and political suppression, it acted as a place of relaxation for the political elite. Gitana and Dalė joined some seventy protesters in a peaceful march. People carried placards "Russians go home", "Gorbi give us freedom" and "Brezhnev's Villa belongs to Lithuanians!" The march was followed by rousing speeches, delivered by the members of freedom movement Sąjūdis, denouncing Lithuania's occupation since 1940. People applauded and cheered the speakers, united in the assurance it was time for the country to return to pre-war independence.

Gitana even surprised herself as she moved from being apolitical to attending more protests, reading the papers and listening to her friends. Lithuania was reviving its independence! People were protesting in Vilnius, Kaunas, and Klaipėda against the Soviet totalitarian regime they had lived under for half a century!

At the end of the month hundreds of people gathered at the beachfront, joining thousands across Lithuania and two million others across the Baltic States, holding hands to make a six-hundred-kilometre human chain in anticipation of regaining their independence. Mixing among the strangers, trampling the sand, Gitana tried to catch the unfamiliar words of the Lithuanian National Anthem. She, like others, became emotional, shedding tears while listening to strangers sharing their family deportation stories. She wanted to embrace them in celebration of this "Baltic Way". The Parliamentarians, standing on a hastily-erected stage, spoke of the hand-holding, symbolising fifty years since signing of the Molotov-Ribbentrop Treaty between the Soviet Union and Nazi Germany. Gitana learned that the secret protocol of the treaty granted authority to Germany and Russia to invade Poland, and executed Russian control over Estonia, Latvia and Finland. But what surprised her most was that, as part of the secret protocol, Lithuania and Danzig fell under German control until the German-Russian war changed the course of history.

The speed of political developments overwhelmed the residents of Kunigiškės, night after night gathering at Rimas' house for discussions. Gitana also went when she could, though feeling some of the uncertainty among the locals as to what might happen to the Baltic people turning against Moscow. Nobody was sure whether this seemingly innocent hand-holding event might possibly anger Gorbachev, and hoped the momentous solidarity didn't evaporate before the desire for national freedom could prevail. But it did prevail! On the 11th of March 1990, Gitana heard on the radio that Lithuania had declared its independence from the Soviet Union. She recalled her father's words "When our homeland is no longer occupied, you will know what to do." Watching the Lithuanian national flag of yellow, green and red appearing on other houses, she ran into the cellar. She pulled out the tricolour flag tucked behind the shelf she had spotted some time back, taking it into the house, upstairs, and attached it to the balcony rail. She lit a fire behind the shed and ignited it with old Swedish newspapers and damaged magazines. She gathered more literature from the house and didn't hesitate to feed the flames with old schoolbooks praising the Soviet system and obscuring Lithuania's history. She removed the newspaper *Komjaunimo tiesa* from its place on a hook next to the toilet where it had had been used as a toilet paper, and enjoyed watching as it twisted, curled, and crumbled in the flames—the daily edition of the Truth of Komsomol had lost its purpose. Leaving the cellar door ajar, she calmly walked to the edge of the water and threw the key into the dark green waves. The fairytale of nine hundred million Soviet citizens building a classless society lifted into the sky like the spray from the crashing waves, dissolving in the thickening mist. She looked towards the other shore on the horizon where she thought she'd rather be—in a country that had broken away from Russia some seventy years before, and where freedom was a way of life.

Learning of the January 1991 events left Gitana even more disappointed. The proclamation of Lithuanian independence was interrupted on the 13th of January with Soviet troops entering the capital. National television showed a footage of Russian tanks approaching the Television Tower of Vilnius. Gitana watched people standing in front of the tanks defending themselves with their bare hands, singing patriotic songs. She sang along, her heart beating to the meaningful words Lietuva brangi, mano tėvyne— my dear Lithuanian homeland. Then the live broadcast was interrupted by a Soviet soldier who switched the camera off. Outside, people, defending the Tower on a cold winter night were beaten and shot at by special KGB Alfa squad and Pskov Division paratroopers of the 76th Guards Air Assault Division. The rolling tanks squashed and killed fourteen and injured hundreds. The only female victim, Loreta Asanavičiūtė, was twenty-four. Her last words were "Doctor, will I still live?" The tank tracks crushed soft tissues of her small pelvis, and there was nothing can be done to stop bleeding.

*

Rimas passed to Gitana an old diary his brother left with him for safe keeping. Reading Tomas' diary she came across his encounters with foreigners. Her mindset had changed, and she was keen to continue. A captain of one of the Swedish ships he had known for some thirty years, Elias Johansson, used to invite him on board. Tomas met the crew, explored the insides of the ship and received encouragement to stay with them. They made a plan: after reaching Swedish waters, Tomas could jump overboard and ask for political asylum. They were aware of the human rights abuses in the Soviet Union, yet Tomas was aware of the consequences of such an act. Fearful, he spoke of his country, losing a quarter of its population due to the mass exodus to Germany at the end of the war and the Soviet deportations. In an attempt to cheer him up, the crew gave him money, clothing, cigarettes, chewing gum and glossy magazines. Playboy was on the top of the list. He hid the gifts and forbidden literature in a double floor compartment on the bottom of his boat.

Curious, Gitana put down the diary and went to the shed to check his boat. The secret compartment, described in the diary, had a couple of old newspapers, stinking of fish. She wondered how, under the cover of the Communist Party membership, he had never been caught. It must have been the reason he used to change the subject when she or his friends raises the matter of Swedish encounters! She was glad Tomas didn't have to return his boat to the bay after retiring, as his secret floor may have been discovered. Deteriorated and holey, it was declared unsuitable.

Gitana was shocked to learn how the Soviet Lithuanian Communist Party made her father suffer. Someone reported him having an affair with a married woman who worked at the clothing shop in Palanga. Her name was Stasė Rainienė. He had had to stand red-faced in the presence of the Party members while being questioned about his extra-marital affair. He also received a warning letter afterwards. A year later, reaching his pension age of fifty-five, he resigned from the party but continued his liaison with Stasė. She died soon afterwards, and whispers circulated of her husband changing their car tyres the night before, leaving the bolts slightly loose. "Gitana," wrote Tomas, "if there is no love, there is no point in living." As she turned the page, she found the Swedish captain's address. She immediately wrote to Elias Johansson in poor English, trying to share the details of her father's passing.

In a couple of weeks, Elias replied with a sympathy card and a promise to come and see Gitana during his upcoming business trip to Lithuania. He arrived with his son Albin, a widower of Gitana's age. How lucky she was being able to speak to him in Russian, a language he knew and she learned at school. He was amused by her childish laugh, fair hair reaching below her shoulders and her hourglass figure. Taken aback by his hazy brown eyes and erect posture, she was mesmerised by this man in a navy uniform. His blue jacket, white brimmed hat and white belt reminded her of the picture of Charles XIV John she once found in her cellar. She adored Albin's black curly locks that, similar to Charles', partially covered his low forehead.

They stayed at Gitana's house and while Elias was stationed in the port of Klaipėda, she and Albin spent three weeks together. Following their endless conversations, long walks, bathing in the sea, running and exercising together, he admitted he was falling in love with her. Gitana responded with a smile she'd finally managed to perfect. Before they parted, Albin gave her a friendship ring he secretly purchased in Palanga. Soon after they left, she received an invitation to visit the Johansson family. Bringing Albin's ring to her lips, she cried for a long time, but the stream of tears running down her cheeks were tears of joy, as she recalled how she had dreamt of the other shore since the day she wrote the word SWEDEN in the sand.

About the Author

Gražina Pranauskas is a musician turned writer. Formerly a choir conductress from Soviet Lithuania, since her arrival in 1989, she has conducted various choirs in Geelong and Melbourne. She has also made the transition to, and embraced creative writing, using the experiences of her formative years (living under Soviet rule) as inspiration.

Photographer: Olivia Boddeus

As a student at Deakin University, Geelong, she studied journalism and literary studies, obtaining Bachelor, Bachelor with Honours, and Master of Arts by research degrees. In 2015 she was awarded a Doctor of Philosophy degree from Victoria University, Melbourne, for the novel "Torn: the Story of a Lithuanian Migrant".

Gražina is the author of two poetry books: *Eukaliptų tyloj* (In the silence of eucalypts) (2007) and *Abu krantai* (Both shores) (2011), published in Lithuania.

In 2018, in celebration of the Centennial of the Restoration of the State of Lithuania, Australian Scholarly Publishing released Pranauskas' *Lietuvybė Down Under: Maintaining Lithuanian National and Cultural Identity in Australia*.

www.ingramcontent.com/pod-product-compliance
Lightning Source LLC
Chambersburg PA
CBHW051256250626
47155CB00009B/3314